DANTE'S DILEMMA

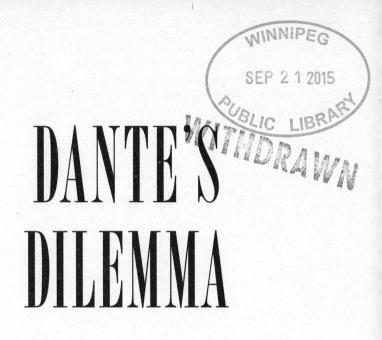

ALSO BY LYNNE RAIMONDO

Dante's Wood

Dante's Poison

DANTE'S DILEMMA

A MARK ANGELOTTI NOVEL

LYNNE RAIMONDO

SEVENTH STREET BOOKS®

AN IMPRINT OF PROMETHEUS BOOKS

59 JOHN GLENN DRIVE • AMHERST, NY 14228

www.seventhstreetbooks.com

Cover image © Matt Frankel
Cover design by Jacqueline Nasso Cooke

Inquiries should be addressed to
Seventh Street Books
59 John Glenn Drive
Amherst, New York 14228
VOICE: 716–691–0133 • FAX: 716–691–0137
WWW.SEVENTHSTREETBOOKS.COM

19 18 17 16 15 • 5 4 3 2 1

Library of Congress Cataloging-in-Publication Data

Raimondo, Lynne, 1957-
    Dante's dilemma : a Mark Angelotti novel / by Lynne Raimondo.
        pages ; cm
    ISBN 978-1-63388-042-9 (pbk.) — ISBN 978-1-63388-043-6 (e-book)
    I. Title.

PS3618.A387D35 2015
813'.6—dc23

2015004945

Printed in the United States of America

To my husband

"Ma ficca li occhi a valle, ché s'approcia
la reviera del sangue in la qual bolle
qual che per violenza in altrui noccia."

(But fix your eyes below, for we draw near
the river of blood that scalds
those who by violence do injury to others.)

—Dante Alighieri, *Inferno* XII
(Translated by Robert Hollander and Jean Hollander,
Doubleday, 2000)

ONE

I was the victim of a thief.

Or a practical joker.

How else to explain that my door lock had gone missing?

Shivering on my porch, I pondered this latest riddle. I was already late for the party and needed to get a move on. The last time I used it, the keyhole was just above the handle. Roughly at chest height and a hand's width from the frame. Was it only my imagination that it was no longer there? Or was I thinking of the one I had recently left behind? For the umpteenth time since the closing, I cursed my dull wits. Why was it so hard to remember where things were?

At last I found it, though it seemed to have jumped several inches from its prior location. After setting the deadbolt, I rattled the door to be on the safe side. My left wrist still ached where it had been shattered a few months before. The townhome had a security system, but it was presently useless, an accessible keypad not being among the amenities insisted upon by the former owners. The alarm company had promised to send someone out to help me with it the first thing Monday morning. In the meantime, I could take solace from the fact that the last household intruder who had tried to kill me was now resting peaceably six feet under.

Moving homes had been more challenging than I'd imagined. My new place was only a block from the old, but that was where the similarities ended. Three stories tall, it stood in a gated courtyard development just north of the Chicago River. It was more room than I needed, but the opportunity to buy had come up quickly, and I'd jumped at the chance to stay in the same neighborhood. In fair weather I could walk to work, and on foul days a cab ride was only a shout away—at least on those occasions when I found one willing to pull over for me.

Still, I was having a rough time of it. As cramped as my former quarters had been, I could sail from one end to the other without scraping so much as a knuckle. In contrast, getting around my new home was like trying to chart a course through the Bermuda Triangle. Adding to the mayhem, the movers I hired must have studied organizational science in a rummage shop. It had taken a solid hour to find the closet where they'd stashed my tuxedo, and I still wasn't sure what they'd done with half my shoes. If the collection of bumps and bruises I was accumulating didn't kill me, going barefoot in a Chicago winter surely would.

I tapped the porch step with my cane and started gingerly down the walk. The storm that began as freezing rain in the afternoon was now turning into a blizzard. If the Eskimos had dozens of different words for *snow*, I thought I deserved my own special glossary. *Sno-Cone*, I decided, as I pulled my foot from another pile of slush. By the time I reached the street, my shoes were soaked and I was sure the creases in my trousers were a thing of the past. The cane was fine for avoiding solid objects, but what I really needed on a night like this was a divining rod.

Fortunately Boris, my driver, was waiting for me just outside the gate.

"You are late," he said in mild rebuke as he rushed to position an umbrella over my head.

"I know. It's been hell sorting out where the movers put everything."

"You should ask Yelena's help."

Yelena is Boris's wife, as well as my office assistant. On fleeting occasions—according to some mysterious alignment of the planets I have yet to divine—she condescends to open my mail, answer the phone, and usher patients in and out of my office. More often, getting her to lift one of her well-manicured fingers for me requires the skills of an experienced hostage negotiator. Understandably, I was skeptical of her eagerness to assist with the unpacking.

"I can't afford to give her any more time off. Besides, I don't want to interfere with your rekindled marital bliss."

Boris grunted in reply. Married and divorced once before, the couple had recently retied the knot in a lavish affair involving a virtual Red Army of guests and enough imported vodka to float the battleship *Potemkin*.

I took hold of Boris's elbow and followed him over to the town car. "If you don't mind my asking, what on earth made you sign up again?"

Boris let out a sigh as he opened the passenger door for me. "Food is better."

This was terse even for Boris, and I took it as a signal that the second honeymoon was already wearing thin. I slid into the car, hauling the cane in behind me and folding the sections so I could store it on the seat next to me.

Boris gunned the engine, and we swung out onto McClurg Court. The drive was only a mile or two, but long enough to get me thinking about the toast I'd been commissioned to give on the unhappy (for me anyway) occasion of my boss's retirement.

I had many reasons to be grateful to Septimus Brennan. A crusty septuagenarian who managed the warring factions in our department with tact, fairness, and the occasional loss of temper, Sep had come to my rescue at some of the darkest moments in my life. I had him to thank for my present job as a clinical psychiatrist in a large Chicago teaching hospital, where I'd fled after losing nearly everything but my license. Other prospective employers might have questioned why a middle-aged shrink in a privileged East Coast practice would suddenly decide to quit and start all over, but Sep had accepted my excuse of needing a fresh challenge, even while suspecting there was a great deal more to my story than I was telling him.

Sep was also the person I'd turned to when I got the second-worst blow of my life.

I frowned, thinking back on the scene in his office three years ago now, on a stunningly beautiful day in September.

"There's no doubt about the diagnosis?" Sep said, eyeing me intently from behind a desk stacked with memos and folders. With his hooked nose and gaunt cheeks, he looked like Uncle Sam without the top hat, which was fitting because I was about to be drafted into a whole new life.

"The blood tests were . . . definitive."

"Tell me again what it's called?"

"Leber's Hereditary Optic Neuropathy." In other words, a disease caused by a defective gene that had just robbed me of the sight in my left eye and was gearing up to do the same thing in the other.

"And there's nothing that can be done, no treatment whatsoever?"

I eased up on the tissue I had been turning into pulp in my lap and shook my head. "They gave me some vitamins that might slow the process down, but . . ." I shrugged my shoulders in a helpless gesture.

Sep sighed wearily and turned his face toward the window overlooking Lake Michigan. "How much time do they reckon?"

I followed his gaze with the eye of mine that still worked. Outside, the sun was shining brightly and wisps of cloud were speeding ultramarine shadows across the water. "No one can say. Maybe a month. Maybe tomorrow."

Sep faced me again, and I thought I detected a shiny spot on his lined cheek. "You know you'll have my full support and that of everyone else here."

I managed a weak smile. "Let's not be dishonest with each other."

Sep smiled too—or tried to. "Perhaps you're right. I've never met anyone who—" He stopped and shook his head. "I should be ashamed of myself. This is hardly the time for another lecture about alienating your peers." He pointed a gnarled finger at me. "But while we're on the subject of honesty, I'll expect you back." He paused and added less sternly, "When you're on your feet again."

For most of the next year, I defined being on my feet as crossing the room to pour myself another shot of bourbon. Once again I had Sep to thank for seeing through my stall tactics and forcing me back on the job. In a perverse way, he was also responsible for the expert-witness work that now took up a third of my time.

I shook off the memory and turned to watch the passing streetlights, which I could still make out, if only as brief flashes in an otherwise impenetrable dusk. In better lighting I could see more. Contrasts and shadows, some shapes and a few, washed-out colors, but nothing to get excited about. Except when I was asleep and dreaming, the world I'd once viewed and effortlessly recorded with my photographic memory was gone, sucked into oblivion by a microscopic strand of DNA. I wasn't reconciled to it—not by a long shot—but I still needed to eat. And now that I was spending time with my son again . . .

Boris broke through my reverie with the announcement that we'd arrived at the "Cliff Hangers" club.

"Cliff Dwellers," I corrected him. "But I think your name is an improvement."

The Cliff Dwellers belongs to the venerable Chicago tradition of private eating clubs, each with its own distinct pedigree. Unlike those that started out as ethnic enclaves, it has a long history of catering to artists and supporters of the arts, most famously the film critic Roger Ebert. It was a natural choice for Sep, whose collection of late-century figurative paintings was said to be the best in the city. The club, once housed on top of Orchestra Hall, now occupied the penthouse of a sky-scraper at the corner of Michigan and Adams.

A footman beat Boris to the town car's door and opened it for me, sending a wintery blast across my face.

"You want I come back later?" Boris asked from the front.

"No. I should be able to find someone who can give me a lift. Go home and keep Yelena company. Maybe it will put her in a better mood next week."

The footman escorted me up a carpeted walk and into the lobby, where from the sound of things only a few other tardy arrivals were waiting for the elevator up. One of them was my colleague of six months, Alison DeWitt, who called my name and came over to peck me on the cheek.

"Thank God I'm not the only one who's late," she said.

"We can always claim we got stuck on an ice floe," I said. "How goes it with the new arrival?"

"Oh, Mark," Alison said, sounding frazzled. "I'm so tired I can barely work up the energy to comb my hair. All he ever does is cry. Or spit up. And I'm not even the one who pushed him out."

Alison and her partner, Gina, had recently welcomed the birth of their first child, a baby boy.

I tried to cheer her up. "It's brutal at first. But it will get better."

"Do you really think so?"

"I know so," I said, though my own history gave little evidence of that fact. "You just need to give it some time. It won't be long before he's smiling at you like there's no tomorrow."

"What really worries me is what it's doing to us," she confessed. "I hardly even recognize Gina these days. All we do is snap at each other—like animals in a cage. I'm starting to think I should have paid attention to all those studies saying childless couples are happier. And I'm feeling so guilty about leaving the two of them alone tonight." She sounded on the verge of tears.

"There, there," I said, moving back in to give her a hug. Up close she smelled of curdled milk and eau de Dreft. "Try to relax. You deserve some time out with friends. And motherhood certainly becomes you. You look beautiful tonight."

She accepted the compliment without surprise. Possibly because she was a member of several minority groups herself—half African American and half Native American, as well as an uncloseted lesbian—Alison belonged to the minuscule population of people for whom my handicap was barely remarkable. It was another one of the reasons we were fast becoming close friends.

"But here I am all wrapped up in my own problems without giving a thought to yours," Alison hastened to add. "Are you nervous?"

"At the moment, the only thing worrying me is whether my tie is on straight. It's been ages since I had to dress up like a penguin. Though it does make me feel more at home in the weather."

Alison stepped back to survey me. "You look fine. But that's not what I meant, Sir Nonchalant. This change has to be rough on you."

I shrugged. "I'm sure the new regime will be a model of truth, liberty, and justice for all."

"Bullshit," Alison said. "Jonathan hates your guts."

"Don't overdramatize the situation. He'd like to see my guts being used to teach first-year anatomy."

"And I'd like to see his—"

"Ssshhh," I stopped her. "We're talking about our new Führer. His spies are everywhere. And if we don't head upstairs soon, it will be another black mark on our already-tarnished records."

We took the elevator to the penthouse and deposited our coats with the coat checker, who nervously asked me whether I wanted to hang on to my cane. In answer, I folded it up and stuck it pirate-style in my cummerbund. Alison steered me over to the nametag table, where a young staff member was waiting.

"Dr. *Dante* Angelotti?" she asked after I had identified myself. Predictably, some overzealous assistant had inscribed the tag with my seldom-used first name.

"If that's the only 'Angelotti' in your stack, I guess that's me," I said.

"I can cross it out for you," Alison offered.

"No thanks. It would only draw further attention to the fact that my father hated me. I'll just attend anonymously."

"Fat chance of that," Alison said, laughing.

We moved out into the ballroom, which was packed as tightly as a subway platform, with me hanging not so discreetly onto Alison's elbow. Here and there I could pick out a snippet of conversation above the partygoers' boisterous roar. *"Has to be good for the department. He'll bring some much needed discipline to the table."* And *"The old boy should have relinquished the chair years ago. Too soft on the dissident faction. Angelotti and DeWitt, for example . . ."*

"You hear that," I said to Alison. "You're already getting a reputation."

"If so, I consider myself in good company."

Halfway over to the bar, we were confronted by my other good friend and comrade in arms, Josh Goldman.

"Where the hell have you been?" he demanded. "They've been asking you to come to the mike for the last thirty minutes."

"Just trying to live up to my reputation as a nonconformist. I'm on my way, but get me a double, will you? I'm going to need it when this is all over."

Moments later, I was stepping cautiously onto a small platform, where one of the event coordinators pushed a microphone in my hand. I tested it and made an effort to appear as though staring blindly into a large audience was something I did every day. Which, in a way, it was.

I pulled my Braille notes from my pocket and got underway. "It's great to see all of you here this evening . . ." There were a few nervous titters. "Sep asked me to keep it short, which is good, because to paraphrase Shakespeare, I am 'no orator but a plain, blunt man'"—heartier chuckles this time—and I'm here tonight 'not to bury Caesar but to praise him.'" More laughter. "As you know, it has been our great good fortune that many years ago a young graduate of a second-rate medical school in . . . where was it again?"—I pretended to consult my notes— "ah yes, Cambridge, Massachusetts, that this young man from Peoria, with job offers from every major hospital in the country, turned them down to return to the state where he was raised . . ."

I proceeded to outline some of the highlights of Sep's career: his decorated service as a trauma specialist in a MASH unit during the Vietnam War; the dozens of cutting-edge studies he authored upon his return; his participation in not one, but three of the committees charged with revamping the *Diagnostic and Statistical Manual*; his numerous awards and recognitions, including the Miriam H. Taub Chair in Clinical Psychiatry at the hospital where we both worked; and last, but not least, the decades spent overseeing, developing, and raising our department to its present status as a leader in the field.

"I know I speak for all of us in praising these accomplishments as the life's work of both a brilliant physician and a great humanitarian. But I would also be remiss in not mentioning what I know for Sep was, and always will be, his greatest achievement: his thirty-year marriage to his beloved wife, Edna, who passed away a few years ago after a long battle with cancer. During her illness, and despite his overwhelming professional obligations, Sep was never absent from her side."

I ended on a personal note. "In closing—because I can hear Sep harrumphing at me to get on with it—let me say that I have 'neither wit, nor words, nor worth' to express what Sep has meant to me personally. Rarely have I had the privilege of working under a superior with such a temperate disposition"—very loud laughter—"or, one who, when confronted with extreme provocation, if not outright mutiny, was so capable of keeping a lid on his emotions. I have Sep to thank for the profound wisdom—some might say, rampant foolhardiness— that led to my finding a home here, and I will be forever grateful to him for the gentle scolding"—Sep, only a few feet away, nearly choked on this—"that prodded me back to work with my friends and . . . er, colleagues." Gales of laughter this time. "Sep has been a true friend and mentor, and I hope you will all join me in toasting this outstanding leader and the finest human being it has been my privilege to know."

The room erupted into thunderous applause.

"Good job," Josh said, coming up to press a glass of bourbon into my hand. I downed it in a single gulp.

"Yes, very," Sep said, announcing his presence with a hand on my shoulder. "Thank you, my boy. I'll be red-faced for the rest of the party."

"I meant every word of it," I said. "You'll be sorely missed." By me, most of all, I thought morosely.

"Perhaps. However, while I shouldn't quibble with such unrestrained encomium, the references to *Julius Caesar* were a tad unsubtle."

"You think he picked up on it?"

Sep lowered his voice. "I doubt it. He's too busy basking in the imagined glory of his new position. But if you'll take my advice, it's time to start mending your fences with him."

"I don't see how—"

"No arguing," Sep said. "Go over there right now and congratulate him. He's standing ten feet to your left."

"Sep, I . . ."

"Just do it," he commanded.

I followed his order—the last he would ever be in a formal position to give me—and went over to shake the hand of my new boss.

My archenemy, Jonathan Frain.

TWO

My father didn't hate me, but he didn't know what to do with me, either: a scrawny, rebellious child who reminded him all too painfully of the wife he had lost to childbirth. In those days, nobody gave any thought to spankings, and we weren't the only warring family in our Queens neighborhood, where the small houses stood so close together that the daily soap operas were as hard to ignore as the smell of *ragù* emanating from a neighbor's kitchen. Especially among Catholics, it was considered a parental virtue to give snot-nosed children their due, and I was far from unique in the number of times I showed up at school with a blackened eye or a swollen lip. Unlike other children, however, I had no mother to wipe away my tears, no siblings to blunt the rage of my father's bitter disappointments. From the time I was small, I was at the mercy of his fists, and it taught me well how to run.

Over the years, this developed into an emotional armor I'm not proud of. It prevented me from ever really knowing him, and later enabled the selfish act that left my own family in ruins. Oddly, though, the same trait that kept me at a distance from my loved ones also proved an asset in my job. If I couldn't look clearly into my own heart, I was nonetheless very good at looking into the hearts of others. Perhaps it was this talent that Sep had instinctively recognized when he took a chance on hiring me. Maybe only the walking wounded are capable of seeing the pain experienced by their fellows. As the old saying goes, it takes one to know one. And on that score, I was as good a psychiatrist as they come.

All of this is a long way of saying that my troubled relationship with Jonathan Frain didn't spring from an absence of skill, much less professionalism, on my part. True, in my self-destructive fashion I often went out of my way to get his goat. Pompous, small-minded people always bring out the worst in me, and I wasn't above reacting negatively when he was trying to impose yet another one of his asinine preferences on the entire department. If there were a prize for making a workplace as joyless as a North Korean labor camp, Jonathan would have taken it every time. But the real problem for me was his elevation of form over substance, his attention to the letter of every rule, and his inability to grasp the conditions under which creativity flourishes and breakthroughs occur.

Exactly the qualities, I figured, that had led to his selection as our new administrator.

Ever since the announcement, I'd been torturing myself with all the ways he could make my life as miserable as a post-downpour slog through the Chicago Deep Tunnel. They weren't difficult to imagine. Assign me to the hospital's diversity committee—a posting I'd only narrowly avoided thus far and that had roughly the same appeal as being named Differently Abled Employee of the Year. Nitpick my grant proposals until they appeared as fresh and enticing as the salad bar on offer in the basement cafeteria. Require me to remove all traces of my personality from my office. (Jonathan's was all glass and steel, and about as welcoming to visitors as the Fortress of Solitude.) The list went on and on.

As it turned out, I had grossly underestimated him.

When I arrived back at my office the following Monday, I was already in a poor mood. The alarm-company representative had proved to be one of those well-meaning but clueless people who equate low vision with a corresponding deficit in brain cells, and it had taken longer than necessary to convince him that all I needed was a keypad with larger buttons I could stick some Braille labels on. On the walk to work, I'd also been accosted by members of a group handing out Bibles, who were keen on me knowing that my blindness would be cured if only I would accept Jesus into my heart. ("Thanks for the tip," I said to the one who insisted on following me halfway down the block. "I'll be sure to try it on my next visit to Lourdes.") To top things off, there was a package waiting for me when I walked in the door of my suite.

"This just came for you," Carol, our receptionist, informed me. "It's from a law office."

"Which one?" I asked, expecting it to be related to one of the cases I was working on.

"Nobody local. Some firm with a fancy-sounding name in Connecticut. And marked confidential."

My insides immediately clenched up. I'd been waiting to hear from Annie, my ex-wife, about an issue concerning our son, and the fact that she'd chosen to communicate through legal channels wasn't a positive sign. My heart sank even further when Carol handed me the envelope and I could judge its thickness—half an inch, at least. Where lawyers are concerned, I'd learned that bad things usually come in big packages.

"Do you need help with it?" Carol asked. "Yelena's downstairs getting a hot wax."

It figured. Yelena's beauty breaks tended to fill the better part of the working day. This time, however, I was relieved to find her AWOL, which prevented the whole office from hearing immediately about the package. Though most of my colleagues were now aware I had a child named Louis, I tried to keep gossip about him to a minimum.

"That's OK," I said. "I . . . was expecting it. It's just some tax forms I need to sign. I'll get to them myself later." And back at home, where I didn't have to worry about the presence of prying eyes.

I slipped the package into my backpack and trudged down the hall to my office, holding my rigid, nonfoldable cane—the one I used for extended travel—in a stationary position a little out in front and to my side. It was different grip than I commonly used outdoors, where I swung the cane from side to side just ahead of my feet. The cane's nearly five feet of length gave me ample time to react to drop-offs without falling and alerted even the dimmest of drivers to the fact I might have trouble spotting them. Indoors, however, I either dispensed with the cane entirely, or employed it as I was then doing, in a mildly defensive capacity.

Which may explain why, just before the door, I collided with something that shouldn't have been there. The hard surface, jutting out some inches above the floor, sent shock waves through my tibia and pitched my upper body onto what initially felt like an oversized punching bag. "What the—?" I swore as I pulled back and righted myself. No one answered, so I moved in to inspect, discovering from a cane and manual exploration that it was the well-worn leather sofa from my office. I'd purchased it and two matching armchairs shortly after my residency and held on to them out of nostalgia throughout the years. Now, for some cryptic reason, they were sitting on top of a dolly.

I maneuvered around the obstruction and headed over to the central administrative station, discovering several similar items—some belonging to me and some not—along the way.

"Would someone be good enough to explain why my sofa is sitting in the middle of the hall?" I called out upon arrival. "You know how I hate it when the furniture gets rearranged."

Lori, Sep's former assistant, answered me apologetically. "I'm sorry. I meant to phone to warn you. Dr. Frain has me running in so many different directions I can't even find time to visit the restroom."

"I'm not blaming you. But what the hell is going on?"

"Office makeover. If it makes you feel any better, you're not the only one. New furniture for all the doctors is being delivered tomorrow."

"You're saying everyone's stuff is being replaced?"

"Uh-huh. But not until the new carpeting is installed."

"You've got to be kidding. The rugs are being torn up, too?"

"Hard to believe, isn't it? But Dr. Frain felt the current decorating scheme didn't project his image for the department."

I could only guess at what image that might be. "Don't tell me," I said. "We're going for the frozen-tundra look."

"Not bad," Lori said. "Pretty much white on white all over."

"I'm surprised we're not repainting the walls, too. Wait, I remember. They're already white."

Lori laughed. "There wasn't enough money for painting left over after the commissioned artwork. The one going over your credenza is against the wall. It's not that bad, actually. Like a Jackson Pollock, but more monochrome."

I wouldn't be missing anything, then. "But how'd he push this through without anyone voting on it? I thought we were all supposed to agree on things like office accents."

Lori lowered her voice to a near whisper. "Well, you didn't hear it from me, but rumor has it that he landed a big donor who agreed to fund the project if his wife got the commission." Lori named a name I recognized as the sole proprietor of a Gold Coast firm that had recently been lauded—or excoriated, depending on your point of view—for a costly renovation of the mayor's office. "Dr. Frain also got the powers that be to agree to the redo as part of his contract. By the way, he wants to speak to you."

"Do you know why?"

"No. But he said, and I quote, 'Kindly inform Dr. Angelotti that I expect to see him in my office the moment he gets in.' I left you a voicemail."

"Did he allow for the possibility that I might have a patient or two to keep me occupied this morning?"

"Yes, but I checked your appointments first. You're clear until two."

"How'd you—" As far as I was aware, Yelena was the only one privy to my schedule, and she was as zealous about guarding her turf as an NFL linebacker. It was one of her better attributes.

"Another change," Lori said. "All personnel calendars have to be uploaded to an executive database twice daily. For keeping track of productivity and so forth. The IT crew was here all weekend getting it set up."

And I thought maybe I'd gone too far in likening Jonathan's take-over to *Julius Caesar*. *1984* was starting to seem more like it.

I ignored the summons and went straight to the coffee lounge, still holding on to my cane, coat, and backpack. It was too early in the day for a real drink, but I was reeling from all the sudden upsets. I didn't particularly feel like surveying the wreckage of my office and thought a cup of tea might steady my nerves.

Alison and Josh were already waiting for me at a table in the corner.

"I guess you heard," Alison said when she saw my face.

Josh got up heavily from his seat and guided me to an empty one. I sat down and put my things on the floor beside me. "'Heard' is putting it mildly. I walked into my sofa just as it was being hauled off to storage."

Josh chuckled. "That's where you think it's headed? Funny, I never took you for an optimist."

"We're talking about my personal property. The last I knew, taking it from me against my will is called theft."

"That's because you couldn't see the memo. It was tacked to our doors this morning. Unless you object in writing, it's all being donated to charity. As a gesture of the institution's commitment to serving the needy. And if you don't mind my saying so, your stuff was looking pretty needy, too."

Alison slipped a cup of something warm into my hand. "Chamomile," she said. "I think you should stay away from caffeine this morning. You look enough on edge as it is."

I shook my head. "This is worse than a horror movie. What's next—*The Stepford Doctors*?"

"Cheer up," Josh said patting me on the back. "Most of the department is as upset about the Stasi tactics as you are. Alison and I are already organizing the loyal resistance."

"I want in," I said.

"Not a chance," Josh said. "This needs to be done on the q.t., and you getting involved would be on a par with Che massing his troops to storm the presidential palace without anyone noticing."

"You two seem awfully blasé about this," I said. "How's Debbie going to feel when you can't even hang pictures of the family ski trip on the wall?"

Josh was as unruffled as always. "I'm not worried. If this keeps up, I figure it's only a matter of time before Jonathan hangs himself."

"If so, I want to be there to kick the chair out from under him."

"Like I said, buddy, no dice."

"You're not even going to let me in on what you two are plotting?"

"Your aura, like Brutus's, would betray you."

Just then Lori reappeared out of the mist with a summons. "Dr.

Angelotti? I'm so sorry to interrupt, but Dr. Frain insisted I come get you. He said . . . well, I'm not going to repeat what he said. I thought it was uncalled for."

"Go ahead," Josh said. "Might as well get it over with. We'll be here waiting with the triage kit when you're through."

"If not with the defibrillator," Alison said merrily.

I got to my feet. "Thanks, guys. I'm glad someone else is finding this as hilarious as I am. 'My master calls me, I must not say no,' to quote a different play. But do me a favor. Keep the funeral arrangements simple. I wouldn't want to give the bastard the pleasure."

THREE

Fifteen minutes later, after an unnecessary trip to the men's room and as much additional dawdling as I thought I could get away with, I was seated on an uncomfortably hard chair in Jonathan's office.

"You're not going to offer me a cigar?"

"Filthy habit," Jonathan said. "They ought to be banned. Along with fast food and soft drinks."

I had a momentary vision of him marching in a modern Christian Temperance Union rally, filled with righteous indignation over the unhealthy habits of his fellow citizens—a soft, undisciplined, and therefore despicable lot. It made me wonder why he'd chosen medicine as a career in the first place. "You wanted to see me?"

"Yes. I've been reviewing your personnel file. There are certain items I need clarified."

I could have predicted this would be the first order of business. I visualized him on the other side of his vacuum-tidy desk, gloating over his newfound license to interrogate me. He was one of those tall people whose heads are too small for their midsections, giving him the appearance of a flesh-colored Michelin Man. A bad hair transplant, tight white jacket, and tortoise-framed glasses completed the picture.

"Which items, exactly?"

"How you came to join us, for instance. I've always wondered what prompted the career move."

"I was getting stale where I was." My stock explanation.

He ruffled some papers on his desk. "Really? According to your file, you were making high six-figures, and on the eve of another promotion. Some might find it unbelievable that you departed out of boredom."

"As you point out, I wasn't fired. So what's the issue?"

"Only that I have the department's interests to consider now. If there's a skeleton in your closet—one that might emerge to cause us embarrassment—I have a responsibility to find out what it is."

A skeleton. My thoughts immediately flashed to the small, white headstone resting in a Hudson River estate near Poughkeepsie. But this was no time for wrestling with my demons. "Are you questioning Sep's judgment? Because I'm sure he'd be interested to hear about it."

"Of course not. But my predecessor was sometimes guilty of allowing his sympathies to interfere with sound management. I intend to change all that. Starting with more rigorous background investigations of new hires. The legal department is already drawing up the guidelines."

"If you're in touch with the lawyers, you must know what thin ice you're skating on right now."

"I'm well aware of the rules. Especially as they pertain to . . . certain individuals."

I almost laughed. He'd stopped just short of calling me a cripple.

"Careful," I warned. "Even *your* job's not that safe."

Jonathan quickly realized his mistake and retreated to a safer position. "No one's *forcing* you to reveal anything," he snapped. "Though I had hoped you would share the information voluntarily. As a gesture of your good faith and willingness to put my concerns to rest. Of course, if you have some reason to fear being honest with a superior . . ."

The message was loud and clear. Why would I be reluctant to talk if I had nothing to hide? I briefly considered giving him the finger and walking out. Or tendering my resignation there and then. I'd already been flirting with the idea of finding another job, one that would put me in closer proximity to Louis. But quitting just then would limit my options, as well as give Jonathan a victory he didn't deserve.

"I would have thought it was obvious," I said, looking straight at him—or as straight as I could pull off. "I got divorced."

"And?"

"And that's it. After the papers were signed, I needed a change of scene. Don't tell me you didn't suspect something like it."

"Of course. But I find it hard to believe that's the whole story. There wasn't something else, too—a little too much love for the bottle or sex with an attractive intern, say?"

My patience was nearing an end. "Cut the crap, Jonathan. If you've looked at my file, you've seen all the references." Though I deserved much of the praise, the glowing letters sent on my behalf weren't solely a reflection of my performance. Roger Whittaker, my former boss and ex-father-in-law, had done everything in his power to speed my exit from his employ.

"So you won't have any objection if I contact Dr. Whittaker myself? Just to complete my due diligence?"

"Be my guest." If that's all he wanted, I was in safe territory. Roger hated me with a passion, but he came from the kind of family stock that aired its dirty laundry where it belonged: in the maid's annex. I smiled to myself, anticipating just how expertly he would put an end to Jonathan's snooping. "Is there anything else you wanted to know? Like whether I sleep in my socks or drown kittens for a hobby?"

"We're just getting started. But my time today is short. I have a luncheon appointment with a member of the board in half an hour. So I'll cut to the main reason I wanted to see you."

I lifted an eyebrow.

"You're being relieved of your duties."

"Woo-hoo, you're headed for the big time now," Josh chortled. "Before you know it, the networks will be signing you on to replace Sanjay Gupta."

I scowled at him. "It's just the local stations. But I was informed they'll be airing tapes of the entire trial."

"I thought you loved courtroom work. And it's better than being told to stop because it's cutting into your patient billings."

"Jonathan floated that threat, too. Just in case I needed help understanding that I don't have a choice."

We were seated in a secluded spot of the cafeteria, where Josh had brought me after I emerged in a state of shock from Jonathan's office. Jonathan had been playing me when he suggested I was losing my job. I wasn't—at least for the time being. But I'd been ordered to drop everything I was doing to assist Linda O'Malley, the recently elected State's Attorney for Cook County, with a political hot potato.

I'd heard about the case, of course. You'd have to live under a rock in Chicago not to. Some months earlier, Gunther Westlake, a controversial University of Chicago professor, had been discovered dead on the university's South Side campus—and under circumstances that quickly had the wheels of journalism humming.

"I don't blame you for feeling squeamish, though," Josh said through a mouthful of potato chips. "Just thinking about what happened to the guy makes me want to puke."

"You and me both," I said, resisting a powerful urge to cross my legs.

It wasn't just that Westlake's body showed up on the last day of "Scav," the university's world-famous scavenger hunt, when the campus was overrun with scores of visiting parents and dignitaries. Or that his corpse was found inside one of the colorful exhibits displayed in the school's main quad for scoring by the competition's judges. Or even that Westlake's remains appeared just as one of them—a class of '73 alumna who collapsed and had to be carried away on a stretcher—was looking inside an entry that should have earned its team a whopping fifty points: a giant papier-mâché replica of a woman's vagina.

It was also that Westlake appeared to be missing some anatomy of his own, which had been severed at the root and stuffed down his throat.

"Still, you've got to admit it's an interesting case," Josh said.

"'Interesting' is one way of putting it," I said. "'Media circus' is another."

Under the circumstances, Westlake's murder initially struck some as ideologically motivated: the professor's polemics, appearing in his popular blog and on the op-ed pages of several national newspapers, could always be counted on to provoke someone's ire. A member of the university's Sociology Department, he rarely confined himself to subjects of purely academic interest, penning caustic, in-depth pieces on everything from women in the military (he didn't approve) to stay-at-home mothers (he did), usually drawing enthusiastic applause from the Right and stinging scorn from the Left. Only a month before his death, an article Westlake had written for the *National Review* on the underrepresentation of women in the STEM fields (entirely appropriate in his view) had erupted into chaos when female undergrads stormed the Ida B. Plotkin Sciences Hall dressed as Barbie dolls—the *Chicago Maroon* had humorously captioned the story "Breastageddon"—bringing unwelcome attention to the university's record on promoting women and forcing its president to convene a hasty press conference reaffirming "our commitment to gender equity in all tenure decisions."

The investigation had taken a different turn, however, when the police discovered evidence that Westlake had been killed in his home and that the weapon used to emasculate him was one of the professor's prized Shun hollow-steel chef's knives, then missing (according to his housekeeper) from its section of a wooden block on the kitchen counter. Their antennae were further raised by reports of altercations between Westlake and his estranged wife, Rachel Lazarus. When students returning from a frat party in the middle of the night claimed to have seen a woman fitting Lazarus's description moving a suspicious bundle across campus, the case seemed open and shut. Lazarus was removed to an Area 5 police station and promptly confessed.

Even with all the theatrics, the case might have produced less fanfare had it not been for the public defender assigned to represent Lazarus who, upon researching possible defenses, discovered what appeared to be a long history of domestic abuse. Police logs going back a decade showed several 911 calls from the couple's home, along with tapes in which a clearly distraught Lazarus begged for help. When she finally left Westlake six months before, Lazarus had sought an order of protection. Friends and colleagues at the university—where Lazarus had lately obtained work as an administrative assistant—were quick to rally to Lazarus's side, volunteering accounts of blackened eyes and ill-concealed bruises, while hospital records confirmed at least one instance in which she had sought treatment for broken bones. Though Lazarus herself steadfastly refused to offer any specifics, she did not object when her counsel announced, in a pressroom percolating with reporters and flashing cameras, that Lazarus would be pursuing a Battered Woman's defense.

The trouble this presented for O'Malley was clear to anyone with even the dimmest awareness of local politics. A Republican, O'Malley had barely squeaked by her male opponent in the November polling, a feat only possible in Cook County because the candidate put up by the Machine was caught subscribing to an online child-pornography site mere days before the election. To complicate matters further, O'Malley had run on a strong domestic-violence platform, drawing the support of EMILY's List and other women's advocacy groups. The Lazarus case put her campaign promises front and center—she'd declared in several speeches that her office would be "taking a hard look at any prosecution in which the defendant was beaten, stalked, or raped by her abuser"— while the brutality of the crime produced the usual loud demands for justice among the law-and-order faction in her base. Whichever side she took, it seemed she couldn't win.

O'Malley played it straight down the middle. While other prosecutors might have broadcast their leanings by hiring one of the celebrity psychiatrists who crossed the country testifying in battered women trials, she'd enlisted Bradley Stephens, a less well-known but highly regarded local doctor who'd never seen the inside of a courtroom. O'Malley also instructed him to spare no expense in conducting his psychiatric evaluation of Lazarus, declaring her intention to offer Stephens's expert opinion into evidence even if it favored a verdict of acquittal. It was a brilliant move, and one that was already creating speculation about a run for higher office down the road.

It was therefore doubly unfortunate for O'Malley that Stephens was mowed down in a hit-and-run accident only days before he was to issue his report.

I'd known Brad Stephens, who worked at a rival hospital down the street, and respected his work immensely. So I'd been shocked when Jonathan told me of his death, a few blocks from his Wicker Park home and roughly at the same time I'd been tying one on at Sep's party.

I pushed my uneaten lunch around with a fork. "Eat your mashed potatoes," Josh urged. "Before I do it for you."

"Is that what these are? I thought I was eating reconstituted soap flakes."

"I wish I had your problem—not eating when I'm depressed. And I shouldn't be making light of the situation. Brad was a good man. Do the police know anything more about the accident?"

I shook my head. "You remember how bad the weather was that night. They think he must have slipped on the ice and been run over by a driver who couldn't brake in time or didn't spot him in the whiteout conditions. If you'd seen him recently, you'd know how shaky his footing was getting."

Around my age—that is, just shy of fifty—Stephens had suffered from early onset Parkinson's disease. My thoughts traveled back to the last time we'd met, while sharing a panel at a conference on emerging issues in veterans' healthcare. Stephens had just graduated to a support cane, and we'd traded jokes about two sticks on a stage.

"So now you're supposed to take over for him?"

I nodded. "Apparently our CEO loved the idea when he was contacted personally by O'Malley. More publicity for the hospital and a chance to show how civic-minded we are—helping local officials out of a tight bind. Jonathan also mentioned a concern that I was becoming too one-sided about the cases I was taking on. He thinks I should be doing more to put lowlifes away."

"Is that what's got you so down—besides Brad, I mean?"

"Working for the prosecution? Maybe. Not to mention the timing. The trial starts in the middle of January. That's only a month off."

"But you'll have all of Brad's work to rely on. He wasn't a guy you could fault for lack of thoroughness."

"That's what Jonathan said when I raised the point. Apparently, there's no interest in having me reinvent the wheel. And under the rules, I'm entitled to simply explain Brad's findings and indicate whether I agree with them. I don't even have to talk to Lazarus unless I want to."

"Do you have any idea what Brad was going to say? It's amazing his report hasn't leaked before now, with all of the reporters working overtime to get the inside track."

"O'Malley's doing, again. She's been worried about a defense motion for a change of venue and has been trying to keep the publicity pot from boiling over, though having the case sent elsewhere would certainly solve her public-relations problem. That's the one ray of sunshine in this whole thing. From everything I've read, she's a straight shooter, unlike some of the sharks in that office."

I was thinking of Tony Di Marco, an Assistant State's Attorney I'd crossed horns with before, and whom I trusted even less than I trusted Jonathan.

"So that's who you'll be working for, Mama Cass herself?" Josh said, making reference to O'Malley's nickname in the gossip columns. He stopped and added ruefully, "As though I should be making cracks about someone's size." Josh had finally given in to temptation and was now making short work of the food left on my plate.

"Uh-huh. I'm supposed to be over there getting my marching orders at the crack of dawn tomorrow."

Josh clapped me on the shoulder. "Like I said when we started this discussion. You're in the big leagues now."

FOUR

It was a fitting coda to the day that when I reached home that evening, I found myself locked out.

I didn't understand what was happening at first.

Still, I ought to have figured out right away why my key wouldn't move when I tried to open the courtyard gate. My first assumption was that I'd pulled out the wrong one. But on removing the key and checking the shape, as well as flipping through all the others on my ring, I knew that wasn't the problem. I reinserted the key into the lock and tried again, but it stubbornly refused to budge. I tried once more, taking care not to exert too much force. The last thing I needed was to snap the head from the shaft. Once again, I couldn't get the thing to move as much as a centimeter in either direction.

I stood there in the cold, unsure of what to do. At half past six, it was already pitch black outside, and the wind was causing the temperature to drop seemingly by the minute. There was an intercom, but I couldn't tell whether any of my neighbors was home. And even if a human being was behind one of the doors, who would risk venturing outside to answer my summons? No one in the complex yet knew my name. The whole purpose of a *gated* community was to keep out strangers and other undesirables. I could call a locksmith, but I was loath to appear both blind *and* incompetent. Besides, I realized with mounting concern, I had nothing on me that would prove my new address.

I was considering whether there was any way I could scale the eight-foot fence when I was saved from further embarrassment by the sound of footsteps approaching.

"Lose your key?" a woman said brightly as she came up beside me.

"No, I have it," I said. "I just can't get it to move. Did someone change the locks?"

"Not that I know of. But I bet that's not the problem. Here," she said, pushing a bulky something against my chest. "Hold my groceries for me while I check it out."

I did as she asked, shifting my cane to my left hand while I took hold of the bag with my right. She leaned in to inspect the lock. "I knew it!" she exclaimed, as though I'd just presented her with a delightful puzzle to solve. "Frozen again."

"Frozen?" I said.

"Yeah. Just like the locks on car doors. It happens all the time in weather like this."

I felt like a fool. Granted, it had been a long time since I'd driven a car. In fact, not being responsible for an automobile was one of the few perks of my current situation, and it was almost liberating when I'd finally bitten the bullet and unloaded my Toyota with a dirt-cheap offer on Craigslist. Oil changes, tire rotations, and annual inspections were now a thing of the past, as was hacking away the ice on the windshield on frigid winter mornings. I could also entertain a sense of superiority listening to the drivers I heard swearing and honking their horns in traffic, while I breezed along the sidewalk with my low-maintenance— not to mention very green—cane.

"We'll have to thaw it out," the woman said.

"How will we do that if we can't get in?"

"Simple. I always carry a can of de-icer in my purse. You should start carrying one too unless you're immune to frostbite."

I heard something being pushed into the keyhole and squirted, followed by the sound of the lock opening. "Here we go. Walk on through while I hold the gate."

I followed her in, balancing the cane against the front of the grocery bag. "You're not worried that I might be Jack the Ripper?"

She laughed. "I know who you are. The new neighbor. I watched you moving in last week. I'm sorry I didn't come over to introduce myself. Horribly rude, I know, but it was finals week and I literally had a hundred papers to grade. My name's Candace, by the way. Candace McIntyre."

"Mark Angelotti. I'd offer to shake hands with you but I only have two."

"Oh, hell. Rude of me again. Here, I'll take that bag back. But now I haven't any hands free, either. I suppose we could just sniff each other, like dogs. How come you don't have one, if it's OK to ask?"

"I did, but he developed fleas."

"Oh, but they . . ." She stopped herself and laughed again. "You're just pulling my leg."

"Now that *would* be rude. So you're a teacher?"

"Renaissance literature. At the University of Chicago. I just moved there from McGill. I thought the weather would be an improvement. Obviously wishful thinking on my part."

"Candace from Canada. Has a certain ring to it."

"So long as you don't ever call me Candy, eh?" she said, exaggerating the last syllable in what was clearly intended as jest.

After the miserable day, I was enjoying the banter, so I said, "I've got one of those names, too."

"As in prone to misuse? Give."

"Dante. My first name."

"That's not so bad. Why don't you care for it?"

"Long story, but if you teach literature you might be able to guess. My father made me read the *Commedia* when I was a kid. It scared me to death."

"I'll bet. All those sinners having their flesh torn apart by harpies or being buried upside down in burning mud. Though as horrific fates go, not much worse than your average fairy tale. It's amazing what they used to read to us when we were young," she added, helpfully identifying herself as someone around my age. "But you haven't told me what you do for a living."

"Doctor."

She didn't miss a beat. "Not a surgeon, I trust?"

I was really beginning to like her. "Psychiatrist. But we're both going to need surgical help if we stay out here much longer." We were still standing just inside the gate, where the wind was rasping my cheeks like a scouring pad.

"You're right," she said. "I shouldn't keep you outside on such a wretched night. I don't suppose you have time to stop in for a drink?"

I was sorely tempted. Hallie Sanchez hadn't returned my calls in weeks. And I could tell from Candace's confident manner that she liked men and men liked her, usually a good sign that a woman's looks were nothing to sneer at. But I couldn't take time off for female companionship that night, not with the unopened package from Annie's lawyers still burning a hole in my backpack.

"I'd like that. But I'm afraid I've got to take a rain check. I have a mountain of work to get through myself this evening."

"Understood. But how about on Saturday? I'm supposed to attend an end-of-quarter faculty party and I could use an escort, not to mention an excuse for leaving early if the conversation begins to waver."

I hesitated, thinking again of Hallie. But if I didn't move on to greener pastures, I'd end up one of those pathetic old men staring down the bottom of a bottle each night.

"I think we have a deal," I said.

"By the way, I'm unattached if that isn't already apparent."

"Me too," I said, wishing it weren't so.

Candace and I said our good-byes and I entered my home, removing my Mets hat, overcoat, and scarf before distributing them among the hooks just inside the door. I was determined to shed some of the habits that made my old home look like a "before" photo in *Good Housekeeping*, a resolution aided by the former owners, who appeared to have spent a tidy fortune at IKEA. There were storage bins for everything, including an umbrella stand that held half a dozen canes in various stages of health, and cubbies for all my footwear—assuming it ever came out of hiding. There were even wall racks for my bicycles, though I'd decided that mine were too valuable to be left out where they could be spotted through the foyer window. Instead, they resided in a locked room next to the garage, which I hoped to turn into a shop-cum-exercise room when I could find the time.

I climbed up the short stairway to the first floor, a spacious kitchen/dining/living area with French doors leading to an outdoor deck. Even in its largely unfurnished state, the place felt like a palace, though it didn't begin to compare to some of the residences I'd shared with Annie, the duplex in the Upper Eighties and the restored farmhouse in Fairfield County. Inevitably my thoughts drifted back to those early days, my dawning awareness that marrying my boss's daughter had been the biggest mistake of my life. The strained year following the birth of our first child, Jack, had only amplified our differences, leaving me feeling trapped and desperate. By that time we'd moved to a turn-of-the century Colonial in Cos Cob, and I began using the commute to the city as a pretext for spending long hours away from home.

Jonathan had been off-base with his sneering insinuation about sex with an intern. I'd never been that reckless, either in my choice of sexual partners or their number. All of my affairs had been carefully planned to escape Roger Whittaker's attention, even if I sometimes carried them out within spitting distance of the hospital where we worked. Recklessness, however, didn't do enough to describe the way I'd dismissed Annie's fears when Jack developed what seemed like an ordinary childhood fever. Eight months pregnant with our second child, she hadn't questioned my excuse when I said I needed to work late that night. The ink was still fresh on Jack's death certificate when I confessed my true whereabouts, earning me perhaps a few points for honesty, though they did nothing to lessen Roger's rage.

The divorce settlement presented to me on the day of Jack's funeral was breathtakingly simple: I was to become a virtual stranger to my younger son. Though I'd later come to regret it, I gave in to every one of Roger's terms. Half out of my mind with grief and shame, I was in no shape to argue, and deep within my soul I *agreed* with him. My neglect had ended the life of one child. How could I ever again be trusted with the care of another? When Louis was born a few weeks later, I couldn't even bring myself to hold him, never dreaming that the glimpses I stole of him through the glass wall of the hospital nursery would be the only ones I would ever have.

I trudged over to the kitchen, taking a frozen dinner from the freezer and shoving it into the microwave—one of the few appliances that didn't feel like it had been designed by a Silicon Valley engineer—before pouring myself a shot of bourbon, which I downed in a single gulp. The first floor had only one other room, a small den that I was turning into an office, and I went there next with the package, to get the scanner-printer started on its contents. After feeding the pages into the machine, I headed upstairs to my bedroom to change, counting off the steps to the second floor to reinforce the map that was still in the "Under Construction" stages in my mind.

On the way back, I stopped in the empty bedroom that I vainly hoped might be Louis's someday. It was one of the reasons I'd bought the house, so that he and I could spend time together in surroundings less crowded and shabby than my old apartment. The scanner was still clicking away downstairs, so I sat down on the hardwood floor with my back to the wall, imagining how I would transform it into the kind of space a small boy would love. Nothing over the top, no beds shaped like racecars or hand-painted murals. But a soft carpet and blond wood furniture and brightly colored fabrics. And shelves—lots of shelves—for toys and books and the games we would play together on nights like this, in front of a cozy fire.

I caught what I was doing and climbed clumsily back to my feet. I could hear the coils of embossed paper overflowing the scanner's tray and piling up on the floor below. If their quantity was any indication, Louis wouldn't be visiting any time soon.

As I descended the stairs, my footsteps echoing off the bare walls were only one reminder of the lonely life I had made for myself.

FIVE

The next morning I was on the phone to my lawyer as soon as the hour would permit, catching her as she was driving to her office in New Haven.

"What's the matter? You sound upset," Kay Bergen said into the car's handset. In the background, I could hear the heavy commuter traffic on I-95.

"I slept poorly." In fact, I had practically worn a hole in my mattress with all my tossing and turning the night before. I'd given up the fight around 4 a.m. and made good use of my new home's opportunities for pacing back and forth, before ringing Kay up promptly at 7 EST.

"Uh-oh," Kay said. "I take it your ex wasn't gung ho about our proposal." By proposal, she meant the letter to Annie I had drawn up with Kay's help, asking for changes to the divorce decree. I hadn't let on to Annie that I'd hired a lawyer, hoping to maintain the modest thaw in our relationship that had allowed me to spend time with Louis half a dozen times in the past year. I had hoped to formalize that arrangement, as well as obtain permission for longer visits, both on the East Coast and with me in Chicago.

"That would be accurate," I said.

"I don't understand. I thought you said the last meeting went well."

I'd thought so too, remembering the Sunday the month before, when Annie and I'd shared coffee in the study that used to be mine while Louis was eating lunch with his nanny. I'd never liked the room— Annie had done it up in English squire style, all chintz-covered sofas and hunting prints—and I felt more uncomfortable there than ever, balancing a cup of Limoges in my lap with my cane on the seat right beside me. In keeping with her finishing-school manners, I was sure

Annie's eyes rarely strayed in its direction. I briefly wondered how time had treated her. Annie had always made heads turn with her elegant looks, and if I had to guess, she was as lovely as ever: blond hair done up in a loose chignon and only the barest touch of makeup on her bone-china complexion.

Our conversation was cordial, and I'd even begun to relax a bit when I made the mistake of asking where the third member of our party was.

"He's not coming."

I wasn't sure what to make of this. I hadn't been looking forward to seeing—or more accurately, not seeing—my ex-father-in-law, but Annie was insistent. Involving Roger in the discussion from the outset would lead to less misunderstanding and give him the illusion he still had veto power. Annie had never been this strategic in her dealings with her father, so I went along with a face-to-face meeting, as much to get the ordeal behind me as to further my fragile truce with her. "So he didn't want the pleasure of my company after all?"

"He said that while he was sure he would relish the spectacle, he would rather become an Alzheimer's patient than be found in the same room with you."

I was no longer relaxed. "So where does that leave us?"

"I'll work on him some more." Annie stopped and exhaled deeply, sending the scent of French Roast my way. "This isn't easy for me either, having you here—in our home. But I don't want Louis growing up thinking his father walked out on him without so much as a look back."

Her words bit into me like a drill saw. *So that's what she thought.* I felt myself color rapidly. "You know I was only trying to make things easier on you . . . after everything. I never meant—"

"I'm not interested in your excuses. We can just be grateful Louis has one parent who cares more about his welfare than their own convenience."

I had to fight to keep a level tone. "I didn't fly all the way out here because it was convenient. Today or any of the other times you said I could come."

"I'll grant that. And it's the only reason we're talking right now. To tell you the truth, I was shocked when you finally asked to see him. If it hadn't been for that and—"

I waited for her to say it.

"—the fact that he was asking so many questions, you wouldn't be welcome."

"Is that everything?"

"And . . . that you seem to be good with him," she said grudgingly.

Now, mentally replaying the conversation, it appeared I'd missed something significant. Or maybe it was that when Annie and I fumbled a handshake at the door, I thought I detected a new cut-stone ring on her third right-hand finger.

"Mark, are you still there?" Kay asked over her car phone.

"Sorry. I was drifting. Annie's remarrying."

"So? Usually that puts women in a good mood."

"I don't know about her mood, but it's sure got her making plans." Or was it Roger doing the planning? For the first time, I began to wonder about my former father-in-law's prolonged vendetta against me. Was there something else behind his fury I was missing?

"So what's the bottom line—will she give you more time with Louis or not?"

"Four weekends annually, no Chicago."

"That's not so bad," Kay said. "If that's her first offer, I'm sure we can move the needle a little more in your favor. And it's an improvement over what you have now." Under the current court-sanctioned arrangement, I was technically allowed to see Louis only once a year.

I shook my head in anger. "I haven't told you what the condition is." The night before, my hand had begun to shake when I first realized what I was reading, and I had to force my fingers to continue down the page. "I have to agree to allow Louis's new stepfather to"—I could barely spit out the words—"adopt him."

I knew the fellow, a radiologist with a toney practice in Riverside. According to the papers tendered by Annie's lawyers, his name would replace mine on Louis's birth certificate, and I would cease to exist in any legal sense as my son's father. It wasn't clear what Louis was then supposed to call me—Once In A While Daddy, or maybe just Poor Uncle Mark—but the mere thought of it sickened me.

"Oh dear," Kay said as she took this in. "Well, I guess we *do* have a fight on our hands."

"Is there a way to fight it? I mean, assuming I won't agree?"

Kay was silent for a moment. "I'll have to do some research."

Worse than I'd imagined. "I won't hold you to an answer, but please tell me what you think right now—can Annie go ahead with an adoption over my objection?"

Kay chose her words carefully. "She'll have to petition the court, but there is precedent for it. When there's been abandonment by the biological parent."

Abandonment. I knew enough about how the legal system worked to see immediately how Annie's lawyers would portray me. Louis was nearly three before I'd asked to see him for the first time. Never mind that I'd stayed away because I'd been sick—and not just from having to live with myself. No matter how I tried to explain it, my long absence from my son's life would inevitably raise questions.

"So it's hopeless."

"I didn't say that. But you need to be aware of what fighting this is going to mean. The issue will ultimately come down to what's in Louis's best interests. At a minimum, he'll have to be interviewed by social workers, maybe even a court-appointed guardian. And that won't be the end of it. Everything about your life will become fodder for discovery. Where you live and work, what you do in your spare time—even how you stock your refrigerator. Any fact that might bear on what kind of home you could provide." She stopped there, not needing to spell it out for me.

"I'm not the first blind father in history. I can take care of him."

"I believe that, but we're going to be battling some pretty nasty assumptions. It will be an uphill battle, even without you living a thousand miles away."

"That's not a problem. I can be on the first plane tomorrow." As a matter of fact, it would kill quite a few birds with one stone. I'd quit my job and dust off my résumé, put the new house on the market . . .

"Not so fast. I don't want to take the chance that you'll be between jobs when we go to hearing."

I realized then with another body blow to my ego exactly what else I had to be fearful of: finding some other place willing to employ me.

"You stay put," Kay advised, "at least until I've taken a closer look at some of the law. But before we get underway, I want to be sure you've thought it all through—that you're really ready to go forward with this."

"I don't need time to decide. He's my kid."

"All right. I'll start the ball rolling on our end. The first thing I'm going to do is call Annie's lawyers and tell them they're to deal directly with me from this point forward. And that we're going to move to have the original decree vacated. We're no longer politely asking for a few unsupervised visits. We're going for full parental rights and joint custody."

"Is that possible? I wasn't under any kind of duress when I signed."

"I can't promise anything, but the first thing you learn as a lawyer is to take the offensive. First impressions count, and I want the court to view you as fighting tooth and nail for Louis. In the meantime, painful as it may be, I want you to think back on the night your son died. Is there anything we can use against Annie, anything that might cast some of the blame on her?"

Kay accurately read my hesitation. "Mark, that's what I meant about being sure. If you want to do everything to get your little boy back, you need to be prepared for it to get ugly. And fast."

SIX

I arrived at the County Building that morning a good half hour early for my meeting with State's Attorney O'Malley. If my conversation with Kay meant anything, it was that I could no longer afford to lose my job. Even with my record, I couldn't assume another hospital would be chomping at the bit to hire a doctor my age, let alone one who couldn't read the first letter off an eye chart. Sure, there were anti-discrimination laws, but they were of small consolation to the seventy-five percent of blind Americans who couldn't find work in their chosen fields. I thought back shamefacedly on my behavior with Jonathan the day before. From now on, my marching orders would be to kiss his dimpled ass from sunrise to sunset, even if I had to swallow every last ounce of my pride to do it.

I exited the cab cautiously, feeling ahead with the cane for a safe place to plant my feet. An arctic cold front had moved in the night before, sending the mercury into the single digits and sheathing the city in ice. Fortunately, the Streets and San crews had been out early: the salt on the pavement was as thick as poppy seeds on a New York bagel. I crunched over to the entrance, vowing to redouble my efforts to locate where the movers had put my rubbers. I could only imagine what the chemicals were doing to my shoes.

The heating vents were working double-time when I squeezed through the revolving door. It was only half past eight, but the lobby was swarming with people: slow-moving workers on their way to their desks, citizens arriving to beg, steal, or bribe a favor from an official. There were plenty of bureaucrats to choose from. By some counts, Illinois is home to more than seven thousand separate government units, the highest in the country. People grumbled about their tax bills, but the appetite for patronage jobs was as rich as the silt flowing through the area's rivers, managed (naturally) by several overlapping agencies.

Once inside, I pulled off my winter hat—a knit Mets/Grateful Dead warmer—and stuffed it into my backpack. It wouldn't do to show up for my new assignment looking unserious or in hostile colors. "Silent Night" was playing on the building's loudspeaker, reminding me that Christmas was only two weeks away. Until the package from Annie's lawyers, I'd entertained hopes of spending part of the holiday season with Louis. Now it looked like I'd be playing Ebenezer Scrooge again. I shook off the thought and started off toward the chiming of the elevators at the back of the lobby. Halfway there, I froze at a familiar sound a few yards distant: an unmistakable contralto coming from the center of a shadowy group headed straight my way.

Shit, I thought. There wasn't time to duck into a corner—was there even one? It didn't matter. Hallie had already spotted me.

"Speak of the devil, there's Mark now."

She and her companions reached me in a few seconds.

"Hallie?" I said, feigning a blind man's confusion to explain the silly look on my face.

"Stop pretending you don't know it's me." She took my arm and gave it a subtle turn so I would know exactly which way to face the others, a maneuver learned from growing up with a blind brother. Even through my overcoat, her touch sent a jolt down my spine. "This is Mark Angelotti, the expert I was just telling you about. Don't pay any attention to his act. He doesn't miss a thing."

She introduced me to two other lawyers, Sara Andrews, a senior partner at her firm, and Carter Fawcett, an associate. I held out my hand and we all shook.

"Pleased," Carter said.

"Don't say that until you get to know him better," Hallie said.

She didn't seem to feel anything like my own embarrassment, so I fell in with the jolly mood. "Three lawyers all at once. I'll have to watch out for my wallet." I made a show of patting my breast pocket.

"That one's so old it has cobwebs on it," Hallie said. "You've gotten rusty in my absence."

"You too, unless I miss my mark."

She laughed and turned back to her colleagues. "Did I mention he's also good with puns? Why don't you guys start back and I'll catch up with you at the office." The law firm of Wentworth, Feinstein, and Shaw, where Hallie headed the criminal practice, was only a few blocks away. "We still have hours to go until the press conference and I need a few minutes alone with Mark. Carter, don't forget about that new set of pleadings."

"You're looking good," she said as soon as they'd departed.

"As are you," I replied, imagining her as Josh had described: a curvy Latin beauty with dark hair and laughing, mocha-colored eyes. I didn't have much else to go on, having kissed her only a few times before working up the courage to tell her about Jack.

"Though I might advise dressing more appropriately for the weather. Your ears are as red as beets," Hallie said.

"I forgot to wear a hat this morning." I lied. "So what's up? Sounds like you have a new case."

"I do. But it's all hush-hush for the moment. We're making the big announcement this afternoon. It's a *pro bono* matter, very high-profile. I really had to work the levers to get my partners to agree, but they're pleased with the exposure it will bring to the firm. The only negative is that Tony Di Marco will be heading up the prosecution. We were just upstairs, meeting with him about scheduling. Same shady little prick as always. I'd love to see you wipe the smirk off his face again."

Di Marco was the assistant who had conducted my first, all-too-painful cross-examination. "As I recall, he cleaned my clock pretty good, too."

"You held your own. That's what I wanted to talk to you about. We're taking over from another defense team and I'm not comfortable with the expert they've been using. We videotaped her for practice and it was like watching a kindergartener trying to explain calculus. We could really use your help."

I winced inwardly. So that's all she wanted from me.

"Do you think you could squeeze in some time tomorrow? I could fill you in over lunch. The change of counsel will be public then, and you can tell me what you think. About helping us, that is."

I looked down at my shoes. "I don't know, Hallie. I'm going to be tied up on a new matter myself for a while." More than one if you counted my upcoming custody battle. "And I'm not sure we should be working together. I'm mean, I assumed when you didn't return my calls—"

She touched my sleeve in an intimate gesture. "I know. But I needed time to get used to what you told me. It's . . . well, let's just say it wasn't easy for me, finding out about your son. And you not telling me about it for so long. I didn't call because I wasn't sure. To be honest, I'm still not. But maybe when this new case is behind us, we could have coffee sometime . . ." She trailed off unpromisingly.

I took a deep breath. "I don't think it's wise. Not the part about coffee, but us being on the same case together. It will just complicate things."

I waited to see whether she'd protest, wishing like hell I could read her expression.

She hesitated before patting my sleeve again. "I guess you're right. I'll call you when this new case is finished then?"

"OK." I turned to go.

"And, Mark?"

"Yes?"

"Happy Holidays."

I rode the elevator to the third floor and checked in at the front desk. The receptionist on duty was better than average—I figured state employees were required to take some kind of sensitivity training—and displayed little discomfort in asking for my ID and showing me where to sign the visitor's log. Michelle Rogers, the ASA sent to fetch me, was less composed, introducing herself in an overly loud voice and hanging back awkwardly thereafter.

I put on my Yes I'm Carrying This Big White Cane expression, and asked if there was a place I could hang my coat.

"Sure," Michelle said. "There's a closet right over there."

She sounded young and fearful of making a mistake, so I went easy on her. "You'll have to show me where 'there' is. Don't worry, it's not hard."

I gave her a quick introduction to "sighted guide" by asking her to tap the front of my left hand with the back of her right, which enabled me to locate her elbow without much trouble. I reached up and grasped it from behind. "Just walk at a normal pace and I'll follow. You don't need to pull me along and I'll trust you to stop us before we pitch down a flight of stairs."

Michelle giggled, and we made it to the closet without mishap. While I was disentangling from my backpack and overcoat, I tried to engage her in small talk. "Have you worked here long?"

"Since September. I only passed the bar this past summer."

"Like it?"

"I guess."

"That doesn't sound like a ringing endorsement."

She gave the audible equivalent of a shrug. "It's hard to find work as a new lawyer these days. I couldn't get a job with one of the big firms, so I'm here. I guess I should count myself lucky to be earning a paycheck."

"The experience can't be that bad. From what I understand, associates at big firms aren't exactly trying many cases."

"It isn't that. I know I'm learning a lot, but some of the supervisors here . . ." She stopped herself, as if she'd just spoken out of school. "I really shouldn't be talking about it."

I was curious to know more but decided against putting her on the spot. We resumed our walking routine while I continued to ply her with polite questions. Michelle was from a small town in Indiana, and proud of her Hoosier upbringing. She'd attended Ball State and John Marshall Law School, and recently married her high-school sweetheart, who was getting his business degree at Kellogg. She wasn't sure about raising a family in Chicago, and hoped to return to her home state someday. By the time we'd traveled a series of hallways crowded with filing cabinets, she'd grown perceptibly more relaxed.

"We're here," she announced as we stopped before a threshold. "I mean, at the conference room where you'll be meeting with the boss. We're still early, so I can show you the lay of the land before the others arrive."

Some five minutes later, I was seated comfortably at a seat near the door with my Bluetooth keyboard and phone in front of me and my cane stored unobtrusively on the floor when a bustle outside the door suggested Linda O'Malley had arrived. I rose as she swept through the entrance with what sounded like an army of lieutenants.

I'd never been in the presence of a politician before, but it was like being swept up in a tsunami.

"Doctor Angelotti! So glad you could make it!" O'Malley said, taking my outstretched hand between her two plump ones and shaking it forcefully, like she was hanging wash out to dry. "Thank you for coming. I hope it wasn't an inconvenience so early in the day. Can you believe this awful weather? I hope you took a cab. Just give Michelle the receipt and we'll cover the tab. Michelle, make sure you submit a requisition form for his travel expenses. We can't have the good doctor freezing his patootie off while he's laboring on our behalf. I'm Linda O'Malley, by the way."

"So I surmised from the available evidence."

She laughed, a sound like a bellows heaving, and released my hand. "I'm going to like this guy," she said to the others now filling the seats around the table. "Somebody get me a Coke Zero. And see if there are any of those sweet rolls left. Oops, I forgot. Make it decaf tea, no sugar, and carrots or some other healthy shit. Doctor's orders," she said in an aside to me. "If he had his way, I'd be eating like a hamster. Don't be shy. Sit down, sit down."

I did as I was told while she settled in laboriously at the head of the table, a few feet to my left.

"Don't mind my language. It's been a long morning and the diet's already making me crazy. I should have gotten a lap-band like Chris Christie while I still could. But what can you do? You look like a healthy specimen. What's your secret?"

"We can probably agree it wasn't carrots."

"Hah! That's a good one. They told me you had a sense of humor. I like that in an expert, shows he doesn't take himself too seriously. Juries don't like being lectured to by someone in love with their résumé. Yours is very impressive, by the way. But I'm forgetting my manners. You'll want to meet everyone."

She went around the table, introducing half a dozen assistants whose names I couldn't possibly keep straight or jot down quickly enough with my keyboard. It didn't matter, because O'Malley continued to do all the talking.

"You must have a lot of questions for us," she said immediately after. Her tone had changed from the jollity of moments ago, and was now all business.

"A place to start is what I'm supposed to testify about."

"Post-traumatic stress disorder. The defense claims Lazarus was suffering from Battered Woman Syndrome when she murdered her spouse. I understood from Doctor Stephens—a shame about the hit-and-run, by the way—that the syndrome isn't considered valid by your ilk."

She was right. Despite its considerable traction in the media, Battered Woman Syndrome, or BWS, was considered scientifically suspect by most reputable practitioners. First proposed in the 1970s, its signs and symptoms were based on the observations of a single clinician, Dr. Lenore Walker, and it had never been shown to meet the rigorous criteria for a recognized psychiatric disorder. Worse, because it relied primarily on the self-report of an obviously interested party, BWS was all too easy to fake.

"That's true," I said. "There's no professional consensus on a BWS diagnosis or even any empirical evidence that the syndrome actually exists. That's not to say battered women can't be traumatized—and sometimes severely so—just that there are better ways of looking at the problem. PTSD is one of them, along with other, more generalized anxiety disorders."

"And you're an expert on the subject?"

"I did a year-long fellowship on PTSD after my residency, and I've since treated a lot of veterans suffering from combat stress. It's maybe twenty percent of my clinical practice at the moment."

"Good. Practical experience is good. Current practical experience is even better."

"OK. But perhaps you could explain to this layman how PTSD—or BWS as the defense claims—would excuse Lazarus's actions. I know the theory's often raised as a defense to criminal charges, but on what legal basis?"

O'Malley appeared to think before replying. "It quickly gets complicated, but the short answer is that PTSD is relevant to two defense theories. One, that Lazarus acted in self-defense because she reasonably believed killing her husband was necessary to prevent imminent harm to herself or someone else. Two, that she acted with diminished capacity."

"An insanity defense?"

"Yes. It's a stretch, unless you tell us that her condition rendered her incapable of appreciating the criminality of her conduct. The first theory is more plausible, if the defense can get past the imminence standard. Lazarus wasn't living with her husband at the time, so what made her believe she was in danger when she went to his home to kill him? That's not your issue—it's up to the jury to decide what Lazarus subjectively believed—but the defense will try to push you in the direction of saying fear of imminent death would be a natural consequence of her illness. You'll have your work cut out for you on cross-examination. Lazarus's lead lawyer is a sharp little cookie—an alum of this office, as a matter of fact—and she'll have you swearing on a stack of Bibles that Lazarus is innocent if you're not careful."

I was so caught up in thinking about the intellectual challenges of the case that I failed to register the subtle shift in her presentation—from studied neutrality to prosecutorial one-sidedness—or even to ask the name of the defense lawyer in question.

"Will I have access to Ms. Lazarus?" I asked.

"As much as her lawyers will allow."

"And to all of the material Dr. Stephens collected?" If Brad Stephens had done his homework, a virtual certainty in my book, he would also have sought corroborating evidence from numerous sources in addition to Lazarus—her family, colleagues, and friends, along with police reports and other pertinent data—before forming an opinion. I'd never be able to replicate all his spadework in time, so I'd have to rely heavily on the fruits of his investigation.

"Michelle here was assisting him. She'll make sure all of the case files are sent to you."

"And his final report?"

"It's here, still in an unopened envelope." O'Malley pushed it across the table to me.

"And as of today you really don't know how he came out?" I asked, taking up the envelope and running my fingers over it. The flap was sealed tight with several layers of plastic tape.

O'Malley said, "One thing you'll learn about me, Doctor, is that I don't pull any punches. I've said it publicly and I'll say it again: I view my job as seeking justice, not getting convictions. Yes, I'd like to know where this prosecution is headed, but we'll wait to hear from you. Obviously, only after you've had a chance to review everything and are comfortable offering your own opinion. In the meantime, I've instructed everyone concerned to give you all the information you need."

It was hard not to be affected by her apparent sincerity. "I'll do my best to get up to speed quickly. How do we stay in touch, you and I?"

Just then, I heard the door to the room open and someone slip in.

"That's another reason I asked you to come here today," O'Malley said. "I'm afraid it won't be me. The newspapers haven't gotten ahold of it yet, but it seems I'm five months pregnant after years of failed attempts. My doctor is worried about gestational diabetes and pre-eclampsia, so he's ordered me off my feet for the next several months. It couldn't come at a worse time, but you can imagine the political heat I'd be taking if I ignored his advice and miscarried. Not to mention the fact that my husband and I would really like to have this baby. Instead, you'll be working with one of my most trusted deputies. If I'm not mistaken, you two already know each other."

The anonymous newcomer had come up to stand behind my chair. I swiveled in my seat and tilted my head up quizzically.

"Hello, *Dottore*," Tony Di Marco said. "*Come stai?*"

SEVEN

Assistant State's Attorney Tony Di Marco fell into the rapidly expanding class of people I had never laid eyes on, though Hallie had given me a snapshot during our first case. Back then, she'd called him a "charming pirate." Later, when she wanted to tease me, she said that except for the coloring—Di Marco's hair and eyes were as black as an oil spill—we could be cousins. I hoped the similarities ended there. If I respected Di Marco at all, it was only because he was good at what he did and never pretended to be anything but a rank opportunist. Defense lawyers hated him, and not just because he won over juries like most people win over their mothers. Though no one had ever been able to prove it, Di Marco was said to be as good at making exculpatory evidence "disappear" as Harry Houdini.

After O'Malley and her other lieutenants departed, I was left alone in the conference room with Di Marco and Michelle Rogers, who I now understood would be the only two assistants trying the case. I was only mildly surprised. If I knew Di Marco, his main objective would be grabbing as many headlines for himself as he could.

"Pretty lean staffing," I observed. "Are you sure your ego can handle it?"

Di Marco answered in his usual insolent drawl. "I could do it without any help if I had to. With the confession and everything else we have on Lazarus, trial shouldn't last more than a week. But my last three panels have been eighty percent women, so I need Michelle here to show our sympathy for the ladies."

I was sure Michelle appreciated being treated like a token.

"Unless they happen to be ladies who strike back at their abusers," I said.

Michelle, still sitting beside me, suppressed a snicker.

Di Marco laughed. "Don't tell me you're on Lazarus's side."

"It seems pretty clear she was a victim too."

"Don't believe everything you hear in the media. I've been all over her medical records. Lazarus went to the emergency room once the entire time she and Westlake were married, and then only for a broken wrist she said she got from falling down the basement stairs."

"What about the bruises and black eyes I read about in the papers?"

"Without doctor visits or pictures, it's just somebody's say-so. And the only ones saying are Lazarus's friends, who'd like nothing better than to get her off."

"The 911 calls?"

"We only found two records, both more than ten years old. Lazarus refused to swear out a complaint when the cops talked to her. Said she was sorry she had bothered them."

"That's not inconsistent with domestic abuse. Women in that position are often afraid of taking their husbands to court."

Di Marco shrugged this off. "That's what all you bleeding hearts say. We're not talking about some low-class broad living in a shack. Lazarus was an educated woman with money in the bank. She could have left him anytime. And let's not forget about what she did to him. As far as I'm concerned, it's a shame the death penalty no longer exists in this state."

"So you think she's making the abuse part up?"

"That's what you're supposed to find out, isn't it? I'm just saying it's mighty suspicious that she didn't breathe a word about it until her defense lawyers came up with the idea."

"During her confession you mean?"

"Exactly."

"Maybe she didn't understand her rights. Or was talked into it." I was referring to the first time Di Marco and I had squared off, in a case where the police had coaxed a murder confession out of a developmentally disabled teenager. With the right kind of psychological pressure, practically anyone could be coerced into admitting what the authorities wanted them to.

"I knew you would bring that up," Di Marco said. "But this confession won't give you any qualms. The Chicago PD played it totally by the book. They didn't use any strong-arm tactics because they didn't have to. Lazarus started spilling her guts practically the minute they sat her down in the interview room. If anything, she was anxious to get it off her chest. It's all there on the videotape, which you're welcome to listen to if my word isn't good enough for you. I guarantee the only questions you'll hear are 'What happened next?' and 'Please go on, ma'am.'"

"So what did she say about the murder, if I'm permitted to know?"

"Not much. Just that she thinks she and Westlake were arguing and she lost her temper."

"That's it?"

"And that she got so angry she picked up a fireplace poker and swung it at him. There wasn't a huge amount to go on, but the forensics guys were able to corroborate her story from fingerprint, blood, and DNA samples taken from the poker. The skull fracture would have been enough to kill him instantly."

I was taken by surprise. "I thought he died when she, uh . . ."

"Nipped him in the bud? Uh-uh."

"What time was this?"

"Not clear. By the time they found the corpse in the quad the next day, it had been outside in fifty-degree temperatures all night. Rigor was still present but could have been slowed by the cold. The ME wasn't able to say anything more definite than sometime in the previous twelve hours, putting the murder before midnight."

"And the mutilation occurred right afterward?"

"Based on the amount of blood around the professor's fireplace, it looks that way."

"Did she say why she did it?"

"That's the other part of her story that isn't too coherent. Says she doesn't know—had some kind of blackout and can't remember. But she was clear-headed enough to haul the professor's body over to the university quad where they found it the next morning."

"That's another thing that doesn't make sense. Why didn't she just leave the body where it was?"

"She doesn't have an explanation for that, either. My take is that she was trying to draw attention away from the domestic angle, make it seem like someone else had it in for her husband. Which, as you might remember, is what a lot of people originally supposed."

"Maybe. But lugging a dead body halfway across Hyde Park doesn't seem very consistent with going unnoticed."

Di Marco dismissed this. "I've seen killers do stranger things. A lot of them want to be caught. It's a twisted desire they have, to get credit for their crimes. And don't forget there were scores of people running around that night with dollies and carts hauling things over to the scavenger hunt. Lazarus must have calculated that if anyone did see her, they'd think she was one of the contestants."

"How big a woman is Lazarus?"

"I know what you're thinking, and it doesn't get her off either. Average height for a woman, say five six, and on the slender side. But Westlake wasn't a big guy—about the same size as you and me. She says she wrapped the body in a blanket and put it in a wheelbarrow she borrowed from Westlake's garage. I have a physiologist who will testify that it wouldn't have been that hard for a smaller woman, not to mention someone as pumped up with adrenaline as Lazarus must have been. And don't forget we have witnesses, a group of students who saw her pushing something in a cart across campus."

"And they got a clear view of her face?"

"Enough to positively identify her in a physical lineup. There's also the knife she used to perform the surgery."

"I thought it had gone missing."

"It had, until she led us straight to it, in a dumpster at a construction site west of campus where no one would have found it in a million years. Her prints were all over that, too."

"Anything else?"

"The clothes she was wearing. The boys found them stuffed down the trash chute in her apartment building, covered in Westlake's blood. No, *Dottore*, if you're trying to make the case that Lazarus is innocent, you're barking up the wrong tree. She carved up her man all right, as sure as you and I are sitting here."

When I finally made it back to the lobby, it was snowing again. I figured finding a cab would be as miraculous as regaining my eyesight, so I turned around and rode the escalator at the lobby's rear down to the pedway, a tangled network of tunnels, concourses, and overhead bridges connecting buildings throughout the Loop. I'd discovered the pedway a while back while trying to exit the Daley Center, and quickly caught on to its advantages. Others might find its subterranean passages disorienting, but I was no stranger to blind travel, and I could walk for blocks without having to worry about a single motor vehicle. Best of all, in winter the pedway was always warm, dry, and free of ice.

I tapped down a wide, echoing corridor until it met up with the walkway connecting City Hall to the old Marshall Field's building. A right turn there took me east and through several sets of doors before depositing me at one of the entrances to the Red Line. I swiped my "People with Disabilities Ride Free" card at the turnstile and descended a flight of steps. Based on the volume of sighs and shuffling feet, there appeared to be a large crowd gathered on the platform. I found an open spot near a pillar and listened while the overhead loudspeaker barked a series of service announcements. Predictably, the snowstorm was causing extensive delays. I had a good twenty minutes to wait before the arrival of the next northbound train—assuming it wasn't already filled to capacity—which gave me plenty of time to think.

Could it get any worse? In the space of three days, I'd lost a sympathetic boss, had my office ransacked, and been thrust into what was shaping up to be a nasty custody battle. If that wasn't sufficiently Job-like, I was now being corralled into a partnership with someone who wouldn't hesitate to screw me if it meant the difference between winning and losing a case.

If he even needed that much motivation.

Beyond that, I was trying to sort through everything I'd just heard.

Westlake's butchering had occurred after he was no longer in a position to threaten his wife. Why? And why had Lazarus risked exposure by transferring the body to a public place where it was sure to be found the next morning and cause a huge commotion? And then there was the fact of the castration itself. Was it simply the enraged act of a disturbed personality? Or was it supposed to symbolize something?

Like all psychiatrists over a certain age, I'd been well-schooled in various theories about the penis. To Sigmund Freud, it wasn't simply a pleasurable piece of anatomy but the fundamental cause of all neuroses. Women wanted a penis and couldn't have one. Men lived in constant fear of losing theirs. Freud also posited that in dreams, elongated objects—such as sticks, poles, and umbrellas—and most weapons were a stand-in for the male organ. Coming a little later, Carl Jung disagreed, finding Freud's focus on the penis too narrow to explain most human behavior. Jung also thought Freud's dream theories were too complicated, famously quipping that the penis itself was a phallic symbol.

Whatever belief you subscribed to, it was hard not to read significance into Westlake's castration. In a world where men still dominated virtually every sphere of public life—from politics to business, academia, and just about every profession—the penis stood as a potent reminder of male authority. Was Westlake's mutilation intended to send the message that men are more vulnerable than they think? Or was it tied to the penis's other symbolic association—as an instrument of male aggression? Westlake had reportedly demeaned, threatened, and beaten his wife. Had he also raped her? And if so, was Lazarus taking out her revenge on the very organ used to force her into submission?

The train came then, and I followed the other commuters on board, tapping skillfully across the gap between the platform and the car before finding a place to stand in the crowd.

"You're doing great," one of the passengers near me said.

Somehow, I didn't think so.

EIGHT

I got back to my office a little before noon to find my entry barred again, this time by a pile of banker's boxes. Yelena was yakking at her desk ten yards away, so I leaned my cane against the wall and went over to inquire about the cause of the latest barricade. I had to cool my heels for several minutes while she finished a telephone call, finally ringing off with an effusive "*Tseluyu!*"

"Kisses no less," I said. "Was that Boris?"

"Please," Yelena said.

I was right. They were back to bickering again.

"Is there some significance to the latest Mt. Everest outside my door? I'd like to be able to reclaim my office one of these days."

"The files, you mean?"

"Is that what they are? I thought I'd stumbled across your Christmas present to me. Where'd they come from, if I may be so bold to ask?"

"A person from the State's Attorney's office. Her name is on the receipt." I surmised this was Michelle Rogers and made a mental note to thank her for acting so quickly. It was good to know I had at least one ally on the case.

"And you thought they'd be at home where they are right now?" I said.

"I wanted to bring them inside, but I sprained my back when we were in San Juan. Boris insisted on going parasailing even though I told him it would ruin my hair. And you should have seen the hotel he picked out. Practically miles from the outlet stores."

I needed her help with the boxes, so I asked how her holiday shopping was going.

"Terrible. The lines at the Water Tower were as bad as anything back in Moscow. I had to wait hours to return the scarf I bought for Boris—Hermès was too good for him after Puerto Rico—and they were all out of the cologne I wanted—" She stopped short, growing suspicious. "Why does it interest you?"

"I was just thinking . . . But you're probably not up to it." I turned and strolled casually back to my office. Yelena considered the meaning of this for a full two seconds before following me over.

"Let me help with that," she said, taking the box I had just shifted from the top of the stack.

"No, please. It's not fair with you being in such pain."

"That's why it pays to work for a doctor."

"True. And it's my professional opinion that you need time off to recover—but not until we've figured out what's in all of these, OK?"

"Slave driver," Yelena said.

After Yelena left, I stood for a moment, deciding which of a multitude of chores to tackle first. My office reeked of new carpet smell and sawdust, but a full survey of the damage would have to wait. My desktop computer was probably sitting somewhere, but it would take a while to find and even longer to get booted up. My phone would be much faster.

People were often surprised by what I could do with a phone, especially one with a flat, glass touchscreen. But a series of recent innovations had made the devices the best friend a blind person could have. The majority of apps on my phone were only a few years old, could be downloaded at little cost or for free, and did much more than give me access to the same technology as everyone else. With them I could also recognize colors, ascertain the value of paper currency, and figure out exactly where I was standing on a street—all without having to ask a single soul. About the only thing my phone couldn't do was let me see who I was talking to, though it was only a matter of time before some child genius at MIT came up with an app for that, too.

In this case, I moved my finger around the glass until Weary—my name for the factory-supplied voiceover—told me it was over the icon for my e-mail program. A double-tap got me in, and swiping with three fingers took me down the subject lines of my messages. Jonathan had wasted no time in shifting my patient load, and my in-box contained only a fraction of its usual contents. Unless it was another sign that I was on my way out the door, I wouldn't have to worry about returning to a mountain of work. In a major disappointment, there was nothing from Kay Bergen, but I reminded myself to be patient.

After that, it was time to tackle the mystery that was my redecorated office. I retrieved my cane from its hook on the door and started on a walking tour, crossing from wall to wall in a gridlike pattern so as not to miss out on anything. My old stuff was completely gone, but the floor plan was essentially the same: a desktop in front of a credenza and shelves, a sofa and chair set in the area closest to the window. The upholstery felt like it belonged in a hotel lobby, but at least I could count on Jonathan to have selected an inoffensive color. I reminded myself to compliment him on his taste the next time I ran into him. Though perhaps not, since it would inevitably raise questions about my sincerity.

In a far corner, I found the carton where my personal effects, including my collection of toys and memorabilia, had been dumped. They would all have to be sent home, another victim of my campaign to remain gainfully employed. When I eventually rediscovered my computer—beneath an L-shaped extension of the desk—it was cold, but all of the peripherals had been hooked up: a monitor I kept mostly for appearances' sake, a headset and speakers, a refreshable Braille display for when I tired of listening to synthetic speech, and a QWERTY keyboard that I used for typing, never having fully mastered the six-key Braille counterpart. I flicked the computer on and sat down to work.

Inspired perhaps by the season of giving—if not the full-day spa pass I'd surprised her with as a Christmas present—Yelena had outdone herself. All of the paper records from Brad's executor were already off to the IT department for more rapid scanning, and the digital portion, contained on a portable hard drive, was sitting in the center of my desk. In a further gesture of magnanimity, Yelena had gone down to the cafeteria to fetch me a sandwich, which I opened and devoured before inserting the drive into a USB port and putting my headset on.

I soon discovered that my deceased colleague had indeed been thorough. Altogether, the materials he had gathered represented days of listening material, even with my screen reader turned to its fastest setting. Of course, I could safely assume that any pertinent facts were summarized in Brad's report. But I had already decided to save the report for last. For one thing, it would lend credibility to my testimony. For another, I was worried about confirmation bias, the tendency of people to focus on facts that support their preexisting hypotheses. Given the high esteem in which I held Brad, I wanted my opinion to be as free as possible—if only initially—of his influence. For that reason, I had asked Yelena to find a locked drawer somewhere where the report could rest securely until I was ready for it.

By this time it was late afternoon, and the fatigue from my sleepless night was setting in. I figured I was in no shape to tackle anything technical, so I scrolled down the list of files, looking for something undemanding and eventually coming upon a memorandum to Brad from Lazarus's divorce lawyer. This piqued my interest, so I clicked to open it and began listening:

MEMORANDUM

TO: *Dr. Bradley Stephens*
FROM: *Andrea Poalicerci*
RE: *Lazarus/Westlake*

In connection with your retention as an expert witness for the State of Illinois, you have asked me to respond to certain questions relating to the separation and divorce proceedings between my client, Rachel Lazarus, and her spouse, Gunther Westlake. I understand that any confidential information I provide to you could become the basis of the opinion you render at Ms. Lazarus's trial, and therefore constitute a waiver of the attorney-client privilege. I wish to be on record that I have counseled Ms. Lazarus against any such waiver. Ms. Lazarus has nonetheless instructed me to cooperate with you, and I am bound to honor her wishes.

Ms. Lazarus first visited my office in July of last year. At the time, she had just moved from the home she shared with Mr. Westlake at 5510 South Woodlawn and was hoping to obtain a legal separation. Unfortunately, as I explained to her, orders of separation may only be granted in Illinois at the request of a spouse who has not yet moved out of the marital residence. Ordinarily, such orders are used to shield one spouse's assets from the other's creditors, since debts incurred after legal separation cannot become the basis for seizure. I asked Ms. Lazarus whether she had any concerns in this regard and she replied no. Apart from her clothing, jewelry, and a few other personal items, all of her property was held in joint tenancy with her husband, and she had no other assets of her own.

Ms. Lazarus also inquired about divorce, stating that she wished to proceed on a "no fault" basis. I explained to her that "irreconcilable differences" is only a ground for divorce in Illinois after a two-year waiting period. This requirement can be waived, but only if both parties agree in writing. This information appeared to upset Ms. Lazarus greatly, as she was certain her husband would not agree to any such waiver. We discussed other grounds for divorce in Illinois, including mental and physical cruelty, but Ms. Lazarus was adamant that she wanted a "no fault" decree.

On August 10, 2012, I filed a Petition for Dissolution of Marriage coupled with a request for a preliminary injunction preventing Mr. Westlake from attempting to remove, abscond with, or otherwise deprive Ms. Lazarus of assets belonging to the couple jointly. The petition did not address custody of the couple's daughter, Olivia, since she was over the age of eighteen and could choose where to live for herself.

Mr. Westlake retaliated almost immediately with verbal threats to my client, over the telephone, in writing, and on the street adjacent to the apartment building at 5475 South Kimbark where Ms. Lazarus was living. Over the course of the next several weeks, these threats escalated to the point where I felt it necessary to seek an emergency Order of Protection. Such orders are, unfortunately, quite common in Illinois, and may be granted on an interim basis until a full evidentiary hearing can be held.

After that, Mr. Westlake appeared to have come to his senses, and voluntarily agreed not to come into contact with Ms. Lazarus until the divorce was finalized. As a result, the matter did not proceed to hearing and the fact of domestic violence in the Westlake home was never established in court.

Last, you asked me what I anticipated happening to the couple's marital property now that Mr. Westlake is dead and the divorce action has become moot. It is interesting that you should ask, since Ms. Lazarus also questioned me about estate matters. As I advised her, the answer depends on whether or not Mr. Westlake left a will. If he died intestate, whatever assets he owned in joint tenancy with Ms. Lazarus would go directly to her, and any property in his estate solely owned by him would be divided evenly between Ms. Lazarus and Olivia. If, however, he prepared a will leaving the latter to someone else, Ms. Lazarus would still be entitled to renounce the will and receive her "widow's share"—or one-third. You would have to ask her criminal counsel how these outcomes might be affected by her conviction.

A.P.

Before I could begin to ponder what all this meant, my phone began ringing. When I heard the CID announce Hallie's name, my heart leapt. I reached out for the receiver, only to find that the phone was now a good foot to the right of where I usually kept it. While I hurried to answer, I entertained a brief fantasy that she had relented and was calling because she wanted to set up a date.

"*You!*" she snapped when I'd finally wrestled the receiver from its hook.

"Me?" I repeated foolishly.

"Yes, you!"

"What is it? Did I do something wrong?" I asked, as though that wasn't already apparent.

"You. Lied. To. Me." She sounded worked up enough to blow the lid off a manhole.

I assumed she was referring to my belated confession and wondered why it was coming up again. "I thought we already talked about that. I wasn't lying about Jack—just omitting certain information. OK, important information. I know I should have been honest with you a whole lot sooner, but—"

"That's not why I'm calling."

"All right," I said in genuine confusion. "But maybe you could tell me what you are angry about?"

"You know."

"No, I don't and I won't know unless you tell me."

"Today. At the County Building."

"OK," I said slowly, scrambling to remember what had passed between us in the lobby that morning. Apparently, I'd done something terribly ungallant, but I couldn't begin to guess what it was. "I don't understand. All I did was ask about your new case."

"Exactly," she said, as though I had just pleaded guilty to grand larceny. "What did you tell him?" she demanded.

"Tell who?"

"Tony Di Marco. It just came over the news that you're helping him with the Lazarus trial."

So my new assignment had already penetrated the airwaves. "Is that what's bothering you—me working for the Prince of Darkness? Hey, I'm not happy about it, either. But I didn't have a choice—I was forced into it. Anyway, what does that have to do with me lying to you?"

She gave a snort of impatience. "You must think I'm stupid. Well, don't expect me to pull any punches just because it's you sitting in the witness box. When I get through with your cross-examination, you'll be lucky to be hired by some two-bit divorce hack in Kane County. I can't believe I ever—"

Cross-examination?

"Wait a minute," I interrupted her. "Are you saying—?"

"Bastard," she said.

And hung up on me.

NINE

Driving with Candace to the party Saturday night, I couldn't help thinking once again about Job, along with the Christian martyrs who were a staple of my Catholic-school education. Their stories were always gruesome—the true believers who were shot through with arrows, crucified upside down, torn apart by wild beasts, or turned into human barbecues—but they usually had an upside, meant to impress on us the rewards of faith. Saint Lucy was a good example. According to legend, she had resisted marriage to a pagan by giving all her wealth to the poor, so enraging the local gentry that they ordered her eyes gouged out. For her pains, Lucy received eternal grace and a lifetime achievement award as the patron saint of the blind.

I was no saint, but I was having trouble seeing a silver lining in the Lazarus case.

I didn't want to be Rachel Lazarus's inquisitor, would have gladly traded the job for something more personally and financially rewarding—like scrubbing toilets or picking trash off the streets—but that didn't matter. Nor did it matter that I had done nothing to sucker Hallie into talking about the case. Before our chance run-in at the County Building, I had every reason to believe I'd be working for Linda O'Malley. Becoming Di Marco's spear-thrower was literally the farthest thing from my mind. About the only thing I could be blamed for was not putting two and two together sooner, which only would have prevented a nasty surprise.

To make things worse, I couldn't even exonerate myself.

After Hallie had unceremoniously ended our conversation, I was on the verge of ringing her back to proclaim my innocence when it hit me what being on opposite sides of the Lazarus case really meant:

no contact. As in none, zip, *niente*. For the duration of the proceedings, including trial, sentencing, and the exhaustion of any appeals, we couldn't say a word about the case to each other outside of official channels. Even a casual meeting might be misconstrued. Whatever you might have called us before—friends, colleagues, acquaintances—was over. We couldn't have been thrust any farther apart if our last names were Hatfield and McCoy.

Of course, I reminded myself, our relationship had always been a long shot. Unless they had a masochistic streak, intelligent, accomplished women tended to shy away from admitted adulterers, even (if not especially) those claiming to be reformed. Throw in a dead child I hadn't told her about for the better part of a year, and it was no wonder she'd doubted me. If there were a Yelp rating for fudging the truth, I would have earned a full five stars. And now, if I hadn't already proved my suspect qualifications as a boyfriend, she had every reason to think I'd lied to her once more.

Candace slowed for a red light on Lake Shore Drive and said, "Hello? You're very far away tonight."

Another reason to kick myself. Whatever my current woes, it was unfair to take them out on my companion, who was going out of her way to be pleasant. I turned embarrassedly in my seat to face her. "I apologize. I was just admiring the scenery."

"Yes, it is lovely this time of year in Antarctica. You should see the Lake. It looks like it's frozen solid all the way to Michigan. It won't be long before the polar bears start moving in."

"At least they'll have somewhere to go while their homes are being turned into the tropics," I said. "Really, I was being a jerk. It won't happen again."

"I'm glad. I was beginning to think it was the clothes I picked out."

"I'm sure you're a feast for all the senses." I paused before adding, "Including the one that took a hike on me." After my earlier rude silence, I figured it was only fair to open up to her a bit. "You're probably wondering about my, um . . . problem."

"Guilty as charged. Though you mustn't like talking about it."

"It depends on who I'm with. You wouldn't believe the number of strangers who think it's perfectly OK to pepper me with questions—everything from how I tie my shoes to how I know when to go to sleep at night."

"Why don't you just tell them to bugger off?"

"I do when I'm in the wrong mood."

"May I ask how it happened?"

"It's an inherited thing. I woke up one morning a few years back with a blurred area in the middle of one eye. A little later, the same thing happened in the other. In both cases, it was like a magician waving a wand. Poof. Now you see it, now you don't."

"Just like that?" Candace said in dismay.

"More or less. I had some down time in between, enough to drink myself into a stupor and ponder the meaning of life."

"And what conclusions did you reach?"

"Luck of the draw is underrated."

That drew a laugh. "Yes it is. All right, I'll stop being such a Nosy Parker, except for one last thing. Is there anything special I need to do tonight?

"Just keep reminding me of who I'm talking to. And unless you want to see a grown man cry, don't leave me standing alone in the middle of the room."

"Never fear. I shall cling to you like Saran wrap."

The party was in Kenwood, a neighborhood some five miles south of the Loop. Settled in the 1850s, it took its name from the Scottish birthplace of one of Chicago's first robber barons, who set up housekeeping there to avoid the filth and congestion of the rapidly growing city. More recently, it was famous for being the non–White House home of the Obamas, whose block was cordoned off by concrete barriers and a twenty-four-hour security checkpoint, additions that probably went unappreciated by the neighbors. Most of the lots in the area were oversized and held mansions of baronial splendor, which Candace described to me as we picked our way, arm-in-arm, across the ice and snow from our parking space.

"Neuschwanstein," Candace said, pointing out one of them. "And the one next to it could be Xanadu."

"Perfect," I said. "Just keep us away from mad kings and Orson Welles impersonators."

"And lions and tigers and bears. This neighborhood certainly does have an Oz-like quality to it. It's hard to believe we're this close to Woodlawn."

Woodlawn, and its neighbor, Garfield Park, were some of the poorest urban enclaves in the country. I wondered how the people who lived there felt about the rich man's Disneyland located practically on their doorstep.

"Here we are," Candace said. "At the end of the yellow brick road."

The house she escorted me to was apparently more modest than some, a three-story Richardsonian Romanesque set back from the street on a full acre. We went up a walkway covered in yet more salt and rang the bell. From the light and noise spilling out from the windows, it appeared the party was already in full swing.

"I should warn you about our host," Candace said while we waited for someone to answer. "Dean Oliver Armstrong, usually referred to around campus by the initials DOA. We'll want to avoid getting stuck with him. Simply deadly. And then there's Professor Ziskin, the retired head of the Italian Department. Poor old dear is nearly deaf and refuses to wear a hearing aid."

Meaning we'd make a fine pair. I suddenly had doubts about what I was getting into, walking into a houseful of tedious academics. As it turned out, I needn't have worried about the party being dull.

Candace proved to be a quick study in blind etiquette, expertly steering me across the spacious front rooms of the Victorian and warning me when we came across hazards in the form of sunken steps, carpet edges, and pedestals bearing hothouse plants, of which there appeared to be quite a few. "My God, it's practically *The Little Shop of Horrors* in here," she whispered in my ear after we'd dropped off our coats. "Check this one out." She stopped to guide my hand to a monster that felt like it had been raised on raw steak. "The last thing I would have predicted about our esteemed dean is having a green thumb." She went on to describe the other rich appointments, which included intricately carved moldings, antique tapestries, and enough pre-Raphaelite paintings to fill a gallery at the British Museum.

I asked how a university administrator could afford all this.

"Dead On Arrival? I think it's his wife's money. I heard she's related to the McCormicks. I should introduce you."

Candace took me over to meet our hosts, who were standing aside a buffet table sending off odors of smoked fish and various items *en croute*. "Pleasure to, ah, make your, ah, acquaintance," Dean Armstrong said, offering a small, soft hand. I imagined him as a wizened little figure with owlish features, which Candace later told me wasn't too far off. Before anyone else could get in a word, he launched into a disquisition on the capital fund, punctuated by further "ahs," "uhs," and drawn-out pauses that fully explained his reputation. Fortunately, his wife had better social skills. "Ollie, I'm sure our guests have better things to talk about," she interrupted, just as he was gearing up to tell us about new improvements to the library. "You two must be hungry. Let me offer you something to eat."

After Candace and I had stuffed ourselves to the gills, we proceeded to make the rounds, circulating among groups engaged in lively debate about such topics as Malthusian economics, the Luo people of Kenya, British attitudes toward slavery in the seventeenth century, literary appropriations of the Faust myth, primate osteology, chaos theory, and the filmography of Miyazaki—to name just a few. With my folding cane tucked into my back trouser pocket, people either didn't notice I was blind or pretended not to, a degree of social anonymity I rarely got to enjoy. By my third drink, I was comfortably ensconced on one of the overstuffed sofas with my arm around Candace's shoulder, listening to half a dozen people whose names and departments I could barely keep straight holding forth on socio-evolutionary theory.

"But Bruce, don't you think it's a stretch to say that people's savage instincts actually contribute to a well-functioning society?"

"Erik, I'm saying that current thinking supports what Nietzsche first proposed—that the urge to punish, which originated in spite, was later converted into a mechanism for achieving fairness through the creation of rules and legal systems to enforce them. Without spite, we'd still be stealing each other's livestock and raping each other's wives."

"And let's not forget about the paradigms suggested by game theory," said a third one, producing a spate of groans.

"Hear, hear, people," Erik crowed. "Can there be one faculty party in which game theory does *not* enter into the discussion?"

"At this university? You're dreaming," a fourth quipped. "But to continue on the subject of Nietzsche . . ."

Eventually, one of them asked me what I thought. Drawn into the conversation for the first time, I chose my words carefully. "I don't know about spite making right, but there have been some interesting studies using college students as subjects—"

"A spiteful little lot if ever there was one," interjected a professor whose high, querulous voice I'd come to associate with Charles, an economist.

"Oh, Charles let it go," said the woman seated next to Candace, introduced to me earlier as Amanda. "We were all parodied in the spring musical. Go on," she urged me politely.

"Well, I was going to say that the research seems to show a connection between negative emotions and certain fields of study. Economics, for instance, is strongly correlated with lowered generosity and feelings of persecution."

This met with a round of guffaws, except from Charles, who said petulantly, "Go ahead and laugh. I hardly think I deserve being portrayed as only one step removed from Hitler. There's a reason behind the strict grading curve, after all."

I quickly pointed out that I was only joking. "But in all seriousness, the work I'm familiar with tends to prove that men are more spiteful than women—"

"What a surprise," Amanda said.

"—and that circumstances can provoke spiteful outbursts in otherwise agreeable people. Bitter divorce, for example, which prompts some spouses to hide or even dispose of assets just to keep the other from getting their fair share."

The conversation then turned to gossip about faculty split-ups and eventually—as I'd hoped—to the Westlake-Lazarus affair. My ears pricked up at the first mention:

"And let's not forget about that absolutely horrid incident at Scav in the spring. Completely overshadowed the Nobel Prize nominations."

"Humph," Amanda said. "I shouldn't speak ill of the dead, but if Rachel killed him out of spite, he deserved it. The man was a perfect little pig—to Rachel and everyone else who had the misfortune to come in contact with him. Including that poor girl, Olivia."

"The daughter?"

"Yes, such a sad, awkward thing. In one of my gender-studies classes last spring. Absolutely terrified of speaking in class. When he was killed, I gave her an extension on turning in her final paper until the trial was over. I can't imagine the ordeal she's been through."

"So you believe he abused her, too?" someone else asked with obvious interest.

Charles sniffed. "Why does everyone assume the man was a wife beater? Always seemed the perfect gentleman to me. It's unfair to libel a chap solely because of his honestly offered opinions."

"Honestly offered opinions," Amanda scoffed. "The only thing that interested Gunther was getting himself on Fox News. I doubt he truly believed in anything he said. It was only the notoriety—and the money it brought in—that he cared about. And yes, I think he abused them both."

"Didn't know Westlake all that well, but his speaking engagements were rumored to be bringing in seven figures annually," Bruce offered, as though bothered by the distasteful direction in which the conversation was headed.

"If you ask my opinion," Erik said, drowning him out, "Charles is right. There wasn't any abuse. It's just a fiction dreamed up by the attorneys."

"Why do you say that?" Amanda demanded.

"Just that I saw the two of them quite a bit socially because of my position as chair of the department. Rachel always struck me as a highly intelligent woman. You know she was getting her PhD just before they were married? It makes no sense that she would have stayed with Gunther all those years if she was truly being mistreated."

Amanda snorted. "That's the theory they trot out in all these cases—she couldn't have been abused because otherwise she would have left him. Whereas all the studies show that it's far more complicated than that. Battered women who don't leave their abusers often love their spouses and harbor the hope—however unrealistic—that they can become normal husbands and fathers. That's why they stay."

"Careful now, Amanda," another person laughed. "Someone might begin to think you're a feminist. Are you sure one of your protégés in the Women's Alliance didn't perform the evil deed?"

"Gunther wouldn't have been worth the effort. Though I did have to remind the young ladies not to make a show of dancing on his grave. Whatever you thought of him, no one deserves ending up like something out of an Orwellian farce."

Charles piped in then with his two cents: "I'm surprised the police didn't think it was one of his students. I heard he was very hard on his PhD candidates."

"Did Westlake even have any? I'd be shocked that someone would voluntarily choose to study under the man," Amanda said. "Erik, what do you know about that?"

"Well, there were only two in the last ten years. The first one had a nervous breakdown last winter and transferred to USC. The second is still here, though I believe there was some friction. Fellow's due to defend his dissertation next quarter. I'm one of the reviewers. Quite a nice piece of work, by the way. Which reminds me, has anyone here heard about the commencement schedule . . ."

Which unfortunately put an end to the subject.

Candace leaned over and whispered in my ear, "I need to go off to use the washroom. Is it OK if I leave you alone for a few minutes? I'll get us fresh drinks on the way back."

I told her I'd be fine.

Moments later, the space she left was taken by someone who sat down clumsily, nearly upsetting the drink I was balancing on my knee. From the way the seat cushions deflated, I gathered the newcomer was large.

"Peter Crow, mind your manners," Amanda said from the other side of him. "That seat's taken and you almost crushed me on the way down."

"Who's sitting here?" he said, slurring his words.

"Candace McIntyre. She just went off for a moment. Isn't that right, Mark?"

Before I could reply, the man said, "Well, I'm staying until she's back. Need some rest." He pushed himself even farther into the sofa, practically forcing me onto the armrest with his bulk.

I thought that was rude but didn't want to seem impolite myself, so I gave him my name.

He seemed not to notice, exhaling loudly as though from the exertion of getting himself settled.

I tried again, saying my name a little louder this time.

Still nothing but labored breathing.

"Peter, what's wrong with you?" Amanda asked. "Mark is trying to introduce himself."

"Who?" Peter asked dully.

His behavior was starting to worry me.

"Are you feeling all right?" I asked, nodding meaningfully in Amanda's direction and putting my drink down. I thought to take his pulse and felt for his hand, which I judged to be somewhere to the left of my knee. I was right about him being huge. The thigh I encountered on my first pass felt like a tree trunk. His hand was equally plus-size, and nearly as big as a Ping-Pong paddle. But muscular, not fat, and oddly shaped on the metacarpal side.

That was as far as I got when Peter exited his stupor. "Wha . . . what are you doing?" he said, tearing the hand away as if in panic.

I put on my bedside manner. "It's OK. I'm a doctor. I thought you were acting a little funny so I—"

"Funny, huh? Yeah, I'm hysterical, all right. But I don't need any doctors."

"Are you sure? Your skin felt a little clammy to me."

"Maybe had a few too many," he admitted.

"Are you light-headed?" I asked. "Maybe you should have some water."

Amanda, meanwhile, had risen to her feet. "I can get him some."

"No, s'all right. I can do it myself," Peter said, his speech growing sloppier by the minute. He made motions to push himself up.

I shook my head at Amanda. In the shape he was in, I didn't think our friend could walk two steps.

"Peter, dear," Amanda said, "Why don't you just stay put while I fetch you a glass. It will only take a minute. Stay here and talk to Mark. He's very nice and won't bite."

"Noooooooo, I don't like doctors," Peter said, attempting to rise once more.

Others around us had now caught on to the drama taking place and ceased talking.

Peter tried once more to get up. Halfway to his feet, he spun on his heel, groaning.

And without further ceremony, vomited all over me.

"Will you ever forgive me?" Candace said as we were pulling into her garage.

"I might if you don't invite me to any more parties."

I took a sniff of the air, which reeked of my slacks, shirt and sport coat, now residing in a plastic bag on Candace's backseat. I couldn't fault our hosts for their manners. After I'd been lifted from the sofa, still dripping bits and pieces of vodka-scented smorgasbord, the dean's wife had rushed me to an upstairs room, offering everything from a steam bath to free dry-cleaning. Except for a quick scrub at the sink, a dash of her husband's cologne, and a necessary loan of clothing, I'd declined all her offers, desperate to get out of there as quickly as possible. I was now squeezed into a pair of the dean's flannel trousers, along with a brand-new University of Chicago tee shirt.

"I take full blame. You did ask me not to leave you alone."

"Being turned into an airsickness bag wasn't one of the hazards I had in mind. Who was that asshole, anyway?"

"Peter Crow? He heads up the Student Counseling Center."

"I hope he's not counseling anyone about substance abuse."

"That's what's so odd. I thought he didn't drink. Grew up on a reservation somewhere and hates what alcohol has done to his people. If I had to guess, it was a momentary lapse."

Which would explain why he'd gotten so sick. "Native American?"

"Mmm-hmm. And looks the movie part, too. All dark eyes and craggy features. Handsome if you like them big."

"Never been my thing," I said, testing the waters.

"Nor mine," Candace replied.

"I suppose I smell like I just crawled out of a sewer."

"Actually, I was just going to compliment you—or rather the dean—on the cologne. Who would have guessed such a gnomish man would have such provocative taste. I wouldn't mind if a little of it rubbed off on me."

"His taste or the cologne?"

"I love a man who plays hard to get."

"There are none 'so firm that cannot be seduced.'"

"And one who can quote Shakespeare at will. Though perhaps I should mind being compared to corruption in the Roman Senate."

"I don't know about that. I'm very susceptible to corrupting influences."

Candace laughed. "Shall we go upstairs and work on it?"

"Only if you'll let me use your shower first."

TEN

The elder Dante Angelotti was furious with me. I'd mouthed off that afternoon to Father Mullaney, my sophomore theology teacher at Regis High, and my father had to leave work early to bail me out of detention. He and I were now engaged in another battle about my dismal grades, and as usual I was scrambling to mount a defense.

"*Ti sei disonorato! E mi hai fatto vergognare! Di nuovo*," he thundered at me as soon as we reached home. You've disgraced yourself. And brought shame on me. Again.

"That's all you ever think about," I shot back in English. "How it affects you. Maybe I'd work harder if you weren't always on my case."

"Your mother would weep to hear you speak that way," he said once more in Italian. He quickly crossed himself and added, "Mother Mary pray for her."

I was supposed to feel guilty. "She'd cry even harder if she knew what kind of parent she left me with."

His huge hand was on me in a flash, lashing me across the face and then whipping back for a stinging cuff to my ear. I felt tears of humiliation well up in my eyes but quickly blinked them away. I'd be damned if I let him know how much it hurt. I eyed the back door a few feet away, trying to decide just how fast I could get out of there before the beating really got underway.

"That's all you know how to do, isn't it, Dad? Slap your kid around until he's black and blue."

The rebuke slowed him down momentarily, and his raised arm dropped to his side. "Dante, why must you always be against me?" he said, using the name I despised because it was also his. "You know I want nothing but what is best for you."

"You don't give a shit about me. Not like *she* would if she were alive."

"*Caro*, how can you say such evil things?"

"Because they're true." The pain in his dark, blunt-featured face was almost enough to make me reconsider, but I went on taunting him, relishing the chance to give voice to my seething resentments. "If you loved me, you'd take my side once in a while."

"I am only trying to teach you—"

"*Vattene all'inferno.*" Go to hell.

The disrespect had its intended effect. He reared back for another blow, wild with anger now. My father was tall for an Italian, nearly six feet, and being much shorter, I was able to slip under him just as his knuckles were barreling toward my head. I twisted down and away and bolted for the door, barely making my escape as he lunged unsuccessfully for my waistband. "Fuck you!" I shouted as the screen door slapped shut behind me.

The scene abruptly switched to later that night. I was back in our tiny kitchen, holding something wet and slippery in my hand. I held it up to the flickering florescent bulb to see what it was, puzzling over the slender, triangular shape. Outside the house, a wail of sirens was drawing near. My eyes traveled down to the floor, only then seeing what I had done. With horror I registered my father's body, the dark stain spreading from his midsection onto the linoleum. "No, *papà!*" I burbled helplessly. "NO!" I sobbed again as the police broke through the door . . .

I awoke to a racing heart in a clammy tangle of sheets.

As nightmares went, it wasn't as bad as my usual, the never-ending cinematic loop of the night Jack died, his labored breathing coming in the same ragged gasps that I now tried to quell by reaching for the water on my nightstand. My fingers closed clumsily around the glass, slopping water onto my bedclothes. I gulped down what was left of the liquid while the tremors subsided, long enough for me to remember that I hadn't in fact murdered my father. Only my son.

Still shaky, I sat up and checked the time on my phone. Three a.m.

Too early to get up and face the day, especially if I wanted to be fresh and alert for my first—and only—meeting with Rachel Lazarus.

Hallie wasn't kidding when she promised to treat me like any other hostile witness, starting with a motion to keep me from meeting Lazarus at all. As she argued, the prosecution's former expert had already been granted full access to her client in interviews totaling more than twenty hours. Further interrogation would only serve to harass Lazarus, whose fragile psychological state was readily apparent from the nature of her defense. The State's new expert—namely me—couldn't claim a reason to *see* Lazarus for himself and could easily gather all the information he needed by listening to the tapes of his predecessor's sessions. If further questions were necessary, they could be posed by written interrogatory and answered under oath, which at this late date was all the prosecution's "hired gun" could reasonably ask for.

Di Marco, of course, had fought back, partially on the basis of arguments I'd supplied him: that the prosecution could not be blamed for the tragic death of Brad Stephens that necessitated the change in witnesses, and that it would be wholly irresponsible for me to render an opinion about the mental state of an individual I'd never met. After listening to both sides in a hearing that bore every resemblance to a World Wrestling Entertainment match, the judge had split the baby down the middle, denying Hallie's bid to shut me out completely, but granting me only two hours with Lazarus.

Thereafter, it had taken what seemed like another full age to get a date fixed. Hallie had made the process as painful as possible, setting up real or imaginary roadblocks at nearly every turn. In the end, she proposed that I meet Lazarus on Christmas Eve, and after getting my permission, Di Marco was all too happy to go along. Hallie probably thought she was punishing me, but the pitiful reality was I had nowhere else to be that day. My plea for a few hours with Louis in Connecticut, delivered in writing by Kay Bergen, had met with stony silence from Annie's lawyers. Josh and his family were off on their annual ski trip in Colorado. Even Candace had deserted me, flying home to Calgary for a weeklong visit with her folks.

I checked my phone again. Three thirty a.m. If I couldn't get back to sleep, I might as well go over my script for the next day.

Ever since its emergence in the late nineteenth century, psychiatry has been criticized as a discipline lacking a scientific basis. Indeed, to some critics, the very concept of mental "illness" is suspect, involving implicit moral judgments about what is "normal" and what is not. Someday, neuroscience may be able to identify a biological cause for most psychiatric ailments, but in the meantime clinicians are stuck with practice guidelines that attempt to divide the sick from the well based on not much more than theory and professional consensus.

By far the most important of these guidelines is the *Diagnostic and Statistical Manual of Mental Disorders* published by the American Psychiatric Association. Often called the Bible of the profession, it is used by practitioners, researchers, regulatory agencies, health insurers, pharmaceutical companies, and the legal system practically to the exclusion of everything else. Then in its fifth edition, the *DSM* had been subject to a barrage of criticism—I'd been known to take shots at it myself—but any psychiatric expert who didn't want to be laughed out of court had better be familiar with its requirements. In Lazarus's case, this meant structuring my inquiry around the six PTSD criteria listed in the *DSM-V*.

First, I had to find that Lazarus had been exposed—either by experiencing it herself or seeing it in person—to a traumatic event, or "stressor," consisting of death, threatened death, actual or threatened serious injury, or actual or threatened sexual violence. Then I had to find that she was persistently reexperiencing it in one of several ways, such as through recurrent, intrusive memories, nightmares, or "dissociative reactions"—the psychiatric term for flashbacks. Lazarus also had to be exhibiting avoidance behavior, alterations in cognition and mood, and changes in "arousal and reactivity," a fancy way of saying that her nervous system was on constant red alert. Finally, all of these symptoms had to have lasted for at least a month and not be the result of medication, substance abuse, or other illness.

The further gloss was that Westlake's murder was now more than six months old. For purposes of my testimony, it wouldn't be enough to decide whether Lazarus was suffering from PTSD today. I had to go back and reconstruct what her thinking may have been on the night she killed her husband. And since all of this depended on Lazarus's self-report, I had to be comfortable that she wasn't malingering—faking symptoms in order to mislead me.

It would have been a tall order even if the court had given me more than two hours with her.

Fortunately, as Hallie had been quick to point out, I was able to listen to all of Brad Stephens's recorded sessions before our meeting. And just as well—or not, depending on your point of view—what I had heard left me with little doubt about what I would find.

ELEVEN

Cook County Jail is the largest correctional facility in the United States. It is also the country's largest mental-healthcare provider. Fully a third of its prisoners are mentally ill. Their medical treatment consists mainly of triage: ensuring inmates are stabilized and back on their meds before returning them to the streets. Since most of them can't afford their prescriptions—let alone a roof over their heads—they're soon back to committing the petty crimes that landed them there in the first place. It's a cruel system that often has me thinking more charitably about the state-run bedlams it replaced. Whatever you may think of involuntary commitment, it has to be better than sleeping in a cardboard box or foraging in a trash can for your next meal.

According to Boris, Division IV of the jail, which houses all of its female prisoners, was a windowless brick structure surrounded by a sixteen-foot razor-wire fence. Boris pulled up to the visitor's entrance on South Sacramento and idled the town car while we waited for Hallie's associate to show up. Under the court order, I was not entitled to meet with Lazarus alone, a courtesy extended to Brad Stephens before Hallie assumed command of the case. The only good news was that Hallie wouldn't be making an appearance. If I had to bet, she was already at her parent's place, helping to prepare mouthwatering dishes for the family's Christmas feast, a bitter contrast to the takeout I planned on ordering for myself.

So it was a shock when Boris informed me a few minutes later that the person exiting the cab pulled up behind us was a diminutive woman wrapped in an ankle-length fur coat.

"You sure?" I said to him, feeling my insides clench. I remembered just such a coat, bought on a fall shopping expedition to the Water

Tower when Hallie and I were still on good terms. "What else can you see?"

"Like Yelena when she is mad."

A moment later, Hallie rapped harshly on the curbside window and told me to get out.

I hopped like a coolie to her summons, completely forgetting about the season. Two steps out the car door, my heel slipped on a slick sheet of ice. Before I knew it, I was sprawled on the ground face up with my backpack still attached to my shoulders and my cane rolling off in another direction. Probably because she knew how much I hated being helped, Hallie watched without comment while I attempted to right myself, offering assistance only when my slapstick efforts appeared to be going nowhere.

"C'mon, Yertle," she said, taking me by the arm and yanking me back to my feet. "Don't you know better than to wear loafers in this weather?"

I was too embarrassed to tell her about the missing shoes. "Thanks for rushing to my aid. Why are you here? I thought Carter would be doing the babysitting this morning."

"He came down with the flu, and all the other associates were already flying off someplace or pretending not to hear their cell phones. Here's your cane."

I used it to steady myself while I leaned down to pat my trouser leg, which felt torn and a little damp. Beneath it, my knee was tingling.

"Oh, hell," Hallie said. "You're bleeding."

"I'm sure it's nothing." I reached into my overcoat and pulled out a handkerchief.

"Give me that and I'll take a look."

Hallie squatted and rolled up my pant leg to get a better look. I thought the setting was innocuous enough to try to clear the air. "About that time in the County Building—" I began.

She cut me off brusquely. "This isn't the time to discuss it." She dabbed at my leg with the handkerchief. "You'll live. It's only a surface cut."

Hallie patched me up with a Band-Aid—her voluminous purse always seemed to hold more items than a Home Depot—and stood, returning my handkerchief to me. I balled it up and shoved it back into my pocket. "Thanks again. Sorry to be such a nuisance."

"It's your forte. Let's get going. We've wasted enough time and there are a million other places I'd rather be today."

She and I both.

Half an hour and numerous security checks later—my cane, as usual, requiring two x-rays and a manual check before it could be cleared—Hallie and I were seated at a table in a small, chilly room, waiting for Lazarus to be brought in. It was a long wait. As the minutes ticked by, I set up my digital recorder and put a fresh CD in, tested the table top, aligned my cane along one edge, folded and unfolded my arms, roamed my eyes unseeingly around the room, and repositioned my backpack several times at my feet, all without prompting a snippet of conversation from Hallie.

When I could stand the silent treatment no longer, I said, "If we were alley cats this would be a staring contest."

"Don't flatter yourself that I'm looking your way."

I was about to reply with something equally snotty when the door buzzed open and Rachel Lazarus was brought in.

Hallie introduced us, we shook, and I frowned.

It's been said that Ray Charles sized up women by feeling their wrists, from which he was able to deduce critical details like breast-to-hip ratio and willingness to join him in the sack. I was no such wizard, but I'd learned to gather what I could from a handshake. Rachel Lazarus's fingers were thin to the point of emaciation, like twigs wrapped in a layer of cellophane. Her skin was dry, cold, and flaky. As she sat down, she was overcome by a fit of coughing that lasted several minutes.

I sent a quizzical look in Hallie's direction. "Rachel, are you ill?" Hallie said.

Rachel apparently nodded yes. "It's just the cold. I always get bronchitis this time of year." Her voice was low, hoarse and barely audible.

"Have they given you something for it?" I asked.

"I'm taking a round of antibiotics."

"Is that all?"

"That's it. And some Tylenol."

Hallie caught on to where I was going. "Rachel, we don't have to do this today if you're not up to it."

"I'm all right," Rachel said. "Though I wouldn't mind borrowing your sweater."

"Of course," Hallie said. "And you can keep it when we're through. Mark, are you ready to begin?"

I said yes and slid into my standard introduction, explaining who I was, what I was there for, and obtaining Lazarus's permission to use a tape recorder.

I then sought her agreement on some preliminaries. "Usually, when a person speaks to a psychiatrist, what they say will remain strictly confidential. Unfortunately, I can't promise you that today. In fact, it's very likely that whatever you tell me will be talked about a great deal at your trial. I need to be sure you're aware of that, and that you're still willing to go ahead."

"Is that the psychiatric version of a *Miranda* warning?" Rachel asked with a hint of amusement.

I smiled at her. "That's a good question. Actually, it is similar, though I won't be asking you the same questions as the police."

"And if I don't agree to talk to you," Lazarus asked. "What happens then?"

"Nothing. Except that I won't be able to testify at your trial. As Ms. Sanchez has no doubt explained, I may be able to offer a professional opinion that will help you."

"Or not." As one of the Chicago professors had mentioned at the party, Lazarus was no dummy.

"That's true. And it's another thing I need to be sure you understand. I'm not here as your therapist. Much as I may want to help you, that's outside my role."

Rachel sighed. "That's what Dr. Stephens said, too. All right, I'll answer your questions. Just promise me one thing."

"What's that?"

"Don't judge me too harshly."

There wasn't much chance of that.

I established that she wasn't taking any medications other than the Tylenol and antibiotics she'd already mentioned, and that she felt clearheaded enough to proceed. I also gave another part of my usual speech—that because I was blind and couldn't see her, she needed to answer all my questions aloud and not with a shake or nod of the head. Then it was time to get down to business.

I didn't have much time, but there were a few things about Lazarus's childhood I wanted to confirm.

Lazarus was born in 1970, and like me, grew up on the East Coast, in a suburb of Long Island. Her father worked for an investment firm in Manhattan and was rarely at home. Her mother was a homemaker.

"Tell me about your relationship with your mother."

"It was the usual, I guess," Lazarus said matter-of-factly.

From what I knew already, it was anything but usual.

"You told Dr. Stephens that your mother shouted a lot."

"That's true. It wasn't her fault. She had a lot to deal with, raising us kids with my father away on business so much of the time. She didn't make friends easily and was lonely. She always wanted us to stay close to home. We weren't allowed to play at friends' houses or go on sleepovers or things like that. She said we were her best friends."

"What about your own friends? Were they allowed to play at your house?"

"Not really. Mom didn't like having other children around. She said the noise gave her migraines. And besides, she didn't have time to be babysitting someone else's kids."

"You also mentioned to Dr. Stephens that your mother had a lot of rules."

"That's right. But they were all very normal and reasonable. Like making my bed every morning and not letting my room get messy. My mother liked a well-kept home, and she had traditional views, not like some other parents who were too permissive."

"How good were you at following the rules?"

Rachel gave a rueful little laugh. "Not very, I'm afraid. I was an absentminded child—pretty airheaded in fact—so I had to be reminded all the time about what was expected of me."

"What happened when you broke the rules? Did she punish you?"

Rachel tittered nervously. "Oh, sure. But I usually deserved it. I was pretty disobedient, and like I said, always forgetting what I was supposed to do."

"What kind of punishment are we talking about?"

"Oh, you know. Nothing too physical. Back then, a lot of parents hit their kids."

In fact, during her sessions with Brad Stephens, Lazarus had revealed significantly more than an occasional slap on the wrist. On various occasions, her mother had gone after her with a broom handle, a hair dryer, a rolling pin, and a pair of scissors, which she had used to cut off all her eight-year-old daughter's hair. Lazarus had also been locked in her room for hours, denied meals, and been required to keep a diary detailing her transgressions and apologizing for what a "bad" person she was. That she was able to excuse her mother and blame herself was symptomatic of her issues.

Lazarus had one sibling, a sister two years her junior.

"What about your sister, Laura? Did your mother punish her, too?"

"Oh, no. Laura was always good. As my mother used to say, I was the one who needed straightening out."

Laura was killed in a car crash when Lazarus was twelve.

"Tell me about the accident," I said.

"It was after school. Laura and I were fooling around on the backseat, and we got a little . . . rambunctious, as my mother would say. She always wanted us to act like little ladies. She . . . reached around to stop us and I guess lost control of the car. I don't remember too much after that, just a lot of noise and waking up in the hospital the next day."

Lazarus had spent the following year of her life recovering from two broken legs and a shattered pelvis.

"That must have been hard on you."

"I guess it was. I couldn't go to school and missed all of seventh grade. My friends couldn't come over and I was alone a lot. But it was OK because Mom was there to take care of me."

"But it wasn't really OK, was it?" I prodded gently.

"You shouldn't think badly of her. I was frequently disobedient and, well . . ."

"And what?"

"I was responsible for what happened to Laura."

"Is that what you think?"

"Of course. I mean if we—that is, I—hadn't been making a scene in the car, the accident wouldn't have happened and Laura would still be alive today. It should have been me."

According to police reports, Lazarus's mother was over the legal limit when she drove her children home from school that day. Remarkably, she walked away from the accident without a scratch or an apparent sense of guilt, although she was able to play the grieving mother long enough to evade a DUI conviction. And all too typically, she made her bedridden daughter into the scapegoat for the accident. Wrapped up in his work or too cowardly to get involved, Lazarus's father had done nothing to stop the torrent of verbal and physical abuse, even declining to intervene when Lazarus re-broke one of her legs after a "fall" down the stairs.

"And your schoolwork after the accident, how did that go?"

"All right, I suppose. I was able to start eighth grade with my classmates."

In fact, it had gone significantly better than "all right." Five years later, Lazarus was the valedictorian of her high-school class. She attended Smith on a full scholarship, graduating in 1992 *summa cum laude* with a double major in history and European studies. Predictably, her mother didn't attend the commencement ceremony because she was feeling "unwell." Lazarus's father was absent too, on a business trip to Japan. A few years later, when Lazarus was a college senior, he died of non-Hodgkin's lymphoma.

"Are you and your mother in touch today?"

"No. I tried to call her after . . . after I was taken into custody, but they'd confiscated my cell phone and she refused to pay the long-distance charge. It's been so hard for her since Dad died. There wasn't as much money as she thought, and she's had to struggle to make ends meet. She can't really afford to help me out."

"Has she communicated with you in any way?"

"She wrote me a letter saying how upset she was about Gunther's death. She liked him so very much. And the notoriety has caused her so much grief. She can't go anywhere without reporters following her and asking questions. It's very embarrassing to be the mother of a murderess. And now, she won't have anyone to take care of her when she's older. She couldn't even think about visiting me in prison. It's too far away and the shame would be too great."

Given what I surmised about Lazarus's mother, I wasn't shocked.

I'd heard everything I needed to know about Lazarus's upbringing. It was now time to move on to her marriage.

TWELVE

Rachel Lazarus was two weeks into her PhD program at the University of Chicago when she happened upon a flyer in the dining commons advertising a lecture by a then up-and-coming young professor named Gunther Westlake. Being at the university exhilarated her. It was such a far cry from her all-woman's college in the sleepy center of Massachusetts. She adored the school's imposing, gothic-style quadrangles, the bohemian cafés and restaurants of surrounding Hyde Park. It would still be a few years until Hogwarts made its debut in a series of popular books, but to Lazarus the university seemed every bit like an exclusive boarding school, set down in a mythical kingdom and populated by creatures whose brilliance she could only guess at. Even the run-down apartment she shared with two other graduate students in the Shoreland, a gritty former hotel that had once been the domain of Al Capone, seemed like a dream come true.

Drawn to the lecture as much by the topic—"The End of the Cold War: Fact or Fiction?"—as by the photograph of the firebrand who would be giving it—Lazarus had arrived early at Harper on a Thursday evening in October and taken a seat in the front row, where she could take in the full sweep of the leaded glass windows rising up nearly thirty feet in what had once been the university's main library. She had put on what she assumed was appropriate wear for such a serious topic—a modest blouse and skirt, dark hose, low-heeled pumps—but couldn't help adding a bright, multi-colored scarf she'd purchased in Paris the month before, a trip she'd financed by waiting tables all summer. It added, she felt, a touch of sophistication, a sign that she wasn't like the other students now entering the cavernous room and filling the chairs behind her, dressed down in jeans, tee shirts and the ubiquitous Birkenstocks. Tattoos and body piercings were just becoming the rage, but she thought they were low-class. Four years at Smith had left her decidedly cold to the radicalism of her classmates, and Chicago's reputation for civilized, right-of-center discourse was a major reason she had chosen it over other places to study.

Twenty-three years old, slender, dark-haired, and delicately featured, Lazarus felt—and no doubt looked—beautiful.

So it was no surprise to her that, while the talk was going on, she noticed Gunther Westlake's eyes straying several times in her direction, particularly after he had drawn another round of enthusiastic applause with his skillful lampooning of the feckless liberals who dared to imagine that the former Soviet Union was dead and over with. She felt as though she was being singled out for special recognition, invited to share in his well-deserved triumph. Westlake's specialty was sociology, but he seemed as intimately versed in European history as any of the professors she had studied under at Smith. Indeed, there didn't appear to be any academic subject he wasn't conversant with. His scholarship and rhetorical mastery dazzled her. Added to that, she liked his looks. Shorter and slenderer than average, bespectacled, and with the slightly comical halo of hair that would later be caricatured in publications like *The New Republic*, he seemed both physically unthreatening and a bit like her father, whom Lazarus had worshipped when she was a child.

In short, she was ready to be swept off her feet.

"You stayed around after the lecture?" I said.

"Yes. I was hoping to get his autograph. He offered to buy me dinner. I thought he was just being kind, so I made an excuse. But he wouldn't take no for an answer. I was . . . flattered."

"So you went out with him that night?"

"And many nights afterward."

"He—that is, Westlake—was married at the time?"

"Yes, but in the process of getting a divorce. His first wife had left him six months before. She also taught at the university, and Gunther said she was jealous of his success. I wish now . . ."

"Yes?" I prompted.

"I wish I had talked to her, found out more about him before we got so involved. But she had already taken another teaching position across the country and, well, I couldn't very well approach her, a complete stranger. Besides, I had no reason to think Gunther was being dishonest with me."

"Did he pressure you into having sex?"

"No. I wanted it, though I knew it was tricky. This was the early nineties. The university didn't yet have a formal rule banning relationships between professors and students, but it was frowned upon. I didn't care. By that time I was already having doubts about getting my PhD. Gunther thought it was a waste of time, given that there were so few tenure-track positions in history."

The clandestine affair continued into the following spring, when it was discovered by university officials. Westlake was mildly rebuked but fought back: since he taught in a completely different department, any objection was specious. It was only the rabid feminists who thought asymmetrical power relationships were a form of sexual harassment. A private person, Lazarus hated being the subject of campus gossip and sought to put the brakes on the relationship, but Westlake would have none of it. He showered her with gifts and flowers and followed her home every day from her classes. Eventually Lazarus gave in to the pressure, though she was beginning to see a less agreeable, controlling side to his personality.

Then Lazarus discovered she was pregnant.

"I wasn't on the pill. It made me sick. I had a diaphragm, but it failed. I didn't realize until it was too late for an abortion, and I would have kept the baby anyway. I told Gunther, and he proposed. By that time, his divorce had been finalized so there was no obstacle to us marrying."

And marry they did, in a quiet ceremony at a Jamaican resort with only witnesses in attendance.

The months that followed were difficult for Lazarus. The baby was large and she suffered from allergies and back pain. Living with Westlake was also a far cry from dating him. He too had many rules, ranging from the proper temperature of his morning coffee to how his laundry should be folded and put away. Initially, she wasn't troubled. She considered herself a traditionalist, and most of her husband's demands struck her as quaint, like the vests and bow ties he affected as a fashion statement. Westlake was brilliant, a genius. Like all great men, he was entitled to a few idiosyncrasies. Besides, being a newlywed always involved a period of adjustment to someone else's wishes and habits.

Or so she told herself.

Though Lazarus did her best to please him, it wasn't long before Westlake was finding fault with everything she did. The house they moved into after the marriage—a turn-of-the century Tudor on South Woodlawn—wasn't being kept tidy enough. Unless he made them himself, meals were late or overcooked. Lazarus's presence distracted him from his work. Even her appearance failed to satisfy. She had gained too much weight. Her maternity clothes were ill-fitting. Her makeup made her look cheap. Once again, Lazarus felt like she was living in a dream. Except that in this dream she wasn't an apprentice at an elite academy. She was more like one of the scullery maids.

Worn down by the pregnancy, her teaching load, and her husband's incessant hectoring, Lazarus fell behind in her doctoral work, which now seemed more than ever like a selfish and frivolous pursuit. At the end of the fall quarter, she bowed to Westlake's demand and quit. Her work-study grant was canceled, and she was left without financial resources of her own. Westlake applauded the decision, telling her she had always been a borderline PhD candidate to begin with. In her exhausted frame of mind, Lazarus was all too ready to agree with him. What was a degree anyway? A silly piece of paper that would distract her from the more important roles of being a good mother to her child and the supportive wife of a distinguished man.

It was only after Olivia was born that the beatings began.

"He didn't physically threaten you before then?"

"No. Not while I was still pregnant. He was excited about the child. He was expecting it to be a boy and extremely intelligent—just like him. The baby's safety mattered more than putting me in my place."

"Tell me about the first time."

"Olivia was two months old. I couldn't stop her from crying. I was never any good at comforting her. I was walking around the house, bouncing her. He took her from my arms. I thought he meant to bounce her a little himself. Instead, he brought her upstairs to her crib. And then he came back and slapped me. Hard, across the face. I was shocked. By the suddenness of it and . . . the look in his eyes. And then I remembered: it was the same look my mother used to have."

"What happened then?"

"Gunther raised his hand again—and then he stopped and shook his head. He seemed almost as surprised as I was. He apologized at once and said it wouldn't happen again. I believed him. We were both tired from the baby and ready to snap."

"But it didn't stop."

"No."

The violence in the Westlake home didn't end with the first incident and soon settled into a predictable pattern: physical assaults followed by rapid apologies and promises of reform until the next confrontation started the cycle all over again. Westlake may have been a wealthy man and an intellectual giant, but as a spouse he was no better than the lowest criminal, driven to take out his frustrations on a weaker and increasingly isolated wife. But unlike his less well-off counterparts, Westlake had a reputation to protect. He never attacked Lazarus with anything but his hands and kept the noise to a minimum, carrying out his beatings with a ruthless efficiency that terrified her all the more. The two times Lazarus had called the police to their home resulted in the usual skepticism. With a famous professor for a husband and no one to corroborate her account, Lazarus was easily dissuaded from pressing charges.

Throughout the interview, Lazarus spoke in the same low, uninflected voice she had used from the start, never rising, falling, or changing speed. It was as if life had carved such a huge hole in her heart, she had no room left for emotion.

"Were you ever afraid for your life?"

"Yes. Once we were in the kitchen and he took one of those chef's knives he liked so much and held it to my throat. But not enough to draw blood. I thought about calling the police, but what good would it do? It was my word against his."

"I think you mentioned he also pushed you down the stairs."

"Yes."

"More than once?"

"Yes."

"I'm sorry to have to ask this, but did he also rape you?"

Lazarus didn't answer immediately. Eventually she said, "He forced himself on me, if that's what you're asking."

"Did you ever think of leaving him?"

"Not for very long. I was ashamed and didn't want anyone to know. And I was afraid of what would become of us—Olivia and me. I had no skills, hadn't worked at anything but odd jobs during school breaks. How would I ever support us? I knew Gunther would make divorce as difficult as possible, cut off as much support as he could get away with. I wanted Olivia to grow up in a comfortable home. It ... the abuse seemed a small price to pay for her well-being."

"You told Dr. Stephens that your daughter had a good relationship with her father. She wasn't negatively affected by the violence?"

"As I said, Gunther was always careful about not being discovered. He usually saved his anger until she'd gone to bed or was sleeping at a friend's. And I did my best to shield her, explaining it was all my fault. I didn't ... didn't want her to think ill of her father. Then, when she was older, she began to side with him. I think she was ashamed of me."

"Did she say that to you?"

"Not in so many words. But I could tell from the way she treated me. Toward the end—just before I moved out—it became another kind of game for Gunther, encouraging her to join in his ridicule. That and the fact that she was no longer living at home were finally enough for me. A friend from my PhD days offered me a job as an administrative assistant, and the income was enough for me to pay for my own apartment."

"And your relationship with Olivia. What's it like now?"

"What do you think?" Lazarus said. "She hates me. Almost as much as I hate myself. We haven't spoken since . . ."

For the first time, Lazarus seemed on the verge of breaking down, causing Hallie to jump in. "Rachel, you don't need to continue if it's too difficult." I could only imagine the disgusted look she was throwing me.

Lazarus took a few minutes to compose herself. Then she let off another wet cough and said, "No, it's all right. It's just that I sometimes can't believe I did what they say I did."

I flipped the crystal on my watch and felt for the dial. I had used up three quarters of my time.

"Tell me what you remember about that night."

"Very little. I was watching *House Hunters* on television. The show was about a young couple searching for an apartment in DUMBO. It reminded me of a book I liked when I was a girl. *A Tree Grows in Brooklyn.*"

The disclosure struck me as highly significant. Though usually considered a girl's book, I had read *A Tree Grows in Brooklyn* avidly as a youngster, along with everything else the Catholic Church considered sufficiently salacious to ban. If I remembered the book correctly, it might explain something.

Rachel added in evident embarrassment, "I may have forgotten to mention that to Dr. Stephens."

"That's all right," I said. "I'm glad you brought it up now. What happened next?"

"I thought I had a copy somewhere and went looking for it. But it wasn't anywhere in my apartment. I remembered then where I had last seen it—in Gunther's library, along with some other old favorites of mine I had almost forgotten about. I think . . . I think I must have gone back there to get them."

"But you have no memory of leaving your apartment or arriving at your former home?"

"None."

"Was this the first time you experienced a blackout like that?"

"No. Once, when I saw a woman slap her child on the street. I was driving and blanked out for a few seconds. It almost caused an accident. After that, I tried to drive as little as possible. Another time, one of my new neighbors found me standing outside our apartment building in the freezing rain and I couldn't remember how I got there. There were other times too, when I would lose myself for a few minutes, or feel disconnected from everything around me."

"Did you have nightmares as well?"

"I don't remember what it's like to have a normal night's sleep."

"After the blackouts, did you seek medical attention of any kind?"

"I visited a neurologist. But the scans he took were all normal. He suggested I see a psychiatrist and gave me a card. But I never did get around to calling."

"What's the next thing you remember—after *A Tree Grows in Brooklyn*?"

"Standing over Gunther with the poker in my hand and . . . and . . ." Lazarus went through another fit of coughing. "And realizing he was dead."

"What were you feeling then?"

"Nothing really. It was so odd, like I was watching the scene from far away. On a movie or television screen. The only thing I felt was surprise. I remember thinking that Gunther looked surprised, too."

"You don't remember hitting him?"

"Not really."

"Or anything else that happened previously?"

"No. Though we must have been fighting or I wouldn't have struck him. It's funny, isn't it? I'd never fought back before."

"And after you realized he was dead—?"

"The memory is hazy—my thoughts were all jumbled up at the time—but I remember wrapping his body in a blanket and finding the wheelbarrow and putting him in it."

"What about the knife. Do you remember anything about it?"

"The one they say that I used to—no. Except later on, throwing it in the dumpster."

"Two more minutes," Hallie warned.

"Just a few more questions, Ms. Lazarus. How you are feeling today?"

"Tired. Depressed. Anxious about the trial. I just want it to all be over."

"It's Christmas. Will anyone be visiting you?"

"No. I didn't want to impose on any of my friends. And as I said, my daughter and I aren't speaking."

"Are you receiving any counseling?"

"I see a prison psychologist once a week."

"Has that been helping?"

"A little. May I ask you something now?"

"Of course," I said.

"Was I wrong to stay with him all those years?"

"Do you think it was wrong?" I said, dodging the question in true professional fashion. It made me feel like a perfect louse.

"I don't know. All I know is that I brought this down on myself."

"Time's up," Hallie announced.

Sadly, she could have been saying that to both of us.

THIRTEEN

In the end, I was spared a holiday alone with my ghosts. Just as I was leaving the jail, Alison DeWitt phoned, reaching me on my cell. Josh had told her about Louis, and my two colleagues had conspired to prevent further damage to my liver: I was to spend Christmas Day with Alison and her partner at their home in Lakeview. Since my only other plans for the occasion consisted of emptying a bottle and listening to George Bailey triumph over Mr. Potter—because he had *friends*, I reminded myself—I was happy to give in. So instead of going straight home, I asked Boris to drop me off at a toy store on Michigan.

I handed Boris his Christmas tip and we went through our usual ritual of embarrassed protest (Boris) and subtle persuasion (me):

"Boris, if I didn't know better, I'd think you weren't really Russian."

"You already pay for trips."

"True. But I happen to know that you grossly undercharge me. Besides, there's that Coach purse Yelena has her eye on."

"Why you not make a gift yourself?"

"She might get ideas. And you're missing the point."

"What point?"

"It will make her happier if she thinks it's coming from you."

"There is line to get in. I should wait with you."

"I'll be fine. It's barely below freezing. Go on now—the department stores are only open until five."

Twenty minutes later, I was standing inside the overheated emporium, having my ears assaulted by "The Little Drummer Boy." The store wasn't completely virgin territory. I'd gone there several times to purchase toys for Louis and could practically count off the number of steps to the Lego section in the rear. But I had to stop for a moment to remember where the stuffed animals were. The synthetic yipping of a toy dog was one indication, so I struck out in that direction, keeping the sweep of my cane to a minimum so as not to collide with the shoppers racing to snap up the last of the Xboxes. I was just thinking I ought to change my name to Andretti when I heard something that caused me to stop short.

Since going blind, my hearing had undeniably grown sharper. Though some blind people pooh-poohed the idea, brain studies had proved what folklore always insisted: when one sense shuts down, the others take over. But there were limits. While I was better at picking up sounds and where they were coming from, my ability to recall them hadn't radically improved. In contrast to my old photographic memory, which depended on sight, I was still only average at recognizing voices.

Still, I was sure I would have known this one anywhere.

An East Coast accent, slightly aristocratic, scaling upward like the trill of a flute. And just beside it, lower down but still discernible from several yards away, the lisp of a young child.

My heart skipped a beat.

And then another.

I stopped mid-stride, wondering if I was hallucinating. But there it was again: a little boy's voice asking when he would get to see Santa.

Louis's voice.

Within an instant, my mind was at war. My ex-wife and child lived thousands of miles away. What could possibly account for their being in Chicago on the most festive night of the year? Surely, they were back in Connecticut, preparing to leave for her parents' house. Once I had been an insider to their holiday rituals. Trimming the tree in the great room overlooking Long Island Sound. Cocktails and dinner at the Belle Haven Club. Midnight services in the family pew at Christ Church. It was madness to think Annie had forsaken all that out of kindness to me. And yet maybe she *had* relented of her plan to rob me of my son. Maybe their bags were waiting now in a room at the Peninsula or the Ritz. Maybe . . .

I started moving toward them, ears on the lookout. If there was a reunion in the works, wouldn't it be fun to surprise them, emerging suddenly from the crowd? I imagined Louis squealing in happiness when he saw me, how I would kneel down to gather him in my arms, tousle the curls on his little head. And Annie, standing to one side, as amused as ever by my lack of WASP restraint. If she permitted it, I might even peck her on the cheek.

For a few brief moments, I allowed my hopes to soar.

"Mommy," the little boy's voice came again when I was only a few feet away.

"Yes, sweetheart?"

"Why does that man have a big stick?"

With a stab of horror, I realized my mistake.

"Sshhh. I'll explain later."

"But *why*?" the boy whined, louder this time.

The woman spoke sharply. "I said not *now*, David."

Filled with embarrassment, I sidestepped to escape.

But not fast enough.

"Are you all right?" the woman said to me. "You look upset."

At least I hadn't shouted out their names.

I mumbled an apology and kept going.

As I beat a further retreat, I heard her call out, "I'm so sorry. He was only being curious."

The next day, Alison was full of sympathy.

"The same thing happens to me whenever I hear a baby cry. I'm always convinced its Mika."

Mika burped. I had just fed him a bottle of Gina's breast milk, and he was now burrowing into my shoulder, sniffling and shuddering his way into deep sleep. It was late—most of Alison's other guests had already departed—but I was still hanging on, enjoying the company and the little bit of heaven in my arms. I glanced over at the Christmas tree, whose lights periodically brushed my eyes like a sprinkling of fairy dust. The room, in a restored Prairie-style home, was as cozily appointed as my new home was not, filled with soft upholstery, scented candles, and strategically located throws. Alison was curled up in one beside me, happy to be off her feet after the long day of entertaining. Gina was off to the side of the room, chatting with a few other stragglers.

"How did you come up with his name?" I asked.

"We found it in one of those baby-name glossaries. It comes from the Lakota Sioux word for raccoon. We thought it fit him. His eyes are like little black buttons."

I shifted Mika so that his head was resting in the crook of my arm. He rewarded me with a jerky fist to my chest and another contented grunt.

Alison patted me on the shoulder. "You like babies," she accused.

"Should I be concerned that you find that shocking?"

"Not shocking. But you're better with kids than you give yourself credit for."

I kept my shrug to a minimum. According to Alison, Mika was only just getting over his colic, and getting him down after a feeding was a major feat. "You're forgetting that my track record in the children department hasn't been all that great."

Alison was one of the few people with whom I'd shared my history.

"You did pretty well just now getting him to go to sleep. Your ex was crazy to shut you out—then and now."

I tried to lure her off the topic. "Thanks for having me today. I had a great time."

"Oh no, boyfriend. You're not changing the subject that easily. I can tell what happened to you yesterday is really bothering you."

"Wouldn't it bother you to make a mistake like that?"

Alison sighed. "You're having second thoughts."

I could tell Alison wasn't going to be deterred, so I confessed some of my fears. "Not about getting more time with him. But maybe asking for joint custody isn't such a good idea. What if Louis had slipped away from me in that crowd and I couldn't find him?"

"You're not the only blind parent in history," Alison said, echoing what I had told my lawyer two weeks back. "You'll do just fine. And don't forget, he needs his father."

"But what if I can't manage it? What if I can't keep him safe? Hell, if anything ever happened to him while he was with me I'd . . ."

I'd kill myself, no two ways about it.

Alison said, "Every parent has those fears."

But not every parent had seen them materialize.

Alison read my thoughts. "Mark, one day you're going to have to stop taking all the blame for your son's death. Wasn't your ex there that night, too? If you ask me, she was just as much at fault as you were for not getting him to the hospital sooner."

"That's ridiculous," I said. "She was eight months pregnant. She was—"

"Was what? Too exhausted to pick up the phone? If it had been me, I would have been screaming for an ambulance long before you returned. Haven't you ever thought about what Annie was doing all that time you were gone?"

"Sure, but—"

Alison put her hand on my arm to stop me. "No. Shut up and listen. Don't you see what you've been doing all this time? You're an expert. You know all about how guilt plays out in the minds of people who have undergone catastrophic trauma. If you had a patient who experienced something just as terrible—a rape victim, for example—how would you handle it?"

That was easy. First, I'd work to reestablish the patient's feelings of safety, of being in a place where she could control her environment. Then, when she felt secure, we would begin the process of remembering, of retelling everything that happened until the memory no longer held such vicious sway over her thoughts. Dissect it like a rotting corpse until the flesh fell away and it was nothing more than a drafty pile of bones. Only then could we start on the later stages of therapy—reconnecting with loved ones and creating a positive self-image for the future.

Alison congratulated me on a textbook response. "So which of those things have you done for yourself?"

Almost none, to tell the truth. I'd seen another shrink for a while, when it was forced on me to save my job. But I'd stopped going six months later, convinced it was taking up too much time. And I'd needed every ounce of forgetfulness to get me through the crisis of losing my sight.

"Don't you see?" Alison said softly. "You'll never trust yourself with Louis until you go back there."

She was right. And wasn't it the same thing Kay Bergen had asked me to do? To reconstruct everything that happened that night—down to the last gut-wrenching second? Whether or not it would help win my custody battle, I would have to try.

Doctor heal thyself.

But later. After the Lazarus trial was finished.

FOURTEEN

The next day, I was finally ready to read Brad Stephens's report.

Arriving at 10 a.m., I wasn't surprised to find the office almost deserted. Besides being the day after Christmas, it was a Friday, and most of my colleagues had chosen to take advantage of the long weekend for some well-deserved R&R. It's a myth that psychiatric emergencies are more common during the holidays. Though people's moods often worsen—based on the mistaken belief that everyone else in the world is having a better time—they tend to put off harming themselves until the weather warms up. Psychiatrists have no idea why suicides go down during winter, but it's one of the few good things I can say about the season.

I unlocked my office door and proceeded to unravel from the layers I'd used to protect myself during the twelve-block walk from home. My wool Mets hat, a muffler, two fleeces, a down parka, and mittens I'd bought from an adventure-travel outfit specializing in polar expeditions. Typical for this time of year in Chicago, the wind chills were hovering in the forties—below zero, that is—and I had more reason than most to be worried about frostbitten fingers. Some blessed soul had come up with traction bands I could slip on and off my boots, and I removed those too, having just that morning solved the mystery of my AWOL footwear, which the movers, in another triumph of logic, had deposited in a box behind the furnace.

That done, I went looking for the key Yelena kept in the upper right-hand drawer of her desk.

On my way over, I caught the sound of a Rachmaninoff concerto emanating from Sep's new office, a closet-like space to the rear of our suite. I smiled to myself. It was just like the old man not to take any time off. Even though officially retired, Sep had been coming in every day to finish up a research project and attend to a handful of patients he'd been seeing for years. I thought to stop in and wish him a Merry Christmas but decided against it. Rachmaninoff usually meant he was deep in thought and wouldn't welcome the interruption.

Possibly because she never did any real work, Yelena's desk was always a model of tidiness, and I had no trouble locating the key in its usual place under a stack of magazines. Then it was off to the bank of pullout filing cabinets on the far wall. The ones belonging to me were in the middle. The bottom drawer held the files I deemed especially confidential and was labeled Private. I opened it with the key and felt around inside until my hand closed on the envelope Linda O'Malley had passed to me at our meeting. It was still sealed tight with multiple layers of tape.

Before returning to my office, I stopped off in the lounge to make a cup of tea and waited impatiently for the single-brew machine to heat up. I was feeling the sort of mild excitement people have when they expect their opinions to be vindicated, a twin of the confirmation bias that had kept me from opening Brad Stephens's report until now. Based on what I knew about him, I was expecting our conclusions to be roughly the same. Sure, we might approach the problem from separate angles, dwell on some facts more than others, attach varying degrees of significance to the same things. But it didn't even occur to me that we might *disagree*.

The first sign of trouble came back at my desk, after I slit open the envelope and shook out the contents. In addition to a bunch of paper, I was expecting some kind of digital file. But there was none. No thumb drive or CD. No indication that any copy of Brad's report existed beyond what I was holding in my hot little hand. Maybe O'Malley had instructed him to limit the number of copies. Maybe Brad had been paranoid about its contents leaking out. The only sure thing was that it created a pain for me, since I would have to scan all the pages before I could listen to them on my computer. Sighing, I got that process underway, figuring from the size of the report it would take a good half hour.

There wasn't much to do while I waited, so I went over to my box of toys, found my Ohio Art Astro-Ray Gun set, taped the target to a bare section of wall, and spent the next twenty minutes shooting at it and feeling sorry for the children of today who have only video games to play with. I even managed to land a few suction darts on the six-inch cardboard circle.

When the scan was finally complete, I donned my headset and began listening.

While there are no hard-and-fast rules about how much should be included in a forensic report, Brad had done a very thorough job. His report began with a summary of the referral and the legal issues it was intended to address. This was followed by a chronological list of the dates he had met with Lazarus, including the nature of the contact— for example, interview, psychological testing, and so on—and the time spent during each session, all of it cross-referenced to his recordings and the Cook County Jail visitors' log. He identified his sources of information, such as academic, medical, and employment records, along with a list of each test and procedure he conducted. Last, before launching into an interpretation of the facts, he included a neutral, yet detailed description of Rachel Lazarus's background and the events leading up to her husband's death.

It was a well-organized document that up to this point gave no hint of the author's leanings in the best forensic-expert manner.

I read on, especially interested in how Brad had handled Lazarus's claimed inability to remember much about the night her husband died. Amnesia is easily faked and frequently fabricated, especially in legal settings where it may help excuse a defendant's conduct. Although clinicians are trained to ask questions that reveal when a subject is lying, nothing is foolproof and it's often difficult to say when reports of limited memory are genuine.

While not exactly "truth serums," certain narcotics may be helpful in this situation to lower the amnesiac's defenses and permit "lost" memories to surface. Likewise, the examiner may try hypnosis. Both are controversial. Even in individuals like me with strong eidetic capabilities, memory is influenced by a number of factors and can never be deemed completely accurate. In addition, some individuals don't respond to drugs or hypnosis, especially if they have rehearsed a story many times.

With the permission of Lazarus's first attorneys, Brad had first elected to try Brevital, a general anesthetic administered intravenously. The Brevital interview was a complete failure. Even in a completely relaxed state, all Lazarus could remember was seeing her husband with his head smashed in and the poker in her hand, leading to her assumption they had fought. Hypnosis had also failed to elicit any more detailed recollections.

Brad had further tested whether Lazarus was feigning a mental disorder using a psychological assessment tool known as the Structured Interview of Reported Symptoms or SIRS, along with the Minnesota Multiphasic Personality Inventory and several other measures that also tend to reveal, if indirectly, whether or not an individual is mentally ill. The scores obtained from all these tests were consistent with the idea that Lazarus was under severe psychological stress both before and after she attacked her husband.

Pleased with where Brad's report seemed to be headed, I proceeded ahead quickly, setting my ears to browse mode and sending my cursor down the pages at a brisk pace, picking out bits and pieces of information but not giving them my full attention. My thoughts wandered, and I was lazily considering when to break for lunch when I reached the final section of the report.

Even then, I was several sentences into it before I realized what I was hearing.

"...*firmly of the opinion that Ms. Lazarus is prevaricating*..."

I stopped and sat straight up.

Removed my headset and let it drop to my shoulders.

Rubbed my ears.

Put the headset back on and returned the cursor to the top of the page.

But there it was, in stark black and white—or would been if I could have seen it on the screen:

"... *regretfully unable to say that at the time of the alleged offense the accused suffering from a psychological disorder that affected her ability to perceive reality or distinguish between right and wrong. Though such conclusions depend a great deal on the subjective impressions of the examiner, I am firmly of the opinion that Ms. Lazarus is prevaricating about the circumstances surrounding her husband's murder ..."*

I felt the blood drain from my face and read on:

"*During numerous sessions in which I was able to assess Ms. Lazarus's truthfulness through careful observation of her facial expressions, mannerisms, and modes of speech, Ms. Lazarus appeared to me to be a talented, in fact pathological liar. It is, of course, not my role to adjudicate her guilt or innocence, and I leave it to the jury to decide whether she has been coached to tell a story that might bring down a lesser sentence upon her. But as a psychiatrist with many years' experience, the indications that she has consistently misrepresented her mental state, both on the date in question and throughout the period following her arrest and incarceration, are quite unmistakable. Indeed, one would have to be blind not to see them.*"

I felt unmistakably ill.

"*Which is not to say that Ms. Lazarus's reported symptoms lack any resemblance to those of a legitimate PTSD sufferer. To a less-experienced mental-health professional, or one harboring unacknowledged biases, her story might well be regarded as genuine and deserving of sympathy. The reality of psychiatry is that it is not a science. Opinions differ, and some practitioners will see the signs and symptoms of mental illness where none are reasonably present. I can only state my own views in the matter— namely, that Lazarus acted intentionally on the night she went to her husband's home, seeking retribution for what was concededly a lengthy history of domestic abuse, and that she was fully capable of appreciating the wrongful nature of her conduct when she murdered and subsequently mutilated him as a symbol of her deep-seated rage.*"

I was shaken to the core.

So I did the only thing I could think of under the circumstances. I went down the hall to seek Sep's advice.

"Odd," Sep remarked, after I'd finished telling him everything. "And nothing in any of his previous work predicted he would come out that way?"

I shook my head. "If I didn't know better, I'd think the last part of the report was written by an entirely different person."

"I wouldn't rule that possibility completely out."

"You mean that the report was altered? But how? The envelope it was in was taped shut when it was given to me, and it's been sitting here inside a locked file cabinet for all of the last month. Yelena may not be diligent in all things, but she guards my files as if they contained her entire collection of Victoria's Secret."

"I wasn't suggesting it was tampered with. Didn't Stephens have Parkinson's disease?"

I considered this. "You're saying his reasoning may have been impaired?"

Sep said, "It's one hypothesis. The man was in his fifties, wasn't he? It's not unusual for Parkinson's patients to begin showing signs of dementia at that age."

It wasn't beyond the realm of possibility, but I doubted it. "The last time I saw Brad, he seemed as sharp as ever. And the way the conclusion's written—other than coming completely out of left field—sounds professional enough. Take a look for yourself."

Sep took a few minutes to read the pages I'd hurriedly gathered up from the scanner and brought with me. When he got to the end, he harrumphed and set them down on his desk with a disapproving thud. "Yes, he does seem very sure of himself. I didn't know the fellow all that well, but I'm afraid I agree with you. These aren't the words of a dementia patient. Tell me, was Stephens always this arrogant?"

I was quick to come to my dead friend's defense. "Arrogant? No, that's the last word I'd use to describe him. What makes you think so?"

"Presuming he could spot a liar from her body language. Yes, I'm aware that everyone thinks liars give themselves away. Upward eye movements and all that poppycock they teach at police academies and throw around on television. But it *is* a fiction. Or do you dispute that?"

I had—at one time. Though study after study shows that people identify liars no more accurately than a coin toss, there was a time when I was as unconvinced as the rest of the world, certain that if others could detect the lie on my face—if not the gymnastics of my overactive knee—I was equally skilled at interpreting the tics, body postures, and shifty glances that betrayed theirs. It was only when I could no longer see those things for myself that I conceded the possibility—no, the *necessity*—that the studies might be right.

Sep was quick to interpret my silence. "Is that what you're concerned about? That Stephens saw something you didn't?"

"You have to agree it's a legitimate fear."

Sep sighed. A less astute man would have rushed in to offer platitudes and sugarcoated reassurances. Reminded me that I was still as good as I used to be, that a psychiatrist didn't really need his eyes to see what was in a person's heart. Not Sep, who always seemed to understand me better than I understood myself.

"Tell me everything you heard when you were with Lazarus," he commanded quietly.

I took him through my interview, summarizing Lazarus's responses to my questions and describing the way she had phrased them. "She wasn't always eager, but she answered everything I asked—without hesitation or any kind of qualification."

"And she wasn't being theatrical—trying to impress you with the severity of her symptoms?"

"No. If anything, she was downplaying them."

"Inconsistencies in her story?"

"None."

"What about her mood?"

"Somber and serious, but that's exactly what I would expect given the circumstances."

"Any signs of disordered thinking?"

"No. She seemed well-grounded in reality—if showing all the signs of clinical depression. Honestly, I would never have guessed in a million years she was lying."

Sep leaned back in his chair and was quiet for a moment. I visualized his characteristic pose when he was presented with a problem, steepled fingers against pursed lips, eyes fixed absently on some distant object.

"Well, then," he said finally, "it sounds to me like you should trust your judgment. Or resign. There's no shame in backing out. Let someone else take your place."

I considered telling him about Jonathan's implied threat but decided against it. It would only send Sep into a rage, and I couldn't prove anything—Jonathan had been too careful. "It's too late for that. And if I don't speak up for Lazarus, who will? But you see the predicament it puts me in?"

"Yes, that's obvious. You'll have to state your disagreement with Stephens for the record."

"And I can't very well say Brad's opinion is 'poppycock,' to use your phrase. Our entire system rests on the idea that the average man or woman can spot a liar at a glance. That's the whole reason we have juries, so they can decide—"

I stopped in midsentence, remembering something Hallie once told me.

A strategy had just suggested itself.

The only question was—could I make it work?

FIFTEEN

Ten days later, I was seated on one of the scarred benches at Twenty-Sixth and Cal, waiting to be called as a witness in the Lazarus trial. When I arrived at the courthouse that morning, the television crews were out in droves, crowding the entrance like an impromptu carnival. Boris dropped me off next to one of the vans idling on the street, and I used the sound of the motor to find my way around the front bumper and to the curb. Even wrapped in my burka-like winter garb, the cane was a dead giveaway, and I hadn't gotten more than a few yards before I was stampeded by a posse of over-caffeinated journalists. *"Doctor, can you tell our viewers anything about your testimony today? Was Lazarus insane when she murdered her husband? Did she fear for her life?"* I managed to push all of them off except for a WGN anchorwoman who clung to me all the way up the walk to the door. "Have you been blind your whole life?" she asked just as I was about to escape inside. "Not yet," I answered, leaving her to figure that one out.

As Di Marco had predicted, the trial was moving along at a brisk pace. After a mere forty-eight hours, it looked like the proceedings would be over in a week. Most of the first day was taken up with opening arguments, followed by Lazarus's videotaped confession. Lazarus didn't dispute that it was freely given, so there was nothing for the defense team to do but sit by in silence while the tape was admitted into evidence and played for the jury. The second day was devoted to the forensic findings, and again saw few objections from the defense. Lazarus's fingerprints were undeniably present on the poker that killed Westlake, along with the knife used to mutilate his corpse. Though Hallie performed brief cross-examinations of the State's witnesses, it was clear she had little to work with.

Di Marco too was maintaining a relatively low profile. He didn't raise a ruckus when Hallie asked that I be excluded from the proceedings until I took the stand, a purely symbolic gesture since there was no danger my testimony would be unfairly influenced. I'd already listened to the tape of Lazarus's confession and the blood, fingerprint, and DNA analysis were beyond the scope of my expertise. Barring me from the courtroom served only to reinforce the idea that Hallie and I were on opposite sides of a legal Maginot Line.

If anything surprised me, it was that Di Marco had spent so little time on my preparation, leaving the lion's share of the work to Michelle Rogers. She and I had met for several days in a "war room" at the State's Attorney's office, a minefield (for me) of computer cables, stacked paper and half-empty coffee cups. With each meeting, Michelle seemed to grow more comfortable around me, my blindness receding into the background like flowery but forgettable wallpaper. Michelle was grass green but eager to improve her skills. Beneath her diffidence and insecurity, I detected a kernel of ambition, and I gave her as much help as I could, showing her how to frame questions to score the most points with the jury and recover from minor stumbles.

"How did you learn all this?" she'd asked as we were nearing the end of our third day together.

I thought of Hallie with a pang of longing. "I had a great teacher. And to give credit where credit is due, from your boss."

She seemed utterly surprised. "Tony?"

"Sure. There's no better training for a witness than being cut to shreds by a master cross-examiner. You can learn a lot just from watching him."

"I'm not sure I want to know everything he could teach me."

I thought this was an opening I should seize on. "Once before, you mentioned feeling uncomfortable working here. Is there any particular reason?"

Michelle laughed nervously. "Well, for starters, the glass ceiling in this place is as thick as the ice on Lake Michigan."

"Even with someone like O'Malley at the top?"

"Especially with her there. Oh, I don't blame her. For a woman to get anywhere in this world, she has to be as ruthless as all the guys. The stories I could tell you. Don't let all that so-called sympathy for abused women fool you. It was just a campaign slogan, to get herself elected. She's treated me fairly, but . . ."

"But?" I prompted.

Michelle lowered her voice to a near whisper. "You shouldn't trust her. You shouldn't trust anyone around here."

"Even you?" I joked.

Michelle gave a hollow laugh. "I don't matter enough to worry about. I'm just saying be careful."

My thoughts immediately flashed on the contradictions in Brad Stephens's report. *What if . . . ?*

"Michelle," I said in all seriousness, "how much work did you do with Dr. Stephens before he was killed?"

"A lot. I was his main contact here, helping him get everything he needed and organizing the files for him. He was so nice. Like you, a super person to work with. Why?"

"Did he ever let on to you how he was leaning—I mean, in his report?"

"Oh, no. I was completely in the dark—same as everyone else. Dr. Stephens agreed with State's Attorney O'Malley that secrecy was very important. He was worried about how the publicity would affect the trial."

"Because of what he planned on saying about Lazarus?"

"I don't know. Just that he wanted to be sure she got a fair shake."

"And his report. Do you know how it got from him to State's Attorney O'Malley?"

"That I can tell you all about. He called me from his home a few days before his accident to say it was ready and how did we want him to get it to us. We're not usually supposed to use messengers—no money for it in the state budget—but I asked and was told it was OK this one time. I signed the requisition form, and the report was waiting on my desk when I got back from lunch."

"Sealed?"

"Just as you saw it when Linda gave it to you . . . Oh shit, I'm sorry."

I gave her a mildly exasperated look. "I thought we'd gotten past that. But listen to me. This is important. Are you sure the envelope stayed sealed from the time you got it until it was passed on to me?"

"Absolutely. I put it in the bottom of my desk drawer and locked it."

"And no one else knew where to find it?"

"I didn't tell anyone where it was, if that's what you want to know."

Just then, we were interrupted by a knock on the door. Linda O'Malley thumped in, accompanied by Di Marco. They were expected but early.

"Well, look who have we here, Tony," O'Malley bellowed. "It's the good doctor. And looking very well, I might add. Is that the jacket you'll be wearing to court? I like it. And navy is a good color on you." She paused to take further stock of my appearance. "The neckwear will have to go, however."

I held up the end of my Jerry Garcia "Crossroads" tie. "Why, is it too eye-catching?"

O'Malley chortled. "Did I say how much I like this guy? Yes, a less blinding color, if you please. And if you can find it in your closet, something that looks like you didn't pay more than fifty dollars for it. We want you looking fed, but not too well fed—if you see my point."

"Is it OK if I continue to part my hair on the left?"

"As long as it's combed."

O'Malley eased herself with difficulty into the seat across the table from me while Di Marco took the one next to it. "God, this pregnancy is killing me. Be careful what you wish for, I always say. My ankles feel like ripe honeydews. You have kids?"

"One," I said.

"Nice," O'Malley said like the good politician she was, though it was plain the subject held zero interest for her. "How's the prep going, Michelle?"

"He—I mean, Dr. Angelotti—is great," Michelle gushed. "He could give courses on how to be a witness."

Di Marco snickered. "Isn't that cute. You have a fan club." He turned his attention to Michelle: "Watch yourself, doll. The *dottore* doesn't sign your paychecks."

Michelle seemed to wilt under the attack. "I'm just saying he doesn't need very much direction, is all."

"Tony," O'Malley reprimanded good-naturedly. "Stop being an asshole. Ignore him, Michelle. You're doing a fine job. And lest Tony needs to be reminded, I'm the one signing the paychecks. You see what I have to put up with?" she said to me. "Running this office is like herding cats."

That bit of personnel management out of the way, she turned to the reason they were there. "So, I'm on pins and needles. What have you got for me?"

"A Band-Aid?" I said.

"Ha! I guess I had that one coming. But in all seriousness, the time has come for you to cough up your opinion about Lazarus. I've held back from asking up until now to allow you as much time as you needed. But I'll have to have a press release ready well before you climb into the witness stand."

"I understand and I'm ready. In fact, Michelle and I were going over my findings just before you walked in." I winked over at her.

"Excellent," O'Malley said. "Tony, listen up good because whatever he says, I expect you to be behind it a hundred percent."

"Sure, boss," Di Marco said, sounding like he was anything but on board with the program. Not for the first time, I wondered how much control O'Malley had over him—paycheck or not.

I folded my arms and leaned back, in a pose I hoped made me seem both calm and confident. "It's not complicated. I believe Ms. Lazarus was suffering from a significant psychological disturbance at the time of the offense brought on by the recurrent stress associated with her marriage, as well as a childhood marked by repeated physical and emotional abuse. I could go into more detail, but that's it in a nutshell."

It fell on the room like a boulder dropped into a swimming pool.

A moment of uneasy silence followed. Di Marco was too good a poker player to react in any way I could tell, though I was sure his face registered frank disgust. And O'Malley? Even now, I can't say exactly how she felt, only that she seemed untroubled by the news and halfway expecting it.

O'Malley broke the air by clearing her throat. "And your predecessor, Dr. Stephens. Was that his professional opinion too?"

Even though I was ready for this, my pulse quickened.

"No," I said striving for a neutral tone.

"What did he think?"

"Dr. Stephens believed that Lazarus wasn't . . . telling the truth. That she was fabricating symptoms of PTSD."

I waited for O'Malley to seek more detail, but she simply sighed and said, "All right. Not as clear-cut as I would like, but that's the jury's job—to decide who's right. As I said from the start, I intend to let the chips fall where they may. You'll tell the jurors about the conflict with Dr. Stephens, though? It's only fair that they hear from both experts the State's paid for."

"I'll answer whatever questions the court allows," I said, fingers crossed.

"Good. Well then, I'll leave it to the three of you to carry on. I have an appointment with my obstetrician in half an hour. Tony, is there anything you'd like to say while I'm still here?"

"Can't think of anything," Di Marco answered insouciantly. "Except maybe *in bocca al lupo?*"

In bocca al lupo. "In the mouth of the wolf." The traditional Italian phrase for wishing someone good luck. Roughly translated, it expresses the wish that you will safely get through whatever ordeal is ahead of you. The time-honored reply, *crepi il lupo!*—or "may the wolf drop dead"—fairly described how I was feeling while I waited in the courthouse corridor to be summoned inside. I was sure Di Marco had meant the colloquialism as a warning. Now, during the interminable wait in the corridor outside the Lazarus trial, I couldn't help wondering who would outfox whom.

As frequently happened when I was stuck somewhere with nothing to do, I felt my attention wandering. All my old ways of biding idle time—examining my fingernails, counting ceiling tiles, studying unusual faces—were lost to me, and after listening to my inbox a dozen or more times and finding nothing new besides a solicitation for Viagra, I fell to daydreaming. Something about the hallway, perhaps the scent of the cleaning fluid used on the floors, brought back a potent memory of my youth. Before long, I was back in the office of Father Charles, my high-school guidance counselor, where I had been summoned one day in my junior year, ostensibly so I could be chewed out for cutting gym.

"Sit down, Angelotti," he said in a not unfriendly way as I entered his office. "And close the door behind you." New to the school, Father Chuck—as we were encouraged to call him—had a degree in psychology and had been hired precisely to deal with disciplinary problems like me. Now, in addition to whacking us over the head with rulers, our teachers were supposed to try to reach us.

I did as I was told, glancing around the small room, whose walls were decorated with a felt banner proclaiming "Love Is All We Need" and framed photographs of Father Chuck's days as a missionary in Africa. Typical of the post–Vatican II generation of priests, Father Chuck eschewed a Roman collar and wore a necklace with a peace symbol over his short-sleeved shirt. His hair was almost as long as mine. He removed a pack of Newports from his breast pocket. "Cigarette?" he asked, shaking one out and offering it to me.

I assumed this was meant to show what pals we were. Also, that I was in for a heavy lecture. I accepted the smoke, along with the chrome lighter he passed across his desk to me. We lit up and sat quietly for a few moments, puffing and regarding each other like circling hyenas.

"Great photos," I said when the silence finally got to me, gesturing toward them with the tip of my cigarette. "Did you meet any lepers while you were over there? It's supposed to be an act of grace to hang out with them."

Father Chuck pretended this was a serious question. "As a matter of fact, I did. It's a terrible disease, a living hell for those unfortunate enough to be afflicted by it. All of them are pushed out of their communities, left to die without food, clothing, or shelter. Maybe you'll have an interest in helping folks like them someday."

I shook my head. "Uh-uh. People without noses are a drag."

Father Chuck looked at me the way you'd look at a puppy who's just soiled the carpet. "You're a disappointment, Angelotti," he said. "I heard you were funny. What you just said wasn't funny. It was stupid. And I don't think you're a stupid young man."

I shrugged my shoulders like I didn't care.

"Shall we start over?" Father Chuck asked.

I took the last drag from my cigarette and stubbed it out. "Do I have a choice?"

"We always have a choice. Right now, yours is talking to me or spending the next hour in detention with Father Ignatius."

Father Ignatius was as old as a fossil and had a punitive urge that would have been right at home in the Spanish Inquisition. "I guess I'll stay where I am, then."

"All right. So, why do you think I asked you in here today?"

"Got me. I'm passing all my subjects."

"But only barely. Why is that, do you think?"

"Maybe I don't have the aptitude."

Father Chuck rolled his eyes.

I tried a different tack. "I'm sick of school. It's just a waste of time."

"Unless you want to have a real job someday. What are your plans after graduation?"

"Dunno. Have fun for a change. Can I smoke some more?"

"Be my guest." He pushed the ashtray over to me and sat back, studying me with a serious expression. After a while he said, "You think you're a unique case, but you're not. I've met kids like you before."

"Shorter than average?"

Father Chuck smiled in spite of himself. "No, I meant smart kids who play the clown. The ones with IQs off the charts who get Cs in all their classes. There's always a reason for it."

"Could be because they're bored."

"Could be, but it's never the whole story. Nine times out of ten, there's also something happening to them outside of school. Something that's making them miserable that they're too proud to tell anyone about. Am I right?"

I lit one of my own cigarettes and blew a smoke ring in his direction. "You're the psychologist."

"That's right. I'm also a kind of detective. If I were one of those guys you see on TV—Columbo, for example—I'd say your issue has something to do with that shiner over your eye."

I shrugged once more, like it was nothing.

"What's the explanation?" Father Chuck asked.

"Got into a shoving match with some PRs on the train."

"I don't think so. They would have broken at least one of your arms."

"I run fast."

"I bet you do. You ever tell anyone about it?"

"About gangs in the subway? I'm sure the *Daily News* is all over it."

"About how your old man beats the crap out of you."

I felt the heat rise in my face. "What do you mean? We're a perfectly normal American family."

"That's the first honest thing you've said to me so far. Does it bother you?"

No. I enjoy being beaten to a pulp by my only living relative. Why do you ask?

I looked down at my scuffed Wallabees, the only nonuniform attire we were allowed at school, and willed away the tears that were forming at the back of my eyes. The cigarette no longer tasted good, so I put it out.

Father Chuck continued on a philosophical note. "You probably think no one cares, that it will always be this way for kids. But the tide is changing. People are finally starting to understand the effects of violence—how it destroys all of us, whether it takes place thousands of miles away or right here at home."

"You're including the guys you work for in this big change of heart?"

"You're right. For too long the Church hasn't practiced what it preaches. But that's changing, too. In ten or twenty years—maybe sooner—corporal punishment will no longer be tolerated, even in religious schools. And your father would be forced to undergo counseling, if not arrested for what he's doing."

I wasn't sure how I felt about that. "He's just trying to . . . I don't know. I'm difficult."

"No you're not, son. You're just a kid with something eating at you. Like leprosy, only on the inside."

"Is there anything else you wanted to talk about?" I asked, wishing he would just leave me alone.

His next words floored me. "Just this. You seem to have a flair for science. Have you ever thought of becoming a doctor?"

A voice abruptly jolted me back to the present. "Dr. Angelotti?"

"Hmmm?" I said absently, still locked in the memory.

"It's me, Michelle Rogers. They asked me to come get you. The court has just recessed for fifteen minutes, but you're up next."

I checked my watch. It was just after 10:30 a.m. on the third day of the Lazarus trial.

SIXTEEN

"All rise."

I stood stiffly behind counsel table while Judge Sanford Katsoros entered the courtroom, bouncing up to the bench like a beach ball. I'd been told he was a dapper man whose campaign slogan—"Justice with a Compassionate Hand"—could be viewed as false advertising since he always handed down the stiffest sentence the law would allow. On the other hand, "Judge Sandy" fancied himself an intellectual and would listen to arguments other jurists might find preposterous or at best far afield. Though he kept a firm grip on the proceedings, he encouraged healthy skepticism of the rules, leading to a reversal rate that would have gotten an NFL referee fired but failed to dissuade the voters who had thus far awarded him four terms.

"You may all be seated," the judge said after his clerk announced his name. The room was then still, except for the usual hushed coughs and scraping of feet. Judge Katsoros ruffled some papers and said, "Counsel, is there any business we need to conduct before I have the jury brought back in?"

"No," Hallie said, from somewhere off to my left. In the static, florescent lighting of the courtroom, I could see close to nothing, but I knew that Rachel Lazarus would be seated by her side, pale and thin and wearing what the newspapers referred to as a "subdued dark dress." I wondered whether she would come to regard me as her champion or her executioner. Depending on how things went, I could end up being either.

"I have one thing to raise," Di Marco said from his position at my side.

"Yes?" the judge prompted.

"I'm anticipating a lengthy examination of the State's next witness, Dr. Angelotti. Just to keep things moving, I'm wondering if defense counsel would be willing to stipulate to his qualification as an expert witness? That way we won't have to waste the jury's valuable time going over his résumé."

It was an unusual request—and a clever one. Normally, the lawyer who puts on an expert witness will want to spend as much time as possible dwelling on his or her credentials in an effort to sway the jury with their breadth and impressiveness. By foregoing that tactical advantage, Di Marco was already signaling his intentions. Though constrained to put me on the stand, he obviously hoped to keep the jury from paying much, if any, attention to me. I waited to see how Hallie would handle it.

Rising, she said sweetly, "While I appreciate counsel's interest in streamlining the proceedings, I for one would like to hear everything there is to know about Dr. Angelotti."

"That's ridiculous," Di Marco snapped without thinking. "She has a copy of his CV. What else does she need?"

"*Counsel*," Judge Katsoros said sharply. "In my courtroom, lawyers are referred to as 'counsel.' Not as 'he' or 'she.'"

Di Marco hastened to rectify the mistake. "Yes, Your Honor. I apologize for forgetting that. But may I respectfully point out that Ms. Sanchez and Dr. Angelotti are already well known to each other?"

"Why? Are they married?" the judge asked, drawing guffaws from the spectator section.

"No," Di Marco answered. "But she—that is, Ms. Sanchez— has previously retained Dr. Angelotti in a professional capacity. As a witness for one of her clients in a recent matter."

This sparked the judge's interest. "Is that so, counsel?" he asked Hallie.

"Actually, he was forced on me by circumstances," Hallie answered, giving me a telepathic wink. "And performed only adequately on the stand. Frankly, I was surprised to hear that Mr. Di Marco chose him over other available experts. But whatever our past affiliation, my only duty in this case is to Ms. Lazarus. Therefore, I shall have to reserve judgment about Dr. Angelotti's fitness as an expert until I have heard testimony about his qualifications—every last one of them."

"It's her right," the judge said to Di Marco, forgetting his own rule. "All right then, let's hear what the fellow has to say."

The bailiff opened the door and the jurors shuffled in. In Illinois, criminal defendants are entitled to choose the size of the jury, and Hallie had gone for the traditional twelve, no doubt hoping to increase her chances of an acquittal. Of the panel that had been selected, eight were women and two belonged to minorities, a good outcome for Lazarus, though nothing was ever guaranteed.

When they were settled, Di Marco called my name and I stood.

To cane or not to cane? That was the question I'd mulled over on my way to court. Outdoors, leaving my white stick behind required a bravado bordering on lunacy. But inside, on relatively familiar ground, I could get by. Defense lawyers loved the cane and the morbid fascination it generated. They told me jurors never dozed when I was on the stand. But today was not the day to be courting their pity. By this time, I knew the standard setup of courtrooms at Twenty-Sixth and Cal reasonably well. The only challenge was getting myself over to the witness box without appearing drunk or disoriented.

To counteract any such misimpression, I took the folded-up cane, which had previously been hidden in my lap, and placed it prominently on the table in front of me. I then strode as nonchalantly as possible out into the room, using the spatial sense that every blind person eventually develops to cross the short distance. A few tense moments later found me climbing into my seat a few yards away from the jury. To top off the performance, I turned toward them and smiled affably.

My purpose wasn't lost on Di Marco. As soon as I was sworn, he asked me if I'd forgotten something.

"I don't think so."

"I meant this," he said, picking up the cane.

"Oh, that," I said. "Thanks, but as you can see, I don't always need it."

"Are you sure?"

"Positive."

To anyone familiar with trial dynamics, it must have seemed surreal. I was Di Marco's witness, but instead of bolstering my credibility, he was doing his damnedest to call it into question. But I knew the rules. As long as I remained calm and cooperative—in legal parlance *nonhostile*—Di Marco couldn't lead, cross-examine, or attack me outright.

"So you're saying you aren't really blind?"

Hallie rose and objected. "Your Honor, I have to say I'm confused. This sounds like cross-examination. And why is the witness's visual impairment relevant?"

"Yes, Mr. Di Marco," Judge Katsoros agreed. "What is the purpose of these questions?"

Di Marco retreated quickly. "My apologies to Dr. Angelotti. I only wanted to give him the opportunity to explain his condition—to prevent any misunderstanding on the jury's part."

"I'll allow you to proceed, then," the judge said. "But politely."

Di Marco turned back to me. "So, Doctor, are you or aren't you blind?"

"Legally," I answered, using a term I tend to avoid since it has no medical meaning. As I often had to explain, blindness exists along a spectrum—the true *Fifty Shades of Grey*—making the legal definition a more or less arbitrary construct. But to the majority of people, "legally blind" sounds far less incapacitated than "blind," which is why I chose it.

"'Legally blind.' What does that mean exactly?" Di Marco pressed on, still trying to gain an advantage.

"It means I can claim an extra personal deduction when I pay my taxes," I said in all seriousness.

"Is that all?"

"And that I could live off the generosity of the Social Security system if I had to."

Several of the jurors chuckled at this, causing Di Marco to realize the attack was backfiring. He dropped it, and we spent the next thirty minutes on my résumé, with Di Marco asking short, pained questions and me doing my best to supply fulsome, but not boastful answers. When that was finally over, he moved to have the court recognize me as an expert witness on matters pertaining to the mental state of the defendant, Rachel Lazarus.

"Any objection?" Judge Katsoros asked the defense.

"None, Your Honor," Hallie said. "After listening to Dr. Angelotti's many accomplishments, I'd be glad to have him working for me."

"Who says he isn't?" Di Marco muttered under his breath.

The main act was now ready to begin.

Though it wasn't required, in an ordinary situation, Di Marco would have started off by questioning me about everything I had done to prepare for my testimony. Like the lengthy recitation of my credentials, it would have been calculated to impress the jury with the scope and comprehensiveness of my investigation. The more work I had done, the more informed and credible my opinion would seem. And showing the jury that I had left no stone unturned would cut off the most obvious areas for cross-examination.

But this was far from an ordinary situation.

"Doctor," Di Marco said when we were ready to begin, "will you explain for the jury the circumstances under which you were retained."

"I was hired by the State to examine Rachel Lazarus, and to render a professional opinion about her mental health at the time of the incident in question," I said, steering well clear of words like *murder*, *husband*, and *emasculation*.

"Rachel Lazarus, the defendant here?"

"Yes," I said.

"Was this immediately after her arrest last May?"

"No."

"Can you put a time frame on it for us?"

"I first learned of the assignment in mid-December."

"And how did you learn about it?"

"My superior informed me that my services had been specially requested by State's Attorney O'Malley."

"Do you know the reason?"

"I believe it was because, as we covered earlier, I have a specialty in post-traumatic stress disorder."

It wasn't the answer Di Marco wanted. "That wasn't what I was asking. To your knowledge, were you the first expert psychiatric witness retained by the State?"

"No."

"There was someone before you."

"Yes."

"Who was that?"

"Dr. Bradley Stephens."

"Was Dr. Stephens known to you before that time?"

"Yes," I answered.

"How was he known to you?"

"He was known to me professionally through his writing and speaking engagements—and also as a friend." I could have off left the last bit, but in the worst-case scenario I wanted the jury to know that I bore no animosity toward Brad.

"What was your opinion of Dr. Stephens—professionally that is?"

"I held him in very high regard."

"Why isn't Dr. Stephens here today?"

"He was killed in a hit-and-run accident shortly before I was hired."

"Tragic," Di Marco remarked. It was probably sincere. "So you were hired to render a psychiatric opinion about the defendant in his stead?"

"That's correct."

"Before we go any further, why don't you state what that opinion is?"

I realized I had been sitting rather stiffly in my chair. I assumed a more relaxed posture, folded my hands in my lap, and half-turned toward the jury. The courtroom was as hushed as a mortuary while I spoke:

"It is my opinion that Ms. Lazarus's behavior on the day of the crime is reasonably viewed as a reaction to severe and recurring stress, a psychological disorder recognized in the American Psychiatric Association's *Diagnostic and Statistical Manual of Mental Disorders* as post-traumatic stress disorder, or PTSD. One symptom of this disorder is the individual's attempt to 'relive' through thoughts and fantasies the original stressful episodes in an attempt to bring about a more successful—that is psychologically acceptable—result. These attempts are sometimes referred to as 'flashbacks.' During a flashback, an individual may feel detached or estranged from the world around him or her and later have no memory of what transpired. It's as if he or she was in an altered state of consciousness.

"Several features of Ms. Lazarus's conduct suggest that she was experiencing a flashback when she traveled to her estranged husband's home on the evening he died. Lazarus's marriage was an extremely unhappy one, marked by nearly constant verbal and physical abuse. Over the course of many years, her husband had beaten, threatened, taunted, and ridiculed her. On one occasion, he held a knife to her throat; on several others, he pushed her down a flight of stairs. He also forced her to have unwanted sex with him. There were many times when Lazarus feared for her life.

"The painful memories of those years consumed Lazarus. After moving out of the couple's residence, she lost consciousness several times for no apparent reason, once after observing an act of physical violence on the street. She also suffered from repeated nightmares. Shortly before Mr. Westlake's death, she reported watching an episode of *House Hunters*, which reminded her of a favorite childhood book—*A Tree Grows in Brooklyn*. I believe this trigger is both what led her to her husband's home that night and what occurred thereafter."

I stopped there to heighten the suspense.

Di Marco was incredulous. "What does a book have to do with it?" he demanded.

"*A Tree Grows in Brooklyn* contains a famous scene, one that caused it to be banned by the Catholic Church. In it, the young protagonist, Francie, who lives in poverty with her family in Brooklyn, is attacked and almost raped by a child molester. Francie's mother saves her by shooting the rapist." I paused and added for effect, "in his genitalia."

A murmur of appreciation shot through the courtroom.

Di Marco didn't like this. "And that tells you what?"

"It tells me that Ms. Lazarus was remembering the scene in *A Tree Grows in Brooklyn*, which further sparked memories of her husband raping her. When she went to his home that night, she was 'reliving' those memories, hoping to erase them."

"Is that what she told you?"

"No. Ms. Lazarus remembers very little about that night. What I just said is an inference based on my training and years of practice. Flashbacks in PTSD sufferers are often triggered by a trivial or chance happening, similar to what occurred here. The fact that Ms. Lazarus's memory of the events is hazy to nonexistent is also consistent with my opinion that she was reliving prior experiences."

"Let me see if I can get this straight," Di Marco said. "You're saying something she remembered from that book gave her the idea of chopping off his . . . I mean, emasculating him?"

"Not the idea, per se. But in her subconscious mind, she was looking for a savior, someone like Francie's mother, to rescue her from memories that had become unbearable for her."

"Sounds more like an act of revenge to me," Di Marco said.

It wasn't a question, but Hallie didn't object, probably because she thought I was holding my own.

I shook my head. "While the means Ms. Lazarus used to restore her psychological well-being may seem extreme—even shocking—to some, it's important to remember that she was not functioning as a conscious person during the incident in question. Individuals in the throes of flashbacks often have diminished self-control, again because they are disassociated from their surroundings. When I interviewed her in prison, Ms. Lazarus reported feeling very strangely that night, as though she were watching herself from a great distance. That's classic flashback behavior."

Di Marco evidently thought the jury had heard enough about flashbacks and switched gears. "You spoke of the defendant having PTSD."

"That's right," I said.

"But not Battered Woman Syndrome."

"Again, that's true. BWS has been largely rejected by the psychiatric community as lacking a proven scientific basis."

"So if I were to tell you that the expert testimony to be offered by the defense relies exclusively on BWS to explain Ms. Lazarus's actions, you would take issue with that?"

I was a little surprised that Hallie had left herself open to this line of attack. But it was probably explained by the fact that she'd come into the case at the eleventh hour. She'd told me she was unhappy with the expert selected by the public defender. Perhaps there hadn't been time to find another one. With a slight nod in her direction, I replied:

"I would have to. While battering is a serious social problem, at present there is insufficient evidence to show that BWS meets the rigorous criteria for recognition as a bona fide mental disorder. The so-called symptoms of the syndrome are nonspecific—in other words, a wide variety of events can cause them—leaving mental-health professionals without a means of separating fact from fiction. Headaches, for example, are a common complaint of women said to be suffering from BWS, but they can be caused by nearly anything. Further, because it is defined as a syndrome uniquely affecting women, BWS reinforces stereotypes about female passivity and helplessness. For women who have indeed been chronically battered, PTSD offers a more reliable—and gender neutral—means of assessment."

"Let's talk about reliability, then. A large part of your diagnosis rests on the domestic abuse that took place in the Westlake home. How certain are you that it occurred?"

"As certain as I can be, based on Ms. Lazarus's self-report, as well as records of police visits to the home that were in the files furnished to me by your office."

"Was the murder victim, Professor Westlake, ever arrested for these so-called crimes?"

"No. My understanding is that Ms. Lazarus declined to press charges."

"And you don't think that undermines her claims of abuse?"

"It's common to think that battered wives can put an end to the violence simply by removing themselves from an abusive spouse. But for many women in that situation, it's not that simple. Often, they're financially dependent on their batterer and fear losing their homes, custody of their children, or in the worst case, their lives by leaving. The experience of battered women in the courts backs up that fear."

"Ms. Lazarus was a well-educated woman, wasn't she?"

"She had a college degree, yes."

"And the couple was well-off financially."

"Also true, but beside the point. It's a myth that domestic violence occurs only among the poor. In fact, the problem exists at every income level, but a culture of silence in upscale communities has prevented it from being widely recognized. Wealthy women are often disbelieved when they report physical abuse, or their husbands counter with suits for defamation. It becomes all-out legal warfare for the victim, even in the rare case when she can match her spouse's financial resources. That plus the social stigma make it a tremendously difficult thing to do. We shouldn't blame Ms. Lazarus for not having the courage to end her marriage sooner."

"Can we blame her for anything?" Di Marco snapped, forgetting himself again.

"Your Honor—" Hallie began.

"Wait," I said, holding up my hand. "There's more."

Di Marco tried to cut me off. "There's no question pending."

"That's because you didn't let him finish," Hallie retorted quickly.

"I agree," Judge Katsoros said from the bench. "You may continue," he told me.

"Rachel Lazarus was physically and emotionally abused not just as an adult, but also throughout her childhood, by a mother I strongly suspect was suffering from borderline personality disorder, or BPD. Mothers with BPD are characteristically violent and have difficulty controlling intense, inappropriate anger, usually brought about by persistent fears of abandonment. Think *Mommie Dearest*, if you will. The psychological effects on a child growing up in that kind of home can be devastating. Such children tend to blame themselves for their parent's outbursts and to carry a negative self-image into adulthood. Not surprisingly, many of them end up in abusive relationships, for which they again blame themselves. I believe this also explains why Ms. Lazarus had difficulty extricating herself from her marriage."

I shut up then, well pleased with myself. I had scored as many points as I could despite Di Marco's attempts to derail my testimony. My words had laid the groundwork for acquittal and given the jury something to think about besides the shocking state of Westlake's corpse and the monstrous impulse that seemed to lie behind it. Whatever fate ultimately awaited her, someone had finally spoken up for Rachel Lazarus.

SEVENTEEN

Di Marco's next thrust came as no surprise.

"Doctor, earlier in your testimony you said that you were hired to evaluate the defendant in December."

I nodded. "That's right."

"So you had only a few weeks to prepare for your testimony."

"Yes."

"Was that sufficient time for your purposes?"

"It was because of the work done by my predecessor. All of Dr. Stephens's files, including tapes of his sessions with Ms. Lazarus, were furnished to me before I began work on the matter."

"Would you say that Dr. Stephens did a thorough job?"

"Very."

"Please describe the work that he did."

I went through the information Brad had collected, the tests he had run, the archival or third-party information he had relied on, and the psychological literature he had consulted.

"All told, it represented about a week of reading material."

"And you read all of it yourself?" Di Marco asked with a slight sneer.

"Yes. I downloaded it into my computer and listened to it using a specialized software program known as a screen reader."

"I *see*," Di Marco said, to underscore that I hadn't. "How many hours did Dr. Stephens spend interviewing the defendant?"

"Close to twenty."

"Were you also able to interview Ms. Lazarus yourself?"

"Yes."

"How many hours did *you* spend with her?"

"I was only allowed two hours by the court."

"So only a tenth of the time Dr. Stephens spent."

I couldn't argue with the math. "Correct."

"Doctor, before his untimely death, did Dr. Stephens prepare a report of his findings?

"Yes."

"Which you had access to?"

"It was delivered to me along with the rest of his files."

"Presumably, you *listened* to that too."

"Certainly."

"Good," Di Marco said, like this was going to be a piece of cake. "So you'll be able to tell us what those findings were."

The moment for Hallie to act had arrived. "Judge, before this goes any further, may we have a sidebar?"

That's my girl, I thought happily.

Di Marco and Hallie approached the bench, and I leaned over to eavesdrop.

"What's her—I mean, *counsel's*—problem?" Di Marco demanded in a harsh whisper.

Hallie wasted no time answering. "I object to any reference to Dr. Stephens's so-called findings on the ground that they invade the province of the jury."

Di Marco was caught completely off guard. "What? How'd she? I didn't—" he began.

Hallie cut him off. "Doctor Angelotti forwarded a copy of the report to me last week."

"You were in contact with my witness?" Di Marco said shrilly. "Judge, that's sanctionable."

"Pipe down," the judge commanded. "Or they'll be able to hear you as far away as State Street. What's your answer to that, Ms. Sanchez?"

"We didn't communicate *ex parte*, if that's what counsel means. Dr. Angelotti simply forwarded both written reports—his and Dr. Stephens's—with a note saying Mr. Di Marco had instructed him to furnish me with copies. In the interest of full disclosure."

In this instance, full disclosure included the fluorescent Post-It flags I had Yelena stick on various pages of Brad's report to make sure Hallie gave them her full attention. But Hallie had spoken the literal truth: the two of us hadn't exchanged a word since that day in the jail.

"You did ask Dr. Angelotti to send it, didn't you?" Hallie continued in an angelic tone, putting Di Marco on the spot.

Di Marco hadn't, nor as I'd suspected, seen fit to provide a copy to the defense himself, clearly hoping to spring it as a surprise at trial. But he couldn't admit to that without Hallie calling him on a violation of the rules. "Sure," he mumbled in a tight voice.

"In that case," Judge Katsoros said, "let's hear her objection."

"If I may tender a copy of Dr. Stephens's report to the court?"

The judge agreed and Hallie went on. "Drawing Your Honor's attention to pages twenty-eight and twenty-nine, you'll see that Dr. Stephens's 'expert' opinion is nothing more than a statement of his belief that my client is a liar. The law is clear in this and virtually every other jurisdiction that the defendant's credibility is not an appropriate subject for expert testimony. It's not helpful to the jury, which is charged with making its own decision about truthfulness, and is unfairly prejudicial to the accused. For that reason, the admission of such testimony is considered plain error and grounds for automatic reversal."

This couldn't help being of concern to the judge. "I hope you have a good response to that, Mr. Di Marco."

Di Marco scrambled to come up with one. "He didn't say she was a liar. He said she was lying about her mental state. That's well within his psychiatric expertise."

"Same difference," Hallie said. "Either way, the message it sends is that Ms. Lazarus isn't telling the truth. That's for the jury to decide."

I was elated that my strategy seemed to be working.

But even good lawyers can make a mistake.

"And, if that isn't enough, the report is hearsay," Hallie added without needing to.

"It's not hearsay if this"—Di Marco bit his tongue—"this *witness* relied on it."

"He clearly didn't rely on the part we're discussing. What's more, Dr. Angelotti is here and can be cross-examined about his findings. Dr. Stephens obviously cannot."

"All right. Quiet, both of you, while I think about this," Judge Katsoros said.

It gave Di Marco just enough time to regroup.

The judge was on the verge of ruling when Di Marco spoke up again, "Excuse me, Your Honor. I didn't mean to interrupt. But counsel's last few remarks have suggested a compromise."

"What's that?" the judge asked.

"I'd like permission to treat this witness as hostile."

Now it was Hallie's turn to be caught by surprise. "Hostile? On what basis?"

Di Marco rejoined, "Dr. Angelotti's beliefs run contrary to the prosecution's interest in seeing a cold-blooded murderer put away. How much more hostile can you get? I'll agree to leave out any reference to Dr. Stephens's report if I can cross-examine him about weaknesses in his analysis."

"That sounds like a good compromise to me," Judge Katsoros said. "How about it, Ms. Sanchez?"

I didn't dare send her a worried look, not with the jury sitting so close by. From their sighs and murmurs, it was plain they were growing impatient with the prolonged interruption in the proceedings. It's a well-known fact that juries tended to take sidebars out on the attorney requesting them. And really, what did I have to be afraid of? Di Marco had already beaten the blindness horse to death. Carrying the theme any further carried the risk that the jury would come to despise him and side with me.

Hallie evidently reached the same conclusion. Not that she had much choice.

"Ms. Sanchez?" Judge Katsoros prodded. "We're losing time."

Hallie said cautiously, "I guess I can go along. If what Dr. Stephens believed stays well out of it."

"You have my word as an officer of the court," Di Marco said solemnly and with what sounded to me like ill-disguised glee.

"It's settled then," the judge declared. "You may proceed," he told Di Marco.

I took a sip of water to steady my nerves and assumed an attentive expression.

Di Marco began, "Doctor, since you've acted in this capacity before, I assume you're familiar with the ethical rules governing expert-witness engagements."

That was easy. "I am."

"Specifically, with the guidelines put forth by the American Academy of Psychiatry and the Law."

"Yes."

"Would you agree, then, with the guideline stating that forensic examiners should strive for objectivity in their assessments?"

"Of course."

"And with the commentary for that guideline cautioning forensic examiners to be on the alert for unintended bias."

I agreed once more.

"In fact, according to the commentary, even the most conscientious and experienced examiner may be subject to such bias."

"That's what the commentary says."

"And that unrecognized bias can result in flawed reasoning."

"I can't quarrel with that in the abstract."

I wondered where he was going with all this.

"Isn't it also true that forensic examinations frequently involve aspects of human behavior that are quite disturbing?"

"I can't say how frequently it comes up, but when they involve violence against human beings, yes of course."

"What about you? Have any of your expert assignments involved conduct you found difficult to stomach?"

Thinking I understood what was behind this question, I chose my words carefully. "If you're referring to the manner in which Ms. Lazarus, ah . . . treated her husband's corpse, I admit that I found it . . . unsettling. As would most people, I imagine." It was always best to be candid. And to admit the things the jury would find unbelievable if you didn't.

"Actually, I wasn't referring to that," Di Marco said, surprising me. I tilted my head at him quizzically.

"I was referring to the defendant's childhood. Didn't you testify that she was abused by her mother?"

"Yes."

"Systematically and over a period of many years?"

"That's right."

"That kind of childhood must have resulted in a great deal of pent-up rage."

All this did was give me another chance to climb aboard my soapbox. "Not necessarily. More often, victims of child abuse direct their anger against themselves. You have to understand that a young child regards her parents as the most powerful beings on earth. When they turn on her, she can't help but believe that she is to blame. Such children typically view themselves as evil and undeserving of normal human love."

"Very nicely put." Di Marco said. "And you say these feelings characterized the defendant?"

"As I mentioned, I believe they account for Ms. Lazarus's decision to stay in her marriage. Believing herself to be unworthy of her husband's love and respect, she accepted the things he did to her until her psyche finally rebelled and she snapped—to use an unscientific term."

"It sounds like you had some sympathy for her."

"Again, I think most people would."

"But you didn't let that sympathy affect your judgment."

"Not to any significant degree."

"You're sure about that?"

"Absolutely."

I should have seen what was coming.

"A little earlier, we talked about unintended bias on the part of the examiner. You weren't subject to any of that yourself?"

"I don't think so," I said truthfully.

"I was wondering whether your sympathy for the defendant might stem from something personal," was Di Marco's next question.

Caught again by surprise, I blinked. "Pardon me?"

"Like your own childhood."

"I don't understand."

"Oh, but I think you do. What I want to know is whether you have any personal experience of child abuse?"

My face must have blushed the shade of a ripe watermelon. I felt a line of sweat form on my back and telegraphed a silent message to Hallie. *Please shut this down. Now.*

But either she wasn't paying attention or was just as interested in the answer as Di Marco was.

"Child abuse? No, of course not," I said. Exactly what I had always told myself.

"But your father hit you."

How the hell did he find that out? I put as much nonchalance into a shrug as I could. "It was a different time. Many adults believed that hitting was an acceptable form of discipline."

"But not when the defendant was a girl?"

"Attitudes had changed. And you can't compare what happened to the defendant—I mean, Ms. Lazarus—to an occasional swat on the backside."

"That's the only place you were hit—on the backside?"

I couldn't perjure myself. "No."

"How often?"

"How often what?" Against my will, I was growing belligerent, the worst thing a witness can do.

"How often did your father hit you?"

"You're asking me to remember things that happened decades ago," I snapped, trying to clamp a lid on my anger. What right did this bastard have to pry into my past? And why wasn't Hallie doing something about it?

"Just give us an estimate, then. Once a week? Twice?"

The sweat on my back was now a spring torrent. "I . . . I can't put an estimate on it. But it wasn't abuse as you're using that term."

"It was your fault, then—that he hit you?"

"I was a little wild back then. He was just trying to keep me out of trouble."

"So you blame yourself. Just as—according to your learned opinion—Ms. Lazarus blamed herself."

"It's not the same thing," I protested.

"Isn't it?" Di Marco said.

A dam of emotion chose that moment to break. "He was my father. He loved me. And what proof do you have? This is all just insinuation."

"Let me show you something then," Di Marco said as smoothly as a card sharp. He slapped down something in front of me. "Recognize this? Oh, sorry. I forgot you *can't*."

Hallie finally woke from her stupor. "Wait just a minute. Before we go on, I want to know what he's showing the witness."

"My apologies. Ms. Rogers," Di Marco sang out to Michelle, "would you please supply counsel with a copy of the letter I have just put in front of Dr. Angelotti?"

"What is this?" Hallie repeated.

"Just this. In the course of investigating Dr. Angelotti's credentials—you can never be too careful about falsification of résumés these days—I subpoenaed his college records. Naturally, I didn't expect to find anything amiss. I was just trying to be on the safe side. As you'd expect, Dr. Angelotti's academic performance was exemplary. But in the file, I ran across this letter from an old acquaintance."

What old acquaintance? And why was it in my file after all these years?

Di Marco turned to me. "The Reverend Patrick Charles. I assume you remember him?"

Father Chuck.

I mumbled a yes.

"Who was Reverend Charles?"

"He was my high-school guidance counselor."

"Did the two of you know each other well?"

"We talked sometimes."

"When you were applying to college, did Reverend Charles write letters of recommendation on your behalf?"

"I believe so," I said.

"The paper I have tendered to you appears to be one of those letters, written to the dean of admissions at the university you ultimately attended. Do you know what it says?"

"No. I never saw it."

"Your Honor, may I have permission to put this up for the jury?" Di Marco asked, referring to the audio-visual screen all courtrooms come equipped with these days. "And of course, I'll read it to Dr. Angelotti."

He proceeded to do just that. I didn't need to see the jury to know they were hanging on every word.

Dear Monsignor Doyle:

I am writing as a fellow Jesuit and because I know you are always looking for that special admissions candidate, the student most in need of our love and prayers to succeed.

Mark Angelotti is just such a candidate. I have worked closely with him over the last several months and found him to be an exceptionally bright, articulate, and sensitive young man. Regrettably, these attributes have not always been reflected in his scholastic performance at St. Regis Preparatory. Without going into detail, Mark is the only child of a troubled and violent father, a background that has thus far prevented him from achieving his true potential. Only recently, and with my counseling, has Mark begun to sort through the anger and confusion brought about by his unfortunate circumstances.

I am aware that Mark's record as it now stands does not meet your high academic standards. But I beg you to give this boy a chance. Mark's mother died in childbirth, and he has borne the brunt of his father's rage and sorrow for all of his young life. Mark has aspirations to study medicine, and I am confident that he will be a tremendous asset to that field, as well as your institution, once he is no longer living at home.

I hope you will understand the need to protect Mark's privacy and ask that this letter be destroyed after you have considered its contents. If you would be willing to meet with Mark, I will personally provide his transportation to the school so that you can judge him for yourself. I believe you will conclude, as I have, that his is a soul eminently worth saving.

Thank you for your kind consideration of this unusual appeal.
Yours in Christ,
Patrick Charles, S.J.

So much for my privacy.

Di Marco paused to let Father Chuck's words sink in before coming back to me. "A 'troubled and violent father,'" he repeated. "The good priest wasn't lying, was he?"

It was a question that needed no answer. I took a moment to think back fondly on Father Chuck. Before now, I never knew the strings he pulled to get me into a decent school.

I was calm then in the way during childhood I had always imagined the Catholic martyrs were, facing down their enemies in a hopeless situation.

Even if I too was about to be slaughtered.

I squared my shoulders and nodded to Di Marco that I was ready to go on.

"Shall we talk some more about bias?" he said.

EIGHTEEN

Five days later, the jury convicted Rachel Lazarus of murder in the first degree.

It wasn't Hallie's fault. After Di Marco had finished dicing me into a human *mirepoix*, she had done her best to paste the bits back together again. To wit: I hadn't volunteered for the Lazarus assignment. I was commandeered into it. And yes, I was fully aware of my prejudices—as Di Marco had taken to calling them—going in. Nonetheless, I had done my best to render a fair and honest opinion. Psychiatrists often confront similarities between themselves and their patients. It was expected and dealt with in their training. I had treated adult survivors of child abuse before. If I'd felt genuinely compromised, I would have resigned.

Which, in hindsight, is exactly what I should have done.

One of the behavioral oddities of juries is that they can hold several seemingly contradictory notions at once. So while the Lazarus panel had overwhelmingly rejected my testimony that she was suffering from PTSD, they embraced my criticism of Battered Woman Syndrome with an enthusiasm bordering on faith in CIA conspiracy theories. In the post-verdict interviews permitted by Judge Sandy, the jurors were unsparing of the well-meaning but misguided doctor who had allowed his prejudices to color his judgment. On the other hand, I was plainly in the know in pointing out the absence of a scientific basis for BWS. Forced to rely on the expert hired by the public defender—who distinguished herself by suggesting that the *DSM*'s treatment of the issue was based on male hostility to the clitoris—Hallie was left with virtually no ammunition. Though her closing was hailed in the press as an "admirable attempt to expose the tragic aftermath of domestic violence," it didn't sway the jurors, who were sympathetic to Lazarus but unable to overlook the horrific vengeance taken out on Westlake's corpse. As the male foreman explained in a television interview that subsequently went viral, "She went too far."

The only bright spot in all this was that Jonathan was off on one of his speaking junkets when I slunk back to work the following week. I hadn't even sat down before Josh and Alison showed up in my office to offer their condolences.

"Hey, buddy," Josh said, placing a carton on my desk. "I brought donuts from that new place down the block *Chicago Magazine*'s been raving about."

"And I brought you some tea," Alison said. "English breakfast. With extra cream and sugar."

Josh opened the box, nearly bowling me over with the scent. "Try one. It's their signature. Apple, blue cheese, and walnut."

"Is that a donut or a Waldorf salad?" I said, putting my hand out for the tea, which did sound good.

"Salads are the antithesis of comfort food," Josh said. He helped himself to one and went over to sink like a ballast into my couch. "These, however, are loaded with fat and carbs. Exactly what you need right now."

"Yes, Mark," Alison said. "You *are* looking rather wan. Come over and tell us about it. I'll bring the food."

I took the cup she'd given me and followed her to my sofa, feeling ahead with my toe since I still hadn't mastered the new furniture arrangement. Even then, I bumped into one of the side chairs. Tea sloshed over the rim of the cup and onto the upholstery.

"Darn," I said. "I hope I haven't soiled the fabric."

"Don't worry," Alison said. "There's so much Scotchgard on the cushions, you could use them as flotation devices. Jonathan's been fielding complaints about the new décor like you wouldn't believe. Some of our colleagues have suggested changing the name of the practice to the Frain Sensory Deprivation Center."

"On that topic, what's the status of the palace uprising?" I settled into my seat.

"Uh-uh," Jonathan said. "You're not changing the subject that easily. We came to offer aid and comfort to a wounded comrade."

I blew on my tea to cool it down. "You're too late. He died on the battlefield."

"That's not what Hallie said. You know she phoned me on Saturday when you wouldn't answer your cell. She thought you did OK . . . considering. Why haven't you returned her calls? There's nothing to prevent you two talking again, now that Lazarus has decided not to appeal."

I hadn't known that. Which wasn't surprising, since I'd spent the weekend after the verdict throwing myself a gala pity party, wrapped up in a blanket in front of the television, and not stirring to shave, shower, or eat, except when hunger pains drove me to the pantry to open a can of tuna. Wary of being tracked down by reporters, I'd turned off my phone and kept all the lights in the house off. By the time Sunday night rolled around, I had re-memorized the theme song to every sitcom produced after 1960, which had now taken up residence in my head with a whole new set of lyrics. *Just sit right down and you'll hear a tale, a tale of a fateful slip, that started in a court of law and sunk a foolish crip* . . .

"So Hallie's giving up." I said.

"She doesn't want to, but Lazarus is insisting. But you haven't answered my question," Josh said through a mouthful of dough.

I feinted. "Which question?"

"Why you've been avoiding her."

"Maybe it has something to do with throwing her client to the wolves."

"Oh, come on. It's not your fault you were sucker punched."

"It's embarrassing that I let it happen," I insisted.

"What's embarrassing is that monsignor not keeping that letter out of your file like he was asked to. You oughta sue the school."

"Oh sure. Because I haven't achieved enough notoriety already."

"He's right," Alison told Josh. "Best to keep the lawyers out of it. But if it were me, I'd contact them and demand that every last copy of that letter be destroyed."

"Too late for that, too," I said. The icing on the cake had been Kay Bergen's e-mail, late Sunday night, informing me that Annie's lawyers were already on the scent, seeking written assurance that all of my academic records would be preserved for the duration of the custody battle. "I can't throw away so much as a tissue now. Not if I still want a prayer of hanging on to Louis."

"Oh," Alison said, like I'd startled her. "I hadn't considered that. But why is your childhood relevant? It was all so long ago."

Why indeed? But I could already hear the testimony of Annie's psychiatric expert, harping on the statistics showing that child-abuse survivors were significantly more likely to end up becoming abusive parents themselves. In trying to secure justice for Lazarus, I had probably damaged my own case beyond repair.

"So what's your game plan now that the trial is over?" Josh asked.

"Hang on to this job for as long as I can." I didn't need to point out that I was probably finished as far as future expert engagements were concerned. "I can't wait to see what further winning assignments Jonathan will have for me."

Josh reached over and clapped me on the knee. "That, my friend, should be the least of your worries. Right, Alison? You may assume that the two of us are exchanging conspiratorial glances."

"Like *Smiley's People*," Alison added.

"But you still won't read me in?"

"We can't, without endangering the mission. For the time being, your role as Secret Agent Man is to maintain a low profile. And get in contact with Hallie. She's been frantic with worry. And, if I'm allowed to say it, proud as hell of you."

I did want to talk to Hallie. I just didn't know what to say.

Not chomping to reclaim my patient load, I spent the rest of the day fussing with my desk, trying to decide just how much of a personal touch I could still get away with. A worker had come in and put up my new artwork. The two canvasses felt like someone had thrown a jar of paste against a wall, which may have explained the titles "Unglued I" and "Unglued II." No doubt the irony of hanging them in a psychiatrist's office had escaped Jonathan. In the end, I opted to keep only two things handy: a photo of Louis and me at the Bronx Zoo, and a Rubik's Cube with tactile markings that I'd found in the online Braille Superstore.

I arrived home that evening to half a foot of snow and an equivalent stack of unopened mail. I deposited the mail inside the door and went back out to shovel the walk. While I worked, fat, wet flakes landed on my cheeks and stuck to my eyelashes and nose. In short order, I was covered from top to bottom, but the exertion felt good, so when I was done with my own front yard, I decided to clear the walk of the anonymous neighbor who had been doing the same favor for me all winter. Not knowing who that might be, I went down the entire row of houses, pushing the snow against the piles already heaped outside the doors.

I had almost reached the courtyard gate when a tap on the back told me I had company.

"Yuri Zhivago," Candace said. "It's been ages."

I hadn't called or spoken to her in weeks.

I turned around to face her, feeling thoroughly chagrined.

"Don't look so guilty," Candace said. "It's not every woman who gets ignored by a celebrity doctor."

Her tone told me I wasn't in serious trouble, which only made me feel worse.

"You heard about the trial."

"Pardon me for saying this, but I would have had to be deaf, dumb, and blind not to."

I tried to change the subject. "Are you just getting home from work?"

"No, I was inside making supper when I happened to glance out and see you looking like Frosty the Snowman."

"I thought I could use the exercise."

"Then come over to my place, when you're done. There's nothing like shoveling snow to build up an appetite."

"I don't know—" I began.

"C'mon. There's beef stew and a bottle of Burgundy inside. And I'm standing out here in nothing but my socks and slippers."

I figured I owed her an explanation, so after I put the shovel away, I went over to the grocery around the corner to pick up a baguette and some flowers.

"Forget-me-nots," Candace said when she looked inside the bag. "I hope I can count on that."

The stew was beyond delicious. Candace, I learned, had spent several of her summers off taking culinary courses at country houses in France. Her *daube du boeuf* was Julia Child perfect, fragrant with garlic, onion, and bacon and served with a nontraditional side of basmati rice. After days of malnourishment, I soaked it up like a sponge, along with huge helpings of bread, salad, and pears poached in vanilla syrup. Candace was polite enough to avoid the subject of my absenteeism until our plates were clean and I had found my way over to her living-room couch. She followed me with a fresh bottle of wine and our glasses.

"I think I've just been ambushed," I said, sinking comfortably into the cushions. "You didn't make all that food tonight."

"You're right. I had nothing to do the last few weekends, so I whipped up some meals for the freezer. Cooking has always been my way of taking the edge off loneliness."

I winced in discomfort. "I guess I deserved that."

"Yes, you did." She poured more wine for us both. "Though I know you've been busy."

That and ... conflicted. I wasn't exactly back in Hallie's good graces, but I couldn't deny that our clandestine alliance had given me renewed hope.

"I was at the trial, you know," she said, causing me to sit straight back up.

"You were?"

"Mmm-hmm. And I saw you with that lawyer. Well, not with her, but looking at her. Oh, damn, not that either. But she means something to you, doesn't she?"

She was too nice a lady ever to lead on. "Yes. But we're not together right now. Or I wouldn't have . . ."

"It's all right. That's why I invited you over here. I thought it was better than us going around avoiding one another every time our paths crossed."

"You're being too gracious. I—"

"Ssshh," Candace said. "Or I'll reconsider my good intentions. I'd rather have us remain friends, as well as neighbors. Just come over and keep me company now and again, like you have tonight."

"I will if you'll let me reciprocate." I made a wry smile. "Not that I'm much of a cook."

"Then let me teach you. Something tells me you neglect your stomach a good deal of the time."

"You're not worried about letting me handle your knives?"

"So long as you take them *by* the handle."

I slept poorly that night, plagued by vivid dreams. For a change, they weren't about Jack or my father. Or at least I didn't think so when my alarm went off. I almost always greet the day with a sense of trepidation that gradually lessens as I go about my morning routines. But today the feeling was worse, a knob of dread that resisted explanation, like someone had installed a pager in my brain that wouldn't stop beeping. Try as I might, I couldn't shut it down, not until after I had showered and was pouring milk on my cereal, when suddenly in the way dreams sometimes have of exploding into our consciousness, I remembered the one I was having just before I woke up.

I was in woods somewhere, deep north woods filled with pines over-hung with moss, like the ones I had once camped in as a Boy Scout. Overhead a full moon hung high between the branches, lighting the forest almost as if it were daylight, etching inky shadows in the underbrush. I startled at a branch cracking behind me and turned to find a handsome, dark-haired woman I knew must be Alison. "Hurry," she said. "There isn't much time." I looked at her arms and saw that they were empty. "Where's Mika?" I asked. "That's who we have to find," she replied. "But we have to be careful. There are wolves all around." She pointed the way and I followed, stepping carefully between the gnarled roots of the path she showed me. Then we reached a clearing of sorts where the moonlight shone so brightly it blinded me. "Hurry!" Alison said from somewhere up ahead where I could no longer see her. "I can't!" I cried. "I'm stuck." Alison reappeared and scolded me. "No you're not. You only think you are!"

The rest of the dream slipped away then, just as suddenly as it had emerged. I heard something dripping and realized the milk had over-flowed the bowl. *Perfect*, I thought, as I scurried to find a paper towel. It was only after I'd mopped up the mess and could consider the dream's meaning that I understood both its source and my anxiety. It didn't require any special psychiatric training. A child could have figured it out.

I hadn't yet done what my lawyer had asked me to do.

Still in my bathrobe, I turned on the television news. According to Tom Skilling, the Windy City's cheery messenger of meteorological calamity, the snowstorm that had started the day before wasn't expected to taper off until midafternoon. In the meantime, conditions were bleak. Schools were closed and all nonessential city, state, and private-sector employees were being urged to stay home. Sadly, nonessential probably applied to me, too. With the Lazarus trial over and my patients still being handled by my colleagues, I no longer had an excuse. If I was going to be snowbound, I might as well put the time to good use.

It was too early to call Yelena to tell her I wouldn't be in. Breakfast forgotten, I went to my small home office and rooted around in the moving crates for a legal pad and a pencil. I still sometimes doodled, a holdover from my sighted days that helped me think through a problem. I put both down on my desk and sat in the chair. I pushed the pencil down hard against the pad and drew harsh lines back and forth until the first sheet of paper was scored through. I tore it off, tossed it in a ball onto the floor, and started on another. I continued in this way through a few more sheets until the pencil point broke off. Another search through the boxes located my electric sharpener, which needed to be plugged in somewhere. The search for an outlet consumed another five minutes.

I was stalling.

I sat back down with the sharpened pencil and refocused. Like soldiers falling into formation, bits and pieces of that harrowing day began coming back to me.

7:00 a.m.	*Annie, swollen belly bulging beneath her pajamas, telling me Jack was running a fever . . .*
9:00 a.m.	*Me, stranded in traffic on the Hudson, pulling a journal from my briefcase and flicking on the dashboard light . . .*
10:00 a.m.	*Late to work. Patient meltdown. Rounds, meetings, more patients . . .*

Another ball of paper on the floor.

6:45 p.m.	*Annie calling. Jack's temperature up, crying constantly. "Annie, I've told you over and over. Fevers in young kids, even high ones, are nothing to get upset about."*
7:30 p.m.	*Dinner.*
8:45 p.m.	*Sex.*
10:15 p.m.	*Waking in confusion . . .*

More harsh scribbling. More hurled paper.

10:45 p.m.	*Dead battery*
12:00 a.m.	*I-95 backed up for miles. Tapping, tapping my fingers on the wheel*
12:45 a.m.	*Home. Annie hysterical.*
12:50 a.m.	*Take the stairs two at a time and . . .*

That was as far as I got before I broke down.

Time may dull our sins but it never pardons them.

I had rarely let myself to weep for my lost son, but I did so now, allowing the full weight of my crime to engulf me. Without wanting to, I had been no better than my father, causing irredeemable harm to my own flesh and blood. Perhaps it would have been better if I too had died young, under one of his many beatings. Then Jack wouldn't be dead and I wouldn't be here now, blind, impotent, and torn apart by remorse. Would I ever find a measure of peace?

I allowed the tears to come for a long time while the snow, in frigid counterpoint, continued falling outside.

It was only the thought of the living that eventually pulled me out of it. Louis was my son too and might stay that way if I could put aside my grief and think. Feeling hollow and a bit weak, I wiped my eyes on the sleeve of my robe and went back to the kitchen, noting along the way how much progress I'd made in mastering my new living arrangements. Moving from one room to the other was becoming far less treacherous. I filled a teapot and set it on the range, and circled the kitchen island several times while I waited for the water to boil, letting my mind empty of everything except the task at hand. What was it Alison had said to me on Christmas Day? *Haven't you ever thought about what Annie was doing all that time you were gone?*

Sleeping was what I'd always imagined. She was eight months pregnant, worn out from dealing with Jack all day. I had come home to her like that many times before: passed out on the family-room sofa, drained to the point of depletion. Usually I didn't try to rouse her. With the baby pressed up against her diaphragm, deep slumber was hard to come by. I would cover her with an afghan and put a pillow under her head, and she would murmur good night from some faraway place and stay there until morning while I performed guard duty: camped out on the floor of Jack's room so that I could immediately arrest any sound from his crib. When it came to Jack, Annie was like the princess and the pea. His slightest whimper would instantly wake her.

And that's when I realized the flaw in my thinking.

Jack couldn't have rested quietly that night. With the meningitis consuming him, he would have tossed, turned, and at the very least moaned until he fell into the comalike stupor I found him in when I burst through the door. And Annie wasn't sleeping when I came home either. She was pacing the den, red-eyed and strung-out. What else had Alison said? *If it had been me, I would have been screaming for an ambulance long before you returned.* Why hadn't Annie called for help when she couldn't reach me? A memory flooded in on me then, aided by my precision recall. The state of the room when I found her, everything as usual except . . . except for *something.* I put the picture before my mind's eye and scanned it, going from object to object until I saw: the wireless home phone empty of its receiver. Where else had I seen it that night? Damn it, where?

On the nightstand beside Jack's crib.

It didn't necessarily mean anything. I knew that Annie had tried several times to reach me. Later, I could see the calls lined up on my pager like the articles of an indictment. It was only because I had turned it off while sleeping with another woman—and then forgotten to turn it back on—that I failed to heed her frantic summonses. But thinking back on it now, all of her calls to me were before 9:30, a good three hours before I got home. Something had caused her to stop trying. Some*thing*—or was it someone else she had spoken to?

There was a simple way to find out. In theory, anyway, depending on how long the phone company kept records. It was only a few years ago. If I was lucky, they still had them. Whatever the answer, it paid to give them a call. I had written checks to New England Bell often enough, and the 800 number atop the service invoices came back to me easily. I could dial it right now.

If I had the stomach for it.

In a sudden flash of self-recognition, I realized why I had never asked these questions before. It wasn't merely because I was too ashamed of my role in Jack's death. It was also because I couldn't bear to think that Annie—beautiful, bland, and essentially guileless Annie— had kept the truth from me out of spite. If so, it implied a failure of our marriage much worse than I had ever imagined. If she had hated me that much.

But once I had started asking, there was no going back. It took a solid half hour of waiting on hold and the robotic announcement, "Your call may be monitored for quality-control assurance," repeated over and over before a live human being came on the line.

"Hello. My name is Megan. How can I assist you today?"

"You're talking about CDRs," she said after I'd explained what I was looking for.

"CDRs?"

"Call Detail Records. Yes, we keep them for five years."

"If I give you a date, can I get them sent to me?"

"Yes. What is the account number?"

I waited anxiously while she inputted the data into her terminal. It had just occurred to me that Annie might have changed the name on the account after I left.

"Yes," she said finally. "We have a current account with that number, billed to a D. Mark Angelotti."

"That's me," I said, silently thanking my luck.

"I'll need your passcode to activate the request."

Shit, I thought. My memory was good, but not that good.

"Or a Social Security number," she added helpfully.

I listened restlessly while she explained that it would take seven to ten business days for my request to be acted on. "Shall I have the records sent to the address at 850 Maple Lane in Cos Cob, Connecticut?"

Another potential hitch. "Er, would it be possible to forward them to me elsewhere? I'm temporarily based in Chicago."

"Certainly. I'll just need that address."

She took it down and informed me that a ten-dollar processing fee would be billed automatically to my account and appear on my next statement. I decided it would be pushing things to offer to pay it by credit card.

"Is there anything else I can help you with today?" Megan asked.

"No, you've been more than helpful."

I was taking a deep breath to steady myself when my phone started sounding again, to the tune of Jim Croce's "Operator." Thinking it was Megan calling back to say I had just been discovered in a fraud, I nervously punched the answer button.

But it wasn't the phone company.

It was Michelle Rogers.

NINETEEN

"What was so important that we needed to talk about it here?" I said to Michelle.

"Please. I'll tell you, but we have to keep it down."

We were in a tavern on West North Avenue appropriately called the Outpost. To get there, I'd had to take the 'L' to the Loop and the Blue Line to a stop on North Damen, a mere half a mile away from the place Michelle said she wanted to meet. In all, the trip had taken me two hours, not counting the number of times I had to detour around the lawn chairs staking a claim to parking spaces on the street.

I looked around the room—metaphorically speaking. The place was so dark, it could have been a coal mine. That is, if coal mines exuded the odors of perspiration, beer suds, and lard. Scuttling sounds near my feet told me all I needed to know about the booth we were seated in, along with the stuffing jutting out at angles from the Naugahyde bench. If I had to guess, there was more than one video gambling machine on the premises.

"I don't think there's much risk of us being overheard," I said. Besides the bartender clinking glasses on the opposite side of the room, the only other indication of human life was someone snoring loudly in a corner. "You couldn't have picked a nicer location? Like one of the restrooms at Union Station?"

"Please don't be mad at me," Michelle said. She sounded as upset as when I'd answered her call that morning, though I couldn't imagine it was because of anything serious. In my experience, lawyers were prone to hand-wringing and overdramatization. Even levelheaded Hallie tended to view whatever case she was working on as an epic clash between the forces of good and evil, and to be cast into a pit of despair when she found herself on the losing side. No doubt Michelle ascribed similar feelings to me and was concerned I might be taking the Lazarus defeat too hard.

The bartender appeared with our drinks, an on-tap lager some sales whiz had christened the "House Special." Against my better judgment, I took a sip. It tasted like it had been brewed in a Palmolive factory.

The bartender must have caught my expression. "Don't blame me," he said. "I don't do the buying around here. Can I get you guys a bite to eat?"

"A burger would really hit the spot," I said. "Considering I'm going to be sick anyway."

He laughed. "They're salmonella-free. I eat them myself."

"I'll have one of those, then. Well-done, please. Michelle?"

"I'm not hungry, thank you."

"So," I said to Michelle when he'd taken himself off, "what is it you wanted to tell me about—so far away from organized civilization?"

"I . . . I just needed to know you're OK."

Exactly as I suspected. I hastened to reassure her that the patient would live. "My ego has known better days, but that's nothing compared to what Rachel Lazarus must be feeling right now. I heard she decided not to appeal."

"I know. That's why I decided we had to talk. Before the judgment becomes final."

"It's not final already?"

"Not until she's sentenced. Until then, it can be reopened. Well, afterward too, but it's much harder under the law."

It seemed like a forlorn hope. "You think there's any chance of that?"

"I don't know. I wish . . ." She sounded close to tears.

I'd always suspected that Michelle's sympathies lay with the woman she was supposed to be prosecuting, but the emotion in her voice confirmed it. Michelle hadn't reached out simply to comfort me.

"You can't blame yourself for her conviction," I said, thinking I knew how to handle this. "You had a job to do. And it wasn't you calling the shots."

"I was just following orders, is that what you mean?" she challenged bitterly.

I shook my head. "Look, you said to me you weren't comfortable in the job you're in. Maybe it's time to look for something else. Not everyone is cut out to be a prosecutor. I hate the result as much as you do, but Rachel got a fair trial."

"You really think so?"

I backtracked. "Well, as fair as you can get under our system. The jury didn't buy my—I mean, *her* excuse. Partly because I screwed up. I accept that. I should have quit and let someone else take over. But that doesn't mean the verdict was flawed. The jury tried. Hallie, I . . . we all tried. But in the end it wasn't enough." I wondered exactly who I was trying to convince.

Michelle interrupted my lofty sentiments. "That's honestly the way you see it?"

At least we had gotten over the troublesome syntax. "I *see* a young woman who has doubts about her role in sending a battered woman to prison—"

Michelle put a hand on my arm to stop me. "You were set up."

"I know that. But—"

"No," Michelle hissed. "I mean *really* set up." Michelle removed her hand from my arm and sat back, as if waiting for me to catch on.

I took a swallow of the loathsome beer. "How, besides having intimate details of my childhood opened up for public inspection?"

Michelle didn't say anything.

"Michelle," I said in my most disarmingly threatening tone. "I hope you didn't drag me halfway across the city—and through a raging blizzard—just to drop hints. What are you trying to say?"

"If I tell you, no one can know you heard it from me. All right?"

"Will 'cross my heart and hope to die' be adequate?"

"You're not taking this seriously enough. You could be in danger."

"The only danger I'm worried about right now is contracting an infection from being in this joint."

"I mean it. There's a lot you don't know."

"Well, my ears are wide open."

More silence.

This was becoming maddening. "Dammit, Michelle. Just tell me."

Evidently she came to some sort of decision, because she said in a rush, "Tony rewrote Dr. Stephens report to say the things it did—about Rachel lying. Dr. Stephens agreed with you about the PTSD."

I should have been shocked, but I wasn't. And as much as I thought Di Marco capable of it, I didn't want to admit I'd been so easily duped. "How did he get to the report? I thought you said it stayed sealed—locked up in your desk."

"I thought it did, too. But I was wrong. Tony must have gotten to it."

"'Must have'?"

"I can't say exactly how, but he must have forced the lock on my desk. All of the furniture at the office is government-issue—cheap stuff. It would have been easy. You could probably do it with a paper clip."

I was still resistant. "That doesn't prove anything. How do you know the report was altered?"

"Because Dr. Stephens told me what he intended to say. Before he died. While I was helping him get ready."

I nearly exploded. "That's not what you told me before the trial. When I asked, you said you were as in the dark as everyone else."

"I thought I had to. To keep you on the case. I thought you were Rachel's only hope."

She was right about one thing: if I'd had so much as a hint, I would have quit at once.

Michelle had commenced sobbing. I pulled my handkerchief from my pocket and gave it to her. "Michelle, tell me exactly what Brad said to you, in as close as possible to the words he used."

"I really don't remember. It was all so technical. All I remember is that he agreed with what you said at the trial about her having a flash-back and not really knowing what she was doing."

"Did you make notes of the conversation—write it down anywhere?"

"No."

"So there's no way to prove what he said to you."

"Uh-uh."

Just then, the bartender appeared with my burger, but I waved him away.

"Suit yourself," he said. "But I'll have to charge you for it."

I pulled out my wallet and handed him a couple of twenties. "Is that enough to buy us some time alone?"

"You bet," he said. I could almost hear the wink.

I turned back to Michelle. "All right. But what makes you so sure it was Tony who rewrote the report—aside from the high esteem in which we both hold him?"

"There's other missing evidence."

"Go on."

"Notes the police made when they were first investigating the case. Conversations with Westlake's neighbors about who was seen going in and out of the house. I saw them when I first got assigned to the case, but when it was time to hand them over to the defense, the file was gone."

"Did you remember what was in the notes?"

"Not really. After Rachel confessed, we weren't pursuing other suspects."

"And you think . . . ?"

"Tony got rid of them. It had to be him."

I was beyond exasperated. "Michelle, if what you think is true, we're talking about obstruction of justice. You have to go to the authorities. At least bring it to Linda O'Malley's attention."

"I can't," Michelle wailed. "It's what you said. It will just be my word over his. No one will ever believe me. I'll lose my job and . . . and . . ."

Her whining left me without sympathy. "Why come to me, then? What do you expect me to do?"

"I thought, maybe . . . maybe you could tell your friend Hallie. Maybe you two could call for an investigation, get the verdict reopened—whatever."

I shook my head at such foolishness. "Not without proof."

"Please," Michelle implored. "Don't you get it? If someone else was in Westlake's house that night, Rachel might be innocent!"

"Yes, I see that, but—"

"And if I'm right about Tony and the report, it's even worse than that. Haven't you ever wondered what really happened to your friend?"

Her words stopped me in midsentence. A possibility had opened up, like a trap door at my feet.

Brad Stephens believed the same thing I did.

Brad Stephens died an untimely death.

Was it really an accident?

TWENTY

I needed to get to Hallie.

But first, I had some homework to do. So after Michelle left me at the Outpost—with more tearful pleas about keeping her name out of it—I searched my contacts list for a number. Either it wasn't in my phone or I was too worked up to find it. On the slim chance that I would find her there, I tried Yelena at the office.

She surprised me by picking up right away. "It's snowing," she said.

"Is that so? I hadn't noticed."

"I couldn't see two feet in front of me when I came back from the hairdresser."

"Welcome to the club. Can you look up a telephone number for me?"

"Directory assistance isn't working?"

"They fired all their employees. For being uncooperative."

"Some thanks I get for coming to work in a blizzard."

If I knew Yelena, it was only the cataclysm of missing her monthly cut and color that had dragged her downtown that day. "Have you asked Dr. Goldman about leaving early?"

"Of course. He was very concerned about my safety."

Unlike the cruel despot she was presently speaking to. "He's right," I said. "You should go home."

Yelena was too flabbergasted to speak.

"But not until you get me that number."

A few minutes later, I had reached Brad Stephens's former assistant and explained who I was.

"Of course I remember you. Dr. Stephens was a great admirer. What can I help you with?"

I didn't want to raise any alarm bells, so I launched into a story about needing to check a few references in Brad's report that appeared to be missing from the background materials sent to me. "I'm sure it was just an oversight, but I'm getting ready to box up my own files, and I'd like to be sure everything's there and accounted for."

"I'm so sorry, but Dr. Stephens did all his work on the Lazarus case at home. He felt it was inappropriate to use hospital resources when he'd been retained independently."

"So there's nothing you can point me to—no drafts, notes, nothing like it left in his office?"

"They just finished clearing it out last week. It was so sad. Of course, Inga—that's his wife—came in to collect all his personal items. She's such a wonderful lady, even brought along brownies for the staff. She was worried about how we were taking the loss."

I asked how Brad's wife was taking it.

"OK I guess, though it must be just awful for her. Dr. Stephens was a very doting husband. Toward the end, when it was becoming harder and harder for him to get around, he often asked me to run out and pick up flowers or a box of candy for her. But not in the way some bosses do—like it's expected. More like you were doing him an enormous favor. That's the way he was—always making you feel appreciated." She sniffled. "I already miss him so much."

I commiserated a bit before asking my next question. "Do you think Mrs. Stephens would mind it if I contacted her?"

"Mind? Oh no. I'm sure she'd appreciate hearing from one of his friends."

"Does she work during the day?"

"Yes. She's an artist—a sculptor—pretty famous around Chicago, actually. Most days, she's in her studio in Wicker Park. I can't say if she's there now, but it may be worth a try."

She gave me a phone number and an address, which I memorized by repeating it out loud before thanking her and ringing off. I tried the number several times, only to get kicked to an answering machine. Still seated in the grimy booth at the Outpost, I tapped at the table with a finger before calling the bartender over.

"How likely is it that I can get a cab to around here?"

He gave me an insider's chuckle. "Maybe if it was August and eighty degrees outside. But today? You'd have better luck trying to score rink-side tickets to the Hawks."

"That's what I thought. Do you happen to know how far we are from Wicker Park?"

"Not far at all. Where exactly are you going?"

I gave him the address.

"You're in luck. That's only ten or twelve blocks from here. But how're you going to get there by yourself—I mean, with your girlfriend gone and all? Great-looking chick by the way." He stopped suddenly, as if embarrassed by something.

"Yes?" I said, scowling up at him.

"I feel for you, dude. I just hope she's not toying with your emotions."

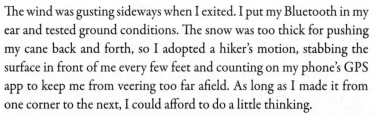

The wind was gusting sideways when I exited. I put my Bluetooth in my ear and tested ground conditions. The snow was too thick for pushing my cane back and forth, so I adopted a hiker's motion, stabbing the surface in front of me every few feet and counting on my phone's GPS app to keep me from veering too far afield. As long as I made it from one corner to the next, I could afford to do a little thinking.

I still wanted to believe that Michelle was imagining things. Di Marco was a snake—as sleazy and underhanded as the worst political attack ad—but he'd always impressed me as shrewd. Too shrewd to open himself up to a murder charge? Evidence could be hidden away with no one the wiser except the cops, who had as big a stake in getting a conviction as he did. Engineering a traffic accident involved a much higher level of risk. And as much as we didn't get along, I thought he had an honorable streak. A few months back, he'd expressed disdain for someone who attacked me knowing full well that I couldn't identify them. It didn't seem like the sentiments of a man who would easily mow down a cripple on a street.

But if Michelle was right and Brad's report was altered, the only other explanation for my friend's death was coincidence, and I didn't put much faith in coincidences either. And if it wasn't Di Marco who had rewritten Brad's report, who else would have gone to such lengths to secure Rachel's conviction? Not Michelle, who seemed as much in Rachel's corner as I was, as well as genuinely distressed by the verdict. And not Linda O'Malley, who had gone out of her way to hire not one, but two independent psychiatrists when there were plenty of experts who would have called Rachel the Demon Barber of Fleet Street if that's what O'Malley wanted.

The more likely scenario was that Brad's report hadn't been monkeyed with, that he believed in good conscience that Lazarus was lying. If I knew Brad, he had entered into the assignment as I did, filled with concern for this depressed, isolated, and broken woman, only to doubt her story over time. Michelle was young and horribly naive. She might have taken something Brad said out of context or mistaken empathy for a belief in Rachel's innocence.

The missing police notes sounded much more likely. Similar rumors about Di Marco had floated around for years. But I wasn't sure how it helped. Rachel never denied she'd killed her husband, and the forensic evidence confirmed it. According to the ME, her fingerprints were on the poker that killed Westlake, along with the knife used to sever his genitals. At most, the notes would show that other people had visited Westlake's house on the night he was killed. It seemed a slim reed on which to proclaim her innocence even if—by some miracle—it could be proved that Di Marco had hidden the notes from the defense.

On the other hand, proving that Brad had reached a different conclusion could conceivably help Rachel. The jury had found my testimony fatally flawed, but they might have been won over by an expert with less skin in the game. At the very least, tampering with the report was a serious business, one that was bound to get the attention of Judge

Sandy. The first order of business, then, was to find out if Brad had left any other indication of what he was thinking. And his widow seemed the only way to find out.

My phone broke in then, announcing that the address Brad's assistant had given me was on the right. I made a ninety-degree turn from the sidewalk and was surprised to find a wooden fence. Since I was looking for an artist's studio, I'd expected something like a warehouse entrance. This appeared to be a residence, older and set back from the street. With some banging of my cane along the posts, I located a gate and then the latch. A short walk brought me to a flight of steps, slippery in the snow but flanked by a handrail. I ascended the staircase, unwound my muffler from my face, and was on the verge of knocking when I was stopped by a low noise inside.

It was the sound of a woman weeping.

I almost reconsidered what I was doing. What right did I have to come barging in on a bereaved woman, bearing the news that her husband's death might not have been an accident? Was I doing it to right a wrong, or to take the sting out of my pathetic performance at Rachel's trial? But I had come this far. And I thought that Brad, if he were still alive, would want me to pursue the truth.

I put a mittened knuckle to the door and was just about to knock when it swung inward of its own accord.

"What are you doing?" a woman demanded shrilly in a voice still thick with tears. "Didn't you see the 'No Solicitation' sign on the gate?"

"I, uh—"

"Are you another one of the Jehovah's Witnesses? I told the group that came by yesterday to please leave me alone."

"No, I—"

She must have noticed then. "Oh bother, I'm sorry. I didn't see . . . But *of course* you're not one of them." I detected a hint of the South in her accent, though I wasn't familiar enough with the region to place it.

I hoisted my cane smiled. "This isn't a Bible, if that's what you mean."

"But what are you doing out all alone in the snow?"

I had a business card in my pocket, but it took some seconds to get it out with my mittens still on. I handed it to her and asked, "Are you Inga Stephens?"

She perused the card and said, "No. My name is Duckworth. I kept my maiden name so as not to be confused with *The Farmer's Daughter*. But Bradley was my husband. Your name is familiar. Did you know him?"

"We were professional colleagues. And friends of sorts. I seem to have found you at a bad time, but would you mind if I came in for a few minutes? There's something I'd like to ask you about."

"Something important enough that you came all this way on foot in a blizzard. Please excuse my manners. I'm not really myself today. Do you need . . . ?"

"If I might just take your arm."

She led me through a chilly vestibule and into a parlor of some sort, where the air was only slightly warmer.

"These old houses," she apologized. "When the wind is whipping around like this, they're almost impossible to keep warm.

"Victorian?"

"Queen Anne," she said. "Eighteen eighty-five. One of the oldest houses on the block."

"I was expecting something different. Brad's assistant—that's how I got your address—said it was your studio."

"Back of the house. In fact, why don't we go there to talk? I have a space heater going and it will be far more comfortable. Please, let me take your coat. Cup of tea?"

I removed my outerwear, and she led me back through a series of wood-floored rooms to a kitchen, where she stopped to put a kettle on the stove and apologized once more for the welcome. "I've been working on something, a bust of my husband to remember him by. I thought it would help—to recall his features with something more concrete than a photograph. With each passing day, it's harder and harder to remember exactly what he looked like. Did you ever . . . ?" She stopped embarrassedly. "But I'm being rude again."

"No. I understand. I have a similar problem. I remember faces, but in a slightly skewed way, like pieces of a mosaic that don't quite come together. I can still see your husband that way."

She seemed surprised. "Then you haven't been . . . ?"

I shook my head. "Just a few years. I knew Brad before."

"Then perhaps you'll appreciate what I've done."

When the tea was ready, she put cups and saucers on a tray, and I followed her to the back of the house and down a short flight of steps into what I guessed was a glassed-in sun porch.

"It's an old solarium," she explained. "Tacked onto the house in the teens. I work very small pieces, mostly in ceramic or soapstone, so it's all the space I need. Though now I'm thinking of selling the house and buying a condo. I'm lonely without Bradley, and there are just too many memories here—"

Her voice caught, and I wondered whether I should offer my handkerchief.

"Do you have family nearby?"

"No. I'm a transplant. From Memphis originally. And Bradley and I have only one child, a daughter who lives on the West Coast. But my friends have been wonderful. In fact, it's been hard shooing them away. I'm only now finding the private time to mourn. But enough of my self-pity. Come, you're welcome to touch it."

She guided my hand to a smooth, oval-shaped object around the size of an egg sitting atop a nearby workbench. I examined it, turning it this way and that, just making out the eyes, nose, and mouth carved from the stone.

"What do you think?" she asked eagerly after a few minutes.

"It's . . . it's a very good likeness." I didn't have the heart to tell her how little my fingers could tell me about a full-sized face, let alone a miniature like this. "You mind if I hold it while we talk?" It seemed to give her comfort that I could appreciate and admire her work.

She settled us in canvas director's chairs near the space heater, which emitted a strong, scorched-smell warmth. I hadn't felt cold walking over, but I felt the chill now. Or perhaps it was the nature of my mission.

"So," Inga said with forced cheer, "you're a psychiatrist. Like my late husband."

"We worked in the same field."

"Maybe that's where I heard your name. Cream and sugar?"

I said yes and tried to find a tactful way to broach the subject I was there for.

She did it for me. "You said you had something to ask me."

"I don't know if you heard that I was hired to replace Brad . . . uh, Bradley in the Lazarus trial."

"No. I haven't paid attention to the news in weeks. Not since the funeral. That poor woman. Bradley said often how sorry he felt for her."

"So you and he discussed the case."

"We always talked about the things he was working on. Oh, not specifics, especially where patients were concerned, but in general. What happened to her—was she let go?"

"Er, no," I said. "The jury found her guilty. Of first-degree murder."

"Why that's just terrible!" She sounded entirely shocked.

My antennae immediately went up. "That's a surprise to you?"

"Not a surprise, necessarily. I mean, the police can do whatever they want, can't they? But Bradley was so excited. You're saying the case was tried after all?"

"Yes, it was tried. I testified on Ms. Lazarus's behalf. Not very successfully, I'm sad to admit. But you're saying Brad thought it wouldn't get that far?"

"That's right. You have to understand. Bradley was a big fan of mystery novels, TV shows, anything involving detective work. He thought he noticed something no one else had."

"What thing, if you remember?"

"I don't know. He wouldn't say, in case he turned out to be wrong. 'I'm not a pathologist, after all,' he said to me. And he always had this fear . . . this fear that he was starting to slip. Because of the Parkinson's, you understand. He didn't want me to worry. 'We'll see if I'm right and then I'll tell you about it,' he said. But I know he told that lawyer, the one handling the case."

"Di Marco?"

"That sounds familiar."

"And that's all you can remember?"

"I'm afraid so. Except that it had something to do with the body being moved."

"Westlake's body?" I asked eagerly, leaning toward her and nearly spilling my tea.

"Yes, if that's the man—the professor, I mean—who was killed."

"Do you know when Brad had this conversation with the lawyer?"

"Not exactly. Though it must have been before he finished his report. I know he was hoping he wouldn't have to complete it."

"Because of what he intended to say about Ms. Lazarus?"

"Because he hoped she'd be freed long before then." She stopped, as though a thought had just crept into her mind. "Why are you asking me all these things?"

It was only fair that I explain. So I did, trying my best not to raise the possibility that Brad's death was other than a hit-and-run.

I failed miserably. When I was only halfway through, she interrupted me angrily. "Stop."

She stood up and went over to stand by the window. A few minutes went by before she spoke again in a low, angry voice. "It was snowing like this that night, too. I thought he was insane to go out. I offered to drive him to wherever he was going. He said driving would be too dangerous, that the exercise would be good for him. I should have put my foot down. I didn't like to make him feel that he was growing dependent. He was entitled to his pride. Then, when the police came, it didn't even occur to me . . . I just accepted what they told me. What you're saying is I shouldn't."

I hastened to backtrack. "Mrs. Stephens, I mean Ms. Duckworth, I—"

"No," she commanded. Steel had replaced the pain in her voice. "Don't play games with me. What else do you know that you haven't told me?"

I shook my head. "Right now, I don't know anything, except that the report given to me may not have been the one your husband wrote. Or that parts of it were changed. And I'm not even sure of those things. Either way, it could still have been an accident."

"No," she said firmly. "No, it couldn't have been."

"What makes you so sure?"

"Because I looked. God help me, I looked!"

I was having trouble following her. "Looked at what?"

"What I told you just now about catering to his pride, that was a lie. I thought . . . when he wouldn't tell me why he was going out in such awful weather, I thought he was having an affair. I was so hurt that I . . ."

I was beginning to get the picture. "You let him leave."

"Yes, and then, after he was killed, I didn't want to know. Where he went. He was already lost to me. But after the funeral, I couldn't help myself. So I checked his phone. He received only one call that night, shortly before he left the house. When I called the number myself, I was so relieved."

"Whose number was it?" I asked, though I thought I already knew.

"It wasn't an individual line. It was the number of a switchboard."

It was all the confirmation I needed. "The switchboard of the State's Attorney's office?"

"That's right. Now what can I do to help you find Bradley's killer?"

TWENTY-ONE

Hallie lived in a stylish Greystone in Bronzeville, bought with her first law-firm paycheck. After years of subsisting on poverty-level wages at the State's Attorney's office, she was ecstatic to have three thousand square feet to herself, and only a stone's throw from Pilsen, where her parents still lived. On the day she moved in, her mother wept. Though Hallie wasn't the only one of her siblings to earn a college degree, none of the others could match her present salary. In that respect we were alike, having both risen from humble beginnings to the outsized rewards of our respective careers. But whereas I had grown up an only child in an emotionally impoverished home, Hallie's family was as big and happy as the Waltons.

Family obligations were on my mind as I inched my way forward through another snow drift. Calling ahead would have been the sensible thing to do, but I knew Hallie would have insisted on coming to get me. At 4:30 p.m., the storm was finally winding down, only to be followed by perilously slick roads and plummeting temperatures. The streets were all but deserted. Apart from the occasional crunch of anti-lock brakes, the only sounds were the shrieking of the wind and the clicking of solitary traffic signals. Each step was a battle to stay upright against the blasts pummeling my sides.

By the time I got to Prairie Avenue, my nose was a running faucet and my limbs were numb. I located the flight of steps leading up to Hallie's door and rang.

No one answered.

I tried again, pressing the button longer this time. Still no sounds of life.

Feeling like an imbecile, I flipped the crystal on my watch. It was now after five, but still too early for Hallie to have come home if, as I now suspected, she'd braved the short journey to her office that morning. Perhaps she hadn't driven. Perhaps she, like me, had judged public transportation to be the better bet and was now following in my footsteps, taking the 'L' south to 35th Street and only now squeezing through the turnstile to begin the bone-chilling mile I'd just traveled myself. If so, should I phone her? Or flirt with exposure by turning around and trying to get home?

Just then, an overhead light switched on, flooding my indecision with hope.

"You idiot!" I heard Hallie say.

I almost collapsed across the threshold in relief.

A short while later, I was cocooned in a quilt on Hallie's sofa with a tumbler of bourbon in my hand, basking in the heavenly warmth of her fireplace. Hallie was seated a few feet away, giving me a proper scolding.

"Let's see," she said. "First, you don't answer my calls for almost a week."

"I was hiding from the press."

"You never heard of caller ID?" She went on, ticking off my transgressions like they were items on a grocery list.

"Then, you ignore all my messages."

"Not ignore. I was waiting for the right time to call back."

"Which was when? After the next millennium? Then, unlike every other sensible human being in Chicago, you go traipsing outdoors in the middle of a polar vortex to take the train down here—"

"Two trains actually. I wasn't home when I started out. I was in Wicker Park."

"Is that supposed to make me feel better? Why didn't you take a cab?"

I gave her a look of incredulity.

"Or call Boris?"

"Yelena said he was tied up. And I can only guess how she'd take it out on me if he got stuck somewhere."

"All right. But you could have phoned me."

"I didn't want you out on the roads in this weather. Besides, I can take care of myself."

"I wouldn't press that point right now. You're still shivering like an aspen."

"Only because it took you close to a century to answer the doorbell," I said.

"I was upstairs taking a bath. I came down as soon as I could get a bathrobe around my shoulders."

I desperately wanted to know if that was all she was wearing. "Aren't you even mildly interested in what I was doing all the way up in Wicker Park?"

"No, because that would mean you're even more reckless than I thought."

I waited an appropriate interval for her curiosity to get the better of her.

"All right, mystery man. Tell me."

"I will. But first, is there anything around here to eat?" I hadn't had a bite all day and was starting to feel the effects of the alcohol on an empty stomach.

"I could probably rustle up some cheese and crackers." Hallie never found time for the supermarket and subsisted largely on snack food and the care packages periodically supplied by her mother. "Or, if you're really hungry we can order from Chinatown."

"Will they deliver on a night like this?"

"They'd deliver in the middle of a typhoon if we had any in Chicago."

After Hallie had phoned Barbecue King, I told her about the events of the day, starting with the call from Michelle Rogers.

Hallie was miffed that Michelle had gotten ahold of me so easily. "That mousy little thing cowering behind Di Marco during the trial?"

"I've been told she's rather attractive."

"Maybe. If you like the timid and palely loitering look."

But her dismissive attitude quickly turned to ire as I went on. "Wait. Michelle thought Stephens's report had been edited and did nothing about it? Did she realize lawyers have lost their licenses over less?"

"Don't go too hard on her," I said. "She thought Lazarus deserved a champion and was trying to keep me on the case. I would have resigned if I'd known."

"That just demonstrates how stupid she is. If she'd come forward when she should have, I could have gotten a continuance. Not to mention a change in prosecutors. I can't believe that bastard Di Marco thought he could get away with it. On second thought, maybe I can." I could feel as well as hear her foot tapping ever more angrily on the carpet.

"Can you use the altered report to get Lazarus a new trial?"

"It depends. Based on what you've told me, all we have right now is Michelle's word for it. And since Judge Sandy didn't allow Stephens's report into evidence, it's going to be hard to show prejudice. Even with proof, I'm not sure it's enough to undo the conviction."

"And we don't have proof—not yet, anyway." Inga Duckworth had promised to look through her husband's papers and get back to me if she found anything. "But there's a lot more going on than just mucking with evidence. Give me a refill on the bourbon. And you'd better pour one for yourself, too."

I told her about the allegedly missing police notes. And my visit to Inga. And the phone call that had summoned Brad outdoors on the night he was run down. By the time I'd finished, Hallie had gotten up and was pacing the room.

"So someone got to Stephens before he could testify," she said furiously.

"It's sure starting to look that way."

"Di Marco." It wasn't a question.

"It looks that way to me too. I had a hard time wrapping my head around it at first, but who else would have cared that much about ensuring Lazarus was found guilty?"

"The only thing Tony didn't count on was his boss hiring you to take Stephens's place."

I laughed uneasily. "You mean I'm lucky I didn't become an accident victim myself?"

"No, I'm sure you were on safe ground. But only because two hit-and-runs in the same case wouldn't have gone unnoticed. And once Di Marco found that letter from your guidance counselor, he had another way to take you down. I'm still kicking myself for giving him the opening."

"He would have found a way regardless."

"Still . . ." Hallie said sympathetically.

"Don't," I said.

"Don't what?"

"Don't feel sorry for me."

"Hmmph," Hallie said. "All right. Just to avoid a debate, I won't. Though I think I understand you a little better now. In the meantime, what are we going to do about all of this?"

"We're going to take it one step at a time. Starting with restoring our blood-sugar levels. I just heard a car pull up outside."

I waited until we had cleaned up most of the Peking Duck, Char Siew Pork, and Yeung Chow fried rice to raise what was foremost on my mind.

"Hallie, how much digging into the Lazarus case did you do?" I asked, finally putting my chopsticks down and groping around for something to wipe the grease from my mouth.

Hallie put a foil containing a moist towelette in my hand. "You're asking me that now? Mind if I take the last pancake?"

"If I eat any more, I'll explode. Did you hear what I just asked?"

"I did and the answer is pretty much none."

"Why? That doesn't sound like your usual approach."

"It isn't. But I'm duty bound to follow my client's instructions. I'm told it was hard enough getting Rachel to agree to the Battered Woman's—I'm sorry, PTSD—defense. She was insistent on us not raising any other issues."

"And that's not odd in your experience?"

"More than ninety-five percent of arrests end in guilty pleas. Our justice system couldn't function otherwise. So no, I don't find it odd. Plus, she confessed. And don't get started on the police egging people into confessions. The public defender was very clear with Rachel about her ability to recant if she'd felt any sort of pressure. Rachel was equally clear that she was responsible for her husband's death."

"But then why not just plead that way and be done with it? Or cop to a lesser charge? Surely the prosecution would have accepted an offer of second-degree murder or even manslaughter in exchange for a substantial prison term."

"You don't know prosecutors like I do. Of course her lawyers raised the issue, but the best Di Marco would offer was thirty years."

"Still, that's better than a life sentence. If Lazarus really thought she was guilty, why go to trial and risk everything?"

Hallie paused before replying. "I don't know why. I always assumed it was because she wanted the world to know what a monster Westlake was. To help other women in the same position."

I shook my head. "Rachel didn't strike me as that kind of person. I couldn't see her, obviously, but her entire demeanor when I was questioning her that day in Cook County spoke of reluctance. She was downplaying what Westlake did to her—not building it up the way she would if she wanted to grandstand."

"So what's the answer to your question?"

"I don't know," I admitted. "But what if the police—everyone—has been wrong about her?"

I felt Hallie's eyes on me. "What are you saying—that Rachel is innocent?"

"Brad apparently thought so. I'm just wondering if it's possible."

"I don't see how. Her fingerprints were all over the murder weapon, in addition to the knife used on Westlake's corpse."

"I agree that's what the forensics show. But just for the sake of argument, let's say it wasn't Rachel who killed her husband. Let's say she came upon Westlake when he was already dead. Maybe her fingerprints were on the poker because she picked it up by accident. If you remember, she said she had no recollection other than coming to and seeing the poker in her hand. What if someone else got to Westlake first?"

"Like who?"

"That I can't say. But a woman as psychologically under siege as Lazarus might have easily convinced herself she was the murderer. And believed she should be punished for it. Then, when the Battered Woman's defense was suggested to her, she went along, partly because she was being told she should, and partly out of indifference to what might happen to her."

"What about Westlake's castration? Are you denying she was responsible for that too?"

"No, I think that was her, and for the reason I gave at trial. She was reenacting the scene from *A Tree Grows in Brooklyn*. Hauling the body across campus was her way of ensuring that she'd be caught and punished for what she—and everyone else—assumed was her own act."

"OK, I agree it's theoretically possible. But the ME was quite clear that Westlake's mutilation occurred shortly after his death—no more than half an hour is what I remember him saying. Meaning it was Rachel both times, unless the real murderer had just slipped out the door or was standing by, watching, both of which seem unlikely."

I thought about this. "How easily can you lay your hands on the ME's report?"

"As easily as walking into the next room. The case file is still sitting in my study. All thirty boxes worth."

"Let's go look through them, then. Maybe whatever bothered Brad Stephens will pop out at us too. And while we're at it, let's also go searching for any police notes."

TWENTY-TWO

"I should have my own license revoked," Hallie said. "Or be hauled in front of a firing squad."

It was several hours later. A thorough search through the file pertaining to *State of Illinois v. Rachel Lazarus* had failed to yield a single item resembling a police officer's notebook.

"It doesn't mean you screwed up," I said.

"I'm still disgusted with myself."

I did my best to console her. "You were just going along with your client's wishes. We don't even know that the notes exist, let alone what they might say."

"Oh, they exist all right—or did before Di Marco got rid of them. Of that I'm certain. Even in this day and age of laptops and tablets, most cops—especially the old-school ones—take notes by hand. And they're usually more accurate than their typed reports, which are mainly intended to impress their superiors. Any defense lawyer worth her salt knows to go looking for them."

"Speaking of which, what *do* the typed reports say?"

Not much, as it turned out. Except that, according to the neighbors, there were several people in and out of Westlake's home on the night he was killed, though no one had followed up on their identity. There was also this tidbit about Westlake's daughter, Olivia:

May 16, 11:30 a.m. Visited W's daughter at her dormitory at 5801 South Ellis to notify of suspected homicide. Residential Advisor present. Young lady very distraught, asking after her mother. Daughter cannot say who may have killed father. Believes possible victim of hate crime . . .

"That's odd," Hallie said immediately. "Her first thoughts were for her mother. I thought the two didn't get along."

I remembered that, too. "And according to the news, Olivia didn't show up for a single day of trial."

"That's right," Hallie said. "She wasn't even interested enough to be there for the verdict. If it had been my mother, you would have had to put me in chains to keep me away."

"Did you ever try to contact her?"

"Rachel asked me not to. And I admit I didn't see any reason to before now. Do you think she knows something?"

"No idea." It suddenly struck me as significant that in all the hoopla, no one had heard a peep out of Olivia. Not even the press had managed to hound a statement out of her. I thought back on the night of the faculty party with Candace. What was it her friend Amanda had said about the girl? That she was shy and rarely spoke up in class. Maybe that explained it. Either way, it was high time someone had a word with Rachel's daughter.

Hallie agreed it was worth following up on. "As well as talking to those neighbors. I want to know if any of them saw or heard something that didn't make it into the file."

That settled, we turned to the ME's report, which as usual was dry and filled with detail. Hallie read from a perch on the coffee table while I lounged with my back to the sofa, listening to the steady cadence of her speech above the comforting hiss of the fire. It felt sublime to be back in her orbit again, even if I had to undergo thorough humiliation to get there.

"*Subject is a well-developed white male, approximately one hundred sixty pounds in weight . . .*"

Before long, I was growing impatient with all the tiresome jargon. "Skip to the cause of death."

"*. . . immediate cause of death, blunt force trauma to the head with cerebral contusion, subarachnoid and subdural hemorrhage . . .*"

"Which means that he died from a skull fracture," I said irritably. "Why doesn't it just say that?"

"*Localized injuries, including laceration above the right orbital cavity, suggest decedent struck with a heavy metal object between eighteen*" *and twenty-two centimeters in diameter. Blood samples taken from fire-place poker found at scene will be tested to confirm . . ."*

Several pages and much hemming and hawing later, the report moved on to postmortem injuries.

"Severing of the genitalia produced massive bleeding in situ, approximately 1300 c.m. based on recovered samples. Using regression analysis it was determined that the interval between time of death and the removal of the decedent's penis and testes was no longer than thirty minutes based on the formula established by Spencer-Fleming: amount of postmortem bleeding (cm = .9571 × time since death (h) + 626.659 . . ."

"There," Hallie said. "That's what I was saying before about timing."

I nodded, thinking. As a rule, when the body dies, the heart stops pumping blood to the arteries, so that injuries inflicted on a corpse produce little bleeding. The ME's report indicated that enough blood was found where Westlake fell to suggest his genitals were removed within a short time after his death. The conclusion seemed solid, but I was still mindful of Brad's remark to his wife about the body being moved. And there was something else I wanted to know.

"Hallie, see if says anything in there about lividity."

"Remind me again what that is."

"It's a medical term that comes from the Latin word for *black and blue*. After the heart stops beating, gravity forces blood to settle into the lowest areas of the body, producing patches of purplish discoloration under the skin, except for places where the body was in contact with a hard surface, where the skin remains white, or blanched. Eventually the blanching becomes fixed. It's one way a coroner can tell if a body's been moved postmortem."

"All right," Hallie said. "But everyone knows Westlake's body was moved after his death. Why would it be significant?"

"I don't know. But Brad evidently thought it was, so humor me."

"OK, I'm looking." Hallie flipped silently through a few pages. "Here we go," she said at last.

"Livor mortis blanching most noticeable in the decedent's buttocks, at the backs of the calves, and to a much lesser extent, along the shoulder blades . . ."

As would be expected if Westlake's corpse had been removed from his house shortly after death and then spent the night on its back in the university quad. There didn't seem to be anything there, either. What on earth had caught Brad's eye?

Just then, a log collapsed in the fireplace with a muted crash.

"Do you want me to put another one on?" I asked, half stirring from my place on the sofa.

"No, I'll get it," Hallie said.

As she stood and moved past me around the coffee table, a piece of her robe slipped and grazed my leg. On top of the alcohol I'd consumed, the thought of what her movement may have exposed—and that I couldn't see—sent blood rushing into my groin. I felt my penis begin to stiffen and . . .

"That's it!" I almost shouted, sitting up straight and groping for a pillow.

"What is?" Hallie said, turning around from the fire.

I hastily plopped the pillow over my midsection. "That's what Brad meant about the body being moved!"

"At the risk of being boringly repetitive, so what?

My erection had subsided almost as quickly as it had started, so I stood and moved into the center of the room. "Here, I'll show you. Come over here and hit me on the head with something. Preferably not a fireplace tool."

"Are you sure? It sounds like you could use some sense knocked into you."

I glared at her. "Use my cane. It's over by the door."

When Hallie returned, I asked her to stand a foot or two away from me. "Now, pretend to smash me over the head with the handle right here." I pointed at my temple above the right eyebrow. Hallie complied—using, I thought, a little more force than was strictly necessary—and I mimicked staggering back. I got down to the carpet and assumed more or less the same position I had occupied on the sofa minutes earlier, stretched out with my feet in front of me and my back on the floor. To add even more verisimilitude, I lolled my head to one side like a dead man.

Hallie started to giggle. "Don't tell me I'm now supposed to go and fetch a carving knife from the kitchen."

"I'm not that insane."

Her giggling degenerated into full-blown mirth. "Hell, I know this isn't supposed to be funny, but you look so . . . authentic."

"Probably the glassy-eyed stare. Now, let's assume I've been lying here dead for several hours. Based on what I told you about gravity, where would you expect the blood in my body to settle?"

"Here, beneath your shoulders. And here," she said, nudging my buttock with a toe. "On both sides. And here too, under your calves. Except it wouldn't, because they're all touching the floor. So they'd be white in appearance, not purple."

"That's right. Now go back and read what it says in the ME's report."

She did:

"*Livor mortis blanching most noticeable in the decedent's buttocks, at the backs of the calves, and to a much lesser extent, along the shoulder blades . . .*"

". . . 'to a much lesser extent along the shoulder blades,'" I repeated after her. "Now, looking at me right now, why do you suppose that is?"

"I don't know," Hallie said thoughtfully. "They should all look the same."

"Uh-huh. Unless this isn't how I landed after you struck me. Let's do it one more time."

We repeated the experiment. Only this time, instead of falling to the floor, I reached over and found the wall next to the fireplace and, placing my back to it, slid to the floor in a seated position, like a drunken marionette with my legs splayed out before me. "Where is the blood going to pool now?"

"In your . . ." Hallie stopped. I'd never known her to be shy about naming body parts, but that part of my anatomy was clearly a dicey subject—for both of us.

"That's right," I said, patting my fly innocuously. "So if you came upon my corpse and opened me up, uh, . . . here, a lot of blood might escape my body, even if it was more than half an hour after my death.

That's why it's important that the body was moved. Because it was moved and everybody knew it from the beginning, nobody paid any attention to where the discoloration was strongest."

Hallie caught on quickly. "And, therefore, nobody ever thought to ask what position Westlake's body was in before it was moved. But if you're right about this, he could have been dead for longer than the ME thought and that means—"

I filled in the rest. "—Rachel might not be the real killer after all."

TWENTY-THREE

It was well past midnight when we finally finished scouring the case file and Hallie was busy laying out a plan of attack.

"We need to find out anyone, besides Rachel, who might have wanted to see Westlake dead."

"That won't be easy," I said. "We're probably talking dozens."

"True. But most murder victims are killed by someone close to them. The problem will be getting past the gates of the ivory tower. When it's a scandal like this, institutions always close ranks. I can picture the administration breathing a huge sigh of relief when the police arrested Rachel. They're not going to welcome us showing up on campus and trying to reopen the case." She let out a sigh. "I'll have to call around to my partners tomorrow. One of them has to have donated to the alumni fund this year—enough of a contribution to get us past the door. I give every year too, but not the pots of gold that would earn us an entrée."

I hesitated before volunteering that I might know a faster way in.

"OK, let's have it."

I explained about Candace and the faculty party in December, leaving out my unfortunate encounter with the drunken head of campus counseling and whose bed I'd ended up in that night.

Hallie wasn't fooled in the slightest.

"This Candace is your neighbor?"

"A little more than that," I said, opting for a modest degree of candor.

Hallie let a long minute pass. When she spoke again, it was with strained stoicism. "I guess I couldn't have expected anything else. I mean, I was the one who—"

I had an overpowering urge to jump across the several feet that separated us and ... well, ravage her wouldn't be putting it too strongly. But something I couldn't explain held me back.

"Once you offered to clear the air," I said. "About us. There's nothing I want more. But after we're done with this mess. After we've done what we can for Rachel."

Hallie indicated her assent by reaching over and taking my hand. It burned like a bonfire in mine and almost caused me to chuck my good intentions. I took a deep breath. "I can't let you drive me home tonight, but would it be OK if I slept here—on the couch?"

It was the most gentlemanly thing I had ever done.

And one I would later earnestly come to regret.

The next morning found us on our way to Hyde Park after a brief stop at my place for a change of clothing and a phone call to Candace. Candace, bless her generous heart, had been happy to be of assistance, and we were on our way to meet with Erik Blum, the head of the Sociology Department I'd met at the party, who agreed to grant us an interview in between classes and meetings.

Despite the low mercury reading, the sun was shining like polished steel as we sped down a post–rush hour Lake Shore Drive. While she steered us in her vintage MG, Hallie kept up a running commentary on the scenery, a habit left over from her childhood, when she'd been inseparable from her brother Geraldo, twelve months her senior and blind since birth. In those days, they'd traveled all over the city together, not because Gerry needed the help but because, being so close in age, they were almost like twins. Gerry's nickname for her was Nancy Drew, and it had stuck with her into adulthood. As a trial lawyer, she was renowned for leaving no investigative stone unturned, a reputation that only underscored her chagrin at having dropped the ball—as she kept saying—on the Lazarus case.

I squinted in the glare as we passed (according to Hallie) an icicle-clad Field Museum, the spaceship addition ballooning from the top of Soldier Field, and the windswept lakeshore below McCormick Place, bare of anything but prairie grass and scrub oaks peeking from the snow. We exited near the flattened dome of the Museum of Science and Industry and drove west to the Midway Plaisance, once envisioned by Frederick Law Olmstead as a grand, Venetian-style canal and now essentially a huge, dry moat dividing Hyde Park from its destitute neighbors to the south.

Hallie had attended the law school, and she gave me a brief history of the university while we parked and made our way from the car to the social-sciences building. Founded in 1890 by the American Baptist Foundation, it was originally bankrolled by John D. Rockefeller on land donated by Marshall Field. The school was nonsectarian and coeducational from the start, a rarity at the time that quickly attracted free-thinking academics from all over the country. Rockefeller had opened his wallet wide, and the university's first buildings copied the architecture of Oxford almost stone for stone, with more towers, cloisters, tunnels, and arches than you could shake a slide rule at. Hallie described it all in magical detail as we went up and down slippery steps, through shadowy arcades, and across quadrangles so quiet you could practically hear the minds at work in the adjoining classrooms.

"Was it fun going to school here?" I asked Hallie.

Hallie laughed. "Fun is not an approved term in the U of C lexicon."

"There's the scavenger hunt," I pointed out. "That must be entertaining—at least when dead bodies aren't involved."

"Oh, there are extracurricular activities, and plenty of good-natured competition among students. But most of the playtime is very true to the school's lofty reputation. Like Scav. Has anyone ever told you how it works?"

I said no and she explained.

"Well, it's always scheduled so that Judgment Day—the last day of the contest—falls on Mother's Day. The Wednesday before, a list is released, sometimes running to thirty pages or more, of things the students have to find, design, collect, eat, wear, or do, with point values assigned to each one. The teams, usually associated with one of the residential houses, compete to earn the most points, with a group of judges composed of volunteers being the arbiters of how well they've succeeded. Some of the items in the past have caused a bit of a stir. Like the year the list included building a nuclear reactor."

"Did a team actually do that?"

"Yes. But they missed out on the bonus points for making it edible. Usually it's something simpler, like constructing a laser from ordinary household appliances. Or building an honest-to-God time machine. And then there's all the traditional stuff, like breaking into the Bulls' locker room and stealing a jock strap. Or fashioning an entire wardrobe from Scotch Tape. It's the ultimate nerd challenge."

"And all this happens over three or four days?"

"Yes, with most of the team members running all over the campus day and night."

And therefore a swell time to commit murder if you wanted to maintain a low profile.

At last we arrived at Blum's office, in a far-flung corner of a third floor, where a dour-sounding assistant showed us in.

I introduced us, and Blum invited us to sit down. With Hallie to act as my guide, I had only a folding cane with me, which I made a show of collapsing and placing in my lap to remind him how we had met before.

"Yes, I remember you. Aren't you the fellow that ass Peter Crow—"

"Let's not talk about it," I butt in quickly.

"Very well, though I don't suppose he apologized for it. I got to know Crow quite well, back in the early nineties when I was heading up Magdalen House. You may know that all of our residence halls are divided into multiyear houses, in the fashion of the Oxford colleges. Crow acted as one of the residential advisors. Could hardly be bothered with his duties, but I suppose he needed the free living quarters. Married then, with a toddler and getting his PhD in psychology. Silly discipline," he added, apparently forgetting it was also mine.

"Yes, well, my colleague and I are here to—"

Blum went on as though I didn't exist. "With all that responsibility—for the students, of course, as well as a young family—you'd think he wouldn't have time for campus politics. But there he was, at the head of every rally, front and center with a bullhorn, decrying the treatment of blacks, Hispanics, Native Americans—excuse me, *Indigenous Peoples*—anyone at all so long as they didn't belong to the white middle class. Are you by any chance an alum?"

"I'm not," I said. "But Ms. Sanchez here attended the law school."

"Well, then, perhaps she'll remember the occupation of the administration building in ninety-one. The Vietnam War was long over by then, but a group headed by Crow got it in their heads that the university was unacceptably tied to the military-industrial complex. You're probably aware that it was Fermi's work on this very campus that led to the development of the atomic bomb and . . ."

I let him go on another three minutes before interrupting. "Excuse me. But we were led to believe your time was short."

"Quite right. I have an appointment with a PhD candidate in twenty minutes. What was it you wanted to see me about?" he asked, making no secret of his boredom.

I decided not to beat about the bush. "We're doing some further looking into Gunther Westlake's death. New evidence has come to light suggesting his wife may be innocent."

"Really!" Blum exclaimed. "Why that's terrible! Simply terrible!"

"For who—Ms. Lazarus or the university?"

Blum rushed to cover his mistake. "Well, I meant terrible in the sense of a miscarriage of justice, of course. What new evidence?" he demanded suspiciously.

I kept it vague. "Evidence of a possible other killer. We're here to find out whether Westlake had any enemies among your colleagues."

"A murderer on the faculty? That's preposterous. I'm ending this conversation at once. And notifying university counsel of your inquiries."

Hallie spoke up then. "Do that and there will be a deposition subpoena on your doorstep faster that you can say Herbert Marcuse. You'll have to answer all our questions then—under oath. Or we can have an informal chat right now. Dr. Angelotti and I aren't interested in creating unnecessary publicity for my alma mater. Or hastily accusing anyone. There's been enough of that already."

She was bluffing. With Lazarus already convicted, Hallie had no standing to seek a subpoena. And she was treading on thin ice as soon as Blum mentioned the school's lawyers. But the threat was enough to make Blum reconsider his stance.

"Can I have your word that anything I say will be off the record?"

"No you cannot," Hallie said. "But if you're right and no one here had anything to do with Westlake's murder, you have nothing to lose by being honest with us."

"Oh, all right," Blum said dismissively. "But it's still absurd to think you'll find anything here. The university hasn't spawned a murderer in all its hundred-year history."

"Two actually," I said.

"I beg your pardon?"

"Leopold and Loeb. Weren't they undergraduates when they murdered Bobby Franks?"

Caught in an exaggeration, Blum cleared his throat. "Yes, I suppose so. But they were students. If you ask me, that's who you should be thinking about."

"Let's stick to faculty for the moment," Hallie said. "Was there anyone Westlake didn't get along with?"

Blum seemed to give this some serious thought. "Not really," he said eventually. "Oh, I'll grant that Gunther wasn't shy about wading into controversy, or adopting a position for the pure joy of demonstrating his intellectual superiority. But he was also enough of a rhetorician to know that *ad hominem* arguments rarely achieve their purpose, at least among true scholars. When he attacked those with whom he disagreed, it was always by exposing the paucity of their reasoning, unlike the blatant editorializing that passes for most social commentary these days. Even those on the faculty who despised his work respected its thoughtfulness."

"What about personal conflicts?" Hallie asked.

"There again, I can't really help you. In person, Westlake was polite and rather withdrawn. Hardly the bullying narcissist painted by his critics. I would have to say he was reasonably well-liked by his peers."

"'Reasonably well-liked'?"

"I see that you were well-trained by my brethren across the Midway, Ms. Sanchez. Yes, I can be accused of overqualifying that last remark. Perhaps I should have stated that while Gunther had few friends on the faculty, he wasn't to my knowledge actively *dis*liked. And before you ask, I wasn't personally fond of the man. I'm not sure exactly why. Perhaps it was the bowties."

"When did you last see him?"

"A few days before. Here, in my office."

"Was there any particular reason?"

"Oh, I suppose it can't hurt to tell you, seeing as how you'll find out anyway. Gunther caused an uproar in one of his classes by suggesting that family dysfunction—and in particular, fatherless households—might be responsible for multigenerational crime among African Americans. The theory's hardly new—or limited to conservative thinkers. Moynihan was saying the same thing fifty years ago. But Gunther exacerbated the matter by ridiculing a student who demanded that he 'check his privilege.' The episode was picked up by the *Moron*— excuse me, the *Maroon*—and precipitated a heated debate about racist attitudes on campus. I understand there were upward of a thousand comments on the newspaper's site. I made the modest suggestion that Gunther tender an apology to the student. Not because he was wrong, mind you. But in the interest of calming things down."

"And did he apologize?"

"No. He wouldn't even discuss it with me."

"That must have caused some friction between you."

"I was . . . disappointed in his decision."

Judging from his tone, furious was more likely.

"Were any of the *Maroon* comments of a threatening nature?"

"Not that I recall. Just the usual back-and-forth about victimization—these days, nearly everyone wants to tell you how disadvantaged they are—and anonymous name-calling. You're welcome to sift through it, though I doubt it will do you any good."

I waded back into the conversation. "Back when we first met—at the party with Candace McIntyre. You said Westlake was responsible for two PhD students, one of whom left last year. Isn't that a very small number?"

"When I said earlier that Westlake was well-liked among his peers, I wasn't referring to his students, naturally."

Naturally. "Could your department afford that? You must see training future academic leaders as part of your mission."

Blum let out a studied breath. "You've probably heard the expression 'those who can do, and those who can't teach.' Thanks in part to Gunther, we receive enough grant money to accommodate both types, and it's my job as chair to steer them toward the roles in which they can be most productive. To be perfectly frank, Gunther's talents did not extend to mentoring the next generation. Not that it mattered."

"The current PhD candidate," I pressed. "What's his name?"

"Adam. Adam Lecht."

"Would you mind if we talked to him?"

"If he's willing, I can't stop you. In fact, he's the PhD candidate I'm supposed to be meeting in a few minutes. I believe I just heard him speaking to my assistant."

A knock came on Blum's door, and I turned toward the sound.

And then a strange thing happened.

The newcomer took two steps into the room, turned on his heel, and fled.

TWENTY-FOUR

Of course, I didn't see him. Or the look on his face, which Hallie described as pure panic. But I could hear the alarm in his movements as he skittered back through the door and fled down the corridor, bumping loudly against a wall in his haste to get away. Blum immediately rose from his seat and shouted after him. "Lecht, what in the hell is going on? Are you ill? Come back here at once!" But the PhD student kept running until his footsteps were only a faint patter in the distance.

I raised my eyebrows quizzically at Hallie. In answer, she took my hand and traced a question mark on my palm to signal that she had no idea either.

Blum returned to his seat, grumbling. "The rudeness..."

"What was that all about?" Hallie asked.

"I haven't a clue," Blum said. "Except that the fellow is due to defend his dissertation in two days' time. I've known some of them to get jittery beforehand, but not to such a degree."

"Does he have any psychiatric problems that you know of?" I asked out of professional interest.

"Again, no idea," Blum said. "But I suppose I shall have to find out now. God forbid the fellow should go off and drown himself in the Lake. Another headache to deal with," he muttered to himself.

"Maybe it was me," I said jokingly to Hallie after we had left Blum and were on our way across campus to the Gender Studies Department. "He wouldn't be the first person to worry about it rubbing off on them."

"You're scary, but not that scary," Hallie said. "And I don't think he noticed. I wouldn't swear to it, but I think it was seeing us with Blum."

"I hate to think we cut such a poor picture as a couple."

"Not that, silly. He recognized us."

"That wouldn't surprise me if he watched the trial. Westlake was his graduate advisor. You'd expect him to follow what was happening. And our faces were all over the news."

Hallie motioned for me to veer left onto another ice-bound walkway. "So what accounts for him bolting like a hare?"

"Two possibilities. He knows something. Or he's feeling guilty."

"Either one puts him on our list of suspects. What about Blum?"

"Do I think he could be our murderer, too? Hard to say. Reading between the lines, there was no love lost between him and his star grant-getter. But why kill the goose who's laying all the golden eggs?"

"Maybe the goose was kicking up too much dirt in the barnyard."

"You're talking about the classroom controversy?"

"Right. These days, nothing cuts off grant money as quickly as charges that an institution is racist. I'm not saying the school is hostile to minorities, but Blum couldn't have been happy when Westlake refused to apologize. Or the administration. I'm sure the 'modest suggestion' came as an order from higher up and that Blum was thoroughly embarrassed—if not in danger of losing control of his department—when he couldn't get Westlake to comply. If you recall, this would have been the second time in months that Westlake provoked a firestorm on campus."

I nodded, remembering the news story about Breastageddon. "What about the *Maroon* message boards? Do you think that's worth following up on?"

"Yes. But I'll get Carter to do it. He and the other associates spend ninety-nine percent of their lives gossiping on the Internet, so it'll be right up his alley."

Arriving at Amanda Pearson's office, we were disappointed to learn that she had just left—with apologies about missing our 11 a.m. appointment.

"Emergency meeting of the Women's Alliance," her assistant reported. "On account of the Supreme Court ruling this morning. If it's convenient, she said she could meet with you there."

We obtained directions and crossed the campus again, this time to the Student Center. In contrast to the churchlike quiet elsewhere, it was bustling with activity—the stamp of passing feet, students laughing and calling out to each other, a choral group rehearsing an *a cappella* number off to one side—all rising in symphonic echoes to the vast ceiling overhead. As we threaded through the crowd, I sniffed coffee and food wrappers, the fusty odor of old wood, and the acetone scent of freshly printed flyers. Hallie said the walls were littered with them, advertising everything from a Court Theatre production of *A Doll's House* to free checking at a local savings bank.

The office of the Women's Alliance was to the rear of the lobby, behind a modern, plate-glass door that whooshed on hydraulic hinges as we entered. The floors were carpeted in a bouncy material that smelled brand-new. Subdued lighting shone from overhead, and chamber music emanated discreetly from a speaker system, muting the bustle outside. Student activism had evidently undergone a change since my college days: the place felt more like an upscale corporate headquarters than a gathering place for the politically motivated.

"Wow," Hallie said, echoing my thoughts. "This is a lot nicer than the closet we used to meet in."

"Professor Pearson's doing," came a bright female voice from what I deduced was the reception desk. "She shamed the administration into it after they spent twenty-five million dollars on an upgrade to a locker room for the football team. Like people actually come to this school to watch football. So you're an alum," she said to Hallie.

"Just of the law school. My name is Hallie Sanchez. And this is Mark Angelotti."

"And I'm Taylor. Fourth-year at the college. I know who you are. You're the lawyer who defended Olivia's mom. And you're the psychiatrist who testified for her. Amanda said you might be coming here this morning. We were all so thrilled." She stopped awkwardly. "Do you think . . . would you mind giving me your autographs? I mean, if that's possible," she added in reference to me.

Hallie answered for us, "We'd be glad to—if we knew the reason."

"Are you serious? You guys are total heroes around here. I mean, even though you lost. Not just because of what you did, but also because it was Olivia's mom. A group of us came here every day to watch the trial with her. Amanda organized it and was here every day too. She said Olivia needed the support, to know we were all a hundred percent behind her. And her mom. Olivia's a friend, so I wouldn't have missed it. That prosecutor—what a pig! I don't know how you can stand dealing with him. I mean, it's your job and all, but still. The system's so sexist!"

I raised an eyebrow at Hallie. She caught my meaning and said, "Taylor, can we talk somewhere? If it's all right, I'd like to ask you a few questions."

"Oh sure, of course. Hang your coats on the hooks over there. And I'll get one of the other volunteers to cover the front desk."

We retired to another room containing a television, a kitchen area, and from what I could tell, an abundance of sofas and chairs whose occupants were too absorbed in their laptops to pay us any attention. Taylor offered us cans of soda from the fridge and brought us over to a corner where we might have a little privacy. "This is where we watched, on the DVR, with Olivia."

"Tell us more about that," Hallie said. "To be honest with you, I was surprised that Olivia never came to court. Didn't she want to?"

"Oh, more than anything. But they told her not to."

"Who told her not to?"

"Her mom. And Amanda."

"Do you know why?"

"I only know what Amanda thought—that it would be too upsetting for Olivia to be there. And that she'd just be a show for the TV reporters who'd be shoving microphones in her face all the time. They're a bunch of pigs, too. Did you know that male anchormen on television outnumber women two to one? Amanda just did an amazing course on gender stereotypes in the media. It's all part of the culture of oppression and belittlement women face. And the LGBT community. And persons with disabilities," Taylor added after a moment's thought.

Hallie gently brought her back to the subject of Olivia's absence at the trial. "It wasn't because Olivia and her mom were on bad terms?"

"Who told you that?" Taylor exclaimed heatedly.

Hallie paused, as if trying to decide just how forthright she could be. "Someone close to the family," she ended up saying.

"Well, I don't know where they were coming from. It's not true. I mean, Olivia and her mom were like sisters. That's why this separation's been so hard on her—on them both. And now that her mom's going to prison for, like, forever . . ." Taylor stopped, sounding tearful. "There isn't anything you can do to help her now, is there?"

Hallie said soothingly, "There's still a possibility of overturning the verdict if people are honest with us. You said you're Olivia's friend. Have you known her a long time?"

"Just since first year. We were in the same house together, in South Campus. Not roomies, but only one suite away. I don't live there anymore. It's considered very uncool to stay in one of the dorms after second year. I'm over in what they call the 'campus ghetto'—on Wood-lawn just north of Fifty-Fifth. I share an apartment with three other students. Pretty big and we all have our own rooms. Olivia wanted to rent with us, but her father wouldn't pay for it. It costs more than a dorm room, but still."

"So there were money issues between Olivia and her father?"

"OMG, yeah. Olivia's mom had to pay all her expenses. Except for her tuition, which was practically free because he was a professor. Books, clothes, everything. Olivia said it was because her dad hated her."

This was news. "Hated Olivia?"

"Uh-huh. She hated him too."

"Do you know why?"

Taylor was on the verge of answering when Amanda suddenly appeared.

"I don't wish to interrupt, Taylor, but I think your help is needed with the press statement we'll be putting out later. Thank you for keeping our guests company, but I'll take over now."

It wasn't an overt rebuke, but I thought I caught a whiff of disap-proval in her tone. "Sure, Amanda," Taylor said meekly. Then to Hallie and me: "You won't forget about the autographs?"

After Taylor took herself off, I got up from my seat and introduced Hallie.

"I'm so very pleased to make your acquaintance, Ms. Sanchez," Amanda said. "You have been such an inspiration for the young women here. And even more so for coming from the bastion of male privilege that is our law school. I commend you on your closing statement. It literally brought tears to my eyes. And thank you, Mark. I hope I may call you that. I feel we share some camaraderie after that awful episode at the dean's party. It's not often that a male member of the psychiatric community speaks up in support of women's rights."

I wondered if I shouldn't say "aw shucks."

"Though I might take just a tiny bit of issue with your paternalistic dismissal of Battered Woman Syndrome," Amanda continued. "I see that Taylor has offered you refreshments. But how else can I help you? To be frank, I was surprised to get Candace's call. I thought the trial was over and that Rachel had decided not to appeal."

There was no other choice but to level with her. Amanda sat down, and Hallie and I took turns explaining what we had learned about Brad Stephens's report, the missing police notes, and the ME's findings, leading us to believe that Lazarus might not have been her husband's killer.

"Why, that's wonderful news," Amanda said, though her enthusiasm sounded forced. "Have you made any progress in identifying the killer?"

"We were hoping you might be able to help us with that."

"Me?" Amanda said, a little too surprised. "I don't see how. Unless you think *I* had something to do with Gunther's murder."

I was beginning to wonder. "We're not here to wring a confession out of you. Just background information. Back at the dean's party in December, you seemed to know something about the family."

"If I gave you that impression, it was certainly false. No doubt a result of having had too much to drink."

"I think you said Olivia was one of your students?"

"Yes, that's right."

"And that you knew both parents?"

"Yes, but only well enough to say hello to. In this kind of small community—as in any other I imagine—you can't help becoming acquainted with colleagues and their partners."

This was not the chatty Amanda I remembered. "You also said you thought Westlake had abused both his wife and his daughter. Was that based on something in particular?"

"As I said at the party, it was merely a guess on my part. Primarily from the kind of man Gunther was and . . ."

"Go on," I prodded.

". . . It's nothing. I didn't—don't—know Olivia all that well. As I said, she was extremely shy, hardly spoke a word in my class, although I'd made it clear that class participation would count for a third of the grade."

"Was Olivia admitted to the college through the usual process?"

"I didn't mean to imply that she isn't up to the work, if that's what you're asking. No, intellectually she is very much her father's daughter. Her work on paper was thorough, well-researched, and in some respects brilliant."

I thought Amanda was doing a pretty brilliant job herself—of shoveling a load of manure at us.

"So you didn't have any kind of special relationship with her?"

"None, other than the fact that she came here to the Women's Alliance often, for the companionship, I suppose, and also to study. I've tried to make this a haven for the young women, who still unfortunately suffer from the fear that intellectual ability and a desire to succeed will be considered unfeminine. This lounge, for example, frees them from having to do all their study in the residence halls or the library, where unwanted attention from male students is all too common."

I was growing weary of whatever game Amanda was playing. So, apparently, was Hallie.

"Funny," she jumped in. "I don't remember much unwanted attention when I was a student here. Everyone was so serious."

Amanda said, "You're fortunate, then. As was I many years ago, before hookups became all the rage. That's one of the things I'm trying to combat—the idea that sexual promiscuity in young women isn't 'liberating.' All it does is cater to male fantasies and feed their sense of entitlement. As I was saying to the students just the other day—"

"Excuse me," Hallie said sharply.

Amanda stopped talking.

"I'm sorry to interrupt, but as one sister to another, isn't it time we cut the crap?"

"What do you mean?" Amanda bristled.

"We heard all about it from Taylor. We know that you set up a special support group for Olivia. And that you virtually held her hand throughout the trial. That implies something more than the usual professor-student relationship. What are you hiding from us?"

"I can't discuss my students. It's against university policy."

"But only if it's something you learned in an official capacity."

"I see it was a mistake to invite you here. I'd like you to leave now."

Hallie said even more quietly, "It was only a mistake if you don't care about a woman going to prison for a crime she didn't commit. Or the daughter whose life will be ruined because of it."

All at once, Amanda seemed to crumple. "But that's just the problem," she said in obvious distress, "I care about them both."

TWENTY-FIVE

"I've got a blister on my heel as big as the Goodyear Blimp," Hallie said as we trekked across campus for the fourth time that day.

"I'd offer to carry you, but it might be regarded as caveman behavior," I said with a levity I didn't feel.

What Amanda eventually confessed to us amounted to the following: during class the previous winter, she'd observed Olivia holding her torso in an odd manner and repeatedly rubbing her shoulder. As soon as the lecture was over, Amanda had approached the girl and asked her what was the matter. Olivia said it was nothing. Amanda refused to take this for an answer.

"She was clearly in pain—almost white-faced with it," Amanda told us. "I thought she might be going into shock. So I suggested driving to the emergency room at the university hospital. At that, Olivia started shaking even more, and I realized she was badly frightened. Eventually, I talked her into seeing my general practitioner—I go to a doctor outside the university system for privacy reasons—where she could be treated quietly with no questions asked."

"What was wrong with her?" Hallie asked.

"Dislocated shoulder. But that wasn't the only thing. Her entire upper arm was purple with bruises—really shocking in appearance—and there were also bruises on her rib cage. My doctor gave her pain medication and put the arm in a sling and took me aside to discuss the situation. We were both convinced that Olivia was the victim of an assault and should report the matter at once. She—my doctor that is—also wanted to do a vaginal exam, but Olivia swore to us that she hadn't been raped. She also refused to say who had done it to her."

"Who did you suspect?"

"At the time, a boyfriend. I pointed out to Olivia that the abuse was unlikely to stop and might even escalate. That if she wasn't up to pressing charges, she should stop seeing the young man at once. And that she should take advantage of the Student Counseling Center, where she could discuss what had happened on a confidential basis. I stressed how important it was for victims of assault to receive early counseling. Olivia said she would think about it."

"And that satisfied you?"

"No more than it would have satisfied you, I think. I knew Olivia's mother worked on campus as an administrative assistant. I looked Rachel up in the directory and a few days later went to see her. I told Rachel what happened and relayed my concerns about the boyfriend. I didn't mention the possibility of rape because I didn't want to upset her, but I thought she should know about the shoulder and the bruising."

"How did she react?"

"She seemed . . . unconcerned, almost nonchalant about it, actually. She confirmed that Olivia had recently started dating a graduate student a few years older than she. Rachel had a bad feeling about the relationship but didn't think it was her place to interfere. When I suggested reporting the boyfriend, she told me in no uncertain terms to mind my own business."

"Did you?"

"Not entirely. I called Peter Crow at the counseling center." Amanda turned to me. "I suspect you remember him from that party. The fellow who—"

I put up a hand to stop her. "I remember."

"Peter and I were graduate students at the university at the same time and were involved in a few causes together. I called him to alert him to what I had seen. He confided—I suppose he shouldn't have, but it gave me some peace of mind—that Olivia had followed my advice and was receiving counseling. Over the next few weeks, I kept a close eye on Olivia in class, but she seemed well and was even speaking up more, so I had reason to hope for the best. Then, at the end of the spring quarter, when she was no longer my student, her father was killed.

"Like the rest of the world, I was sure the killer must have been one of Westlake's ideological opponents. Then they arrested Rachel, and I thought back on the whole episode. Olivia's insistence that she hadn't been raped, Rachel's apparent complacency. That's when I finally understood: the two of them had been through this before."

I nodded in comprehension. "And were covering for Westlake."

"Exactly. To be frank, I wasn't sure what to do about it. And until the press conference, I felt I should respect Rachel's wish for privacy. But once Rachel's lawyers announced the Battered Woman's defense, it was no longer a secret, so I contacted the public defender's office, thinking I might be useful as a witness. It was hard to get through to the lead attorney handling the case. It took weeks. I suppose it's because they're so overwhelmed. However, when the lawyer finally called me back, she seemed excited by what I had to say. We made arrangements for me to come in and give a statement the following week."

"Why am I only hearing about this now?" Hallie said.

"Because it never happened. The day before I was scheduled to meet with her, the lawyer called me to say that my testimony wasn't needed. 'Cumulative' was the legal term she used. The lawyer didn't say it, but I had the distinct impression it wasn't her decision."

"Was that the end of the matter?" I asked.

"No. A week or so later, not long after you and I met at the dean's party, the lawyer called again, saying that Rachel had asked her to deliver a message. The gist of it was that Rachel appreciated my concern in the past and was hoping I would do her another favor."

"Which was?"

"Watching out for Olivia during the trial. Rachel believed her daughter was in a very fragile state and had to be kept away from the legal proceedings at all costs. The lawyer explained that Rachel had no family she could call on. I was the only person she could think of who might help. I arranged for Olivia to move out of her dorm and into her mother's apartment and did everything else I could to ensure her privacy, including hiring a private security guard to accompany her to and from campus. I also set up the support group Taylor mentioned to you and made sure Olivia wasn't left alone for more than a few hours at a time while the trial was ongoing. I believed—I hoped—I was doing the right thing."

I felt the same way.

Now, en route to the Student Counseling Center, Hallie was expressing doubts about our next move.

"Crow won't tell us anything. He can't."

"You're lecturing a psychiatrist about confidentiality?"

"That and what talking to him will get us."

"The more we find out, the better," I pointed out reasonably. "I'm going to try something and see how he reacts. Your job is to pay attention to his body language. Be my eyes, to use a silly expression."

"Oh, all right," Hallie said with a tug on my sleeve. "But I bet we won't even be able to get in."

"Don't worry. I have a plan."

We located the counseling center in yet another building topped with leering gargoyles—Hallie said there were enough of them around campus to start a drinking game—and handed our cards to the receptionist.

"What is it you want to see Dr. Crow about?" she asked. "I don't see your names among his appointments this afternoon."

"If he's not with somebody right now, tell him we want to see him about a suit."

"A suit?"

"That's right. Tell him I think he owes me a new set of clothes. And that my lawyer here"—I gestured at Hallie—"has advised me to take the matter to court if we can't reach an appropriate settlement."

"What is this all about?" Hallie whispered urgently to me while the receptionist was passing my message on.

"A little matter of a lost supper. Just follow my lead and look threatening."

Moments later, we were being ushered into an office where Peter Crow rose nervously from his desk to greet us. I noticed he didn't offer to shake our hands. "I was worried that I'd be hearing from you," he said immediately. "I should have tried to find you myself. But I wasn't thinking clearly the next day and, well, I'm ashamed to say I hoped I'd just dreamed the whole thing up. Please, please have a seat."

I took the chair Hallie steered me to and assumed an air of righteous indignation. "You were drunk."

"Yes, yes, I know," Crow said in an anxious accent.

"And threw up all over me."

"I'm terribly, terribly sorry."

"And ruined all my clothes."

"Just tell me what you paid for them and I'll write a check."

"A written apology also seems in order."

"Whatever you need."

I turned to Hallie and asked, "Is there anything else I should ask for?"

"Well, damages for emotional distress," she said. "And reimbursement for the extra therapy bills. Oh, and don't forget about the lost wages."

I knew I could count on her.

I pretended to smack myself on the forehead. "How could I forget about the lost wages? It was weeks before I was able to leave the house again. You see, I have emetophobia. As a psychologist, you must know of it—an irrational fear of being vomited on. It's become even worse since I lost my sight. Not knowing when it might be coming, etcetera. Completely crippling at times." I turned to Hallie again. "What do you think? Would six figures be reasonable?"

Crow was evidently taking all this seriously. "Please," he pleaded. "I don't make nearly as much money as you think. And half of it goes to my ex in alimony."

"You should be ashamed of yourself," I said.

"Believe me I am. Thoroughly and completely ashamed."

Having extracted this pound of flesh, I decided it was time to move on. "But that's not why we're here."

"Huh?" Crow uttered in confusion.

"I'm surprised that you don't recognize us."

"Is there a reason I should, apart from the, uh . . . party?"

"Well, you must have been following the trial."

"What trial?"

"The trial of Rachel Lazarus."

In an instant, Crow's begging tone turned. "Wait a minute. Now that you say it, I do know who you are. What do you mean by coming here and pretending to want money? I should have you thrown out!"

I said, "Now that would truly be adding insult to injury. You're right. We're not here to hold you up. We're here about Rachel's daughter, Olivia. We know you've been counseling her. We were hoping you might answer a few questions. As a professional courtesy if nothing else."

According to Hallie, Crow looked at the window and scratched his head, as though he wasn't sure his leg was being pulled again. After some thought, he said, "What kind of questions?"

"We have reason to believe Olivia knows something about her father's death. Something that might prove her mother innocent. We were wondering if the subject had come up in one of your sessions."

"You know I can't discuss that—even as a professional courtesy."

I nodded sagely. "The therapist-client privilege."

"Exactly."

"Though there are exceptions," I pointed out. "The *Tarasoff* rule, for instance." I nudged Hallie's foot to be sure she was paying close attention to Crow's face.

Crow's spoken reaction was instantaneous. "You must be joking."

"I wish I wasn't." I turned to Hallie and explained. "*Tarasoff* is a landmark case holding that a therapist has a duty to notify targeted victims when a client is about to go on a killing spree. It's taught in all the ethics courses. I was just wondering if Dr. Crow had given any thought to it before Olivia's father was killed. And to his potential liability to the Westlake estate if he failed to give a proper warning."

"I thought you weren't here to threaten me with lawsuits," Crow said, maintaining his cool—but only just. "What you just said was libelous. And you're barking up the wrong tree. I knew nothing about Westlake's murder beforehand."

"And you'd be willing to swear to that in a court of law?"

"I would," Crow said with conviction. "And now I really do have to ask you to get out."

TWENTY-SIX

"Nice job," Hallie said as we were slipping and sliding our way back to the Midway to retrieve her car.

"So how *did* he look?"

"Do I really need to tell you? The blood drained from his face the minute we walked in. He's worried about something."

"That's why I started off pulling his chain about a lawsuit. To see how much groveling he would do to keep me from making a bigger stink."

"You weren't just trying to get even?"

"I'm not that childish."

"When did the vomiting thing happen?"

"At the party I told you about. The one I went to with Candace. She was off visiting the restroom and I was sitting alone, minding my own business, when Crow came along and nearly crushed the air from my lungs. Is he as big a man as I think?"

"Huge. When I first saw him, I thought I was looking at the Chief in *One Flew over the Cuckoo's Nest*. So he just sat down and puked all over you?"

"I tried to engage him in conversation first. When he didn't respond, I started to worry that he was ill, but then it became clear he was drunk to high heaven. On my suggestion, he got up to get himself a glass of water and . . . well, let's just say I came away from it looking like a bad run-in with a blender."

"You must have been mortified."

"'Mortified' doesn't begin to cover it. But the incident was more comic than anything else. Most people would have laughed off the idea of a lawsuit."

"Except that as head of campus counseling, he's supposed to be setting an example. I'm sure part of his job is keeping students from drowning themselves in Everclear. Getting blind drunk himself doesn't exactly encourage responsible drinking. Maybe he's been warned about the issue. If so, the last thing he needs is being accused of another lapse. Precisely how does that whatchamacallit rule you brought up work?"

We'd reached Hallie's MG. She fired up the ignition and turned the temperature control to its highest setting. Even the short walk from campus had turned my limbs into Popsicles.

"You can't just have a patient who dislikes someone else. Or has expressed a vague desire to do them harm. They have to say something like 'I hate So-and-So and I plan on taking them out next Tuesday with my trusty automatic rifle and fifty rounds of ammo.'"

"So by reminding Crow of the rule, you were trying to trick him into an admission." Hallie stopped abruptly. "But that means you think . . ." She lapsed into uncomfortable silence.

"It's a possibility we can't ignore. I think it's what Amanda was so worried about, and why she was so unhappy that we got Taylor talking. Amanda's been wrestling with her conscience ever since she agreed to watch over Olivia."

Hallie shifted uncomfortably in her seat. "Hell," was all she said.

"I don't like it any better than you do," I said. "But it would explain a lot of Rachel's behavior. The rapid confession. Her insistence on not raising other defenses. And then lying to us about Olivia's relationship with her father. Even the castration and the dumping of the body at Scav."

"I thought you had an explanation for that."

"I thought so too. But now I'm not so sure. Back when I was first learning about the case from Di Marco—before I convinced myself that Rachel was suffering from PTSD—I wondered why she didn't just leave Westlake's body where it was. Di Marco's theory was that she was trying to draw attention away from domestic strife as a motive. Now I'm wondering if he was right." I shook my head at my own cupidity. "Maybe he was right about me too—I was going out of my way to find a psychological reason for Rachel's conduct when the answer was staring me right in the face."

Hallie said, "Rachel's been protecting her."

I nodded. "She could have come across Westlake's body and seen something—some kind of evidence connecting Olivia to the death. So she went about hiding it. She wiped the poker clean and made sure her own fingerprints were all over the murder weapon. Then she moved the body to confuse things even more. The castration was just a red herring, so that the police and everyone else would think she was a killer—and a pretty depraved one at that. If so, it was a brilliant piece of theater."

"And only a relative of what Di Marco theorized. Rachel wasn't trying to direct attention away from her marriage. She wanted all the focus to be on her."

"And probably had to work hard to be seen by those students with all the folks running around on campus that night."

"That poor woman," Hallie said with feeling. "I wish it didn't sound so plausible." After a moment's thought, she added, "But then why didn't she just cop a plea? As you pointed out last night, it was risky to take the case to trial if all she wanted was to be found guilty."

I didn't have an answer to that. A Hail Mary pass, perhaps?

Hallie again fell silent. Eventually she said, "We could be looking at this all wrong, you know. Maybe Rachel *is* the cold-blooded killer everyone thinks she is, and we just don't want to admit it."

I smiled at her. "This is tragic. You're starting to think like me."

"I'm serious. We both feel guilty about our performance at trial. Who's to say we're not just grasping at straws?"

"For once I prefer to think of it as groping in the dark. And don't forget we now have reason to think that there was a time lapse between the murder and the mutilation of the corpse."

"Rachel could have come back later."

"Hallie," I said, taking her hand and squeezing it. "I know it's brutal to even entertain the thought that Olivia was her father's killer."

"It's not just that it's so awful. It's that it puts me in a real pickle."

I thought I knew what she meant. "Because in exposing Olivia as the murderer, you'd be acting in direct contravention of your client's wishes?"

"Yes. But I wasn't only thinking about my responsibilities as a lawyer. Let's say—heaven forbid—that someone abused Louis and then he turned around and murdered that person. Wouldn't you do everything in your power—even take the fall yourself if you had to—to keep him from being caught and punished?"

I didn't have to think long about that one. The dilemma wasn't hers alone.

I said, "OK, you've turned the tables on me. The question is, where do we go from here?"

"That's easy," Hallie said. "We go to jail. But only after we've done a little more snooping."

It was after 3 p.m. when we parked again on the fifty-six-hundred block of Woodlawn. Except for the rumble of an occasional car on 55th, the area was deathly quiet. In the slanting afternoon light, I was able to make out something of the neighborhood. As always I was struck by the contrast between Chicago and my hometown, where the houses are more vertical than horizontal and the trees jostle each other for breathing room. Here, where prairie once stretched for thousands of miles, flat, open vistas are the rule, and the maples, elms, and locusts lining the parkways barely meet overhead. Even the Midwestern architecture, with its hipped roofs and broad gables, invokes the feeling of real estate to spare.

The Westlake residence stood halfway up the block. Hallie said it was a three-story, brick dwelling with a chimney in the middle where a front door would ordinarily be, flanked by narrow, leaded-glass windows. A driveway led from the street to a side entrance half hidden by a *porte cochere*. Months of neglect showed in the tumbleweeds collected in its depths and the pile of sodden and dirty mail by the door. A smattering of winter leaves made a sound like a tongue clicking in disapproval at the home's scandalous past.

Hallie shuddered beside me. "It reminds me of that Edgar Allan Poe poem. The one where you slowly realize that the haunted house he's describing is a face."

"This one must be weeping," I said.

We started with the residence immediately to the north, which was encircled by a wrought-iron fence. To my dismay, it wasn't the only thing guarding the premises. As soon as we reached the gate, a dog bounded up, letting off a series of high-strung yelps. Hallie reported that a sign by the latch said the animal was friendly and wouldn't bite, but I wasn't about to take any chances.

"Let's save this one for last," I said.

"OK, but what is it with you and dogs? You freeze up every time one comes near you."

"Let's just say I prefer my furry friends belonging to other species. Which house has the best sight line to Westlake's front door?"

"That one. Across the street and to the north."

We went there, but no one answered our ring. The one next door yielded similarly disappointing results.

"Do you think we should come back later, when people might be home from work?" I asked as we continued to make our way down the block.

"Maybe," Hallie said. "But let's try this one here. If I'm not mistaken, there's someone inside watching us. I just saw a shade being pulled back."

We went up a walk that was a minefield of unshoveled snow and congealed footprints. It felt like scrambling up a glacier, and I almost fell several times despite Hallie's steadying arm. By the time we reached the porch, I was sweating from the effort of maintaining my balance. I took a deep breath in.

And almost retched.

"Phew," Hallie said. "That's bad. I have a feeling your preference for other species is about to be stress-tested."

Sure enough, when someone answered the door, the place was crawling with cats.

Hallie introduced herself to the owner as a friend of Rachel Lazarus and asked if we might have a word inside.

A women who I guessed to be well past a certain age asked suspiciously, "Friend?"

"As well as her lawyer," Hallie said. "Though we're not here to cause you any trouble."

"What about him?" the woman asked. "Doesn't look like a lawyer."

I was about to say she should be happy I didn't look like a city health inspector when Hallie silenced me with a kick to the shin. "He's my assistant. May we come in, Mrs. . . . ?"

"Esposito. Mrs. Ralph Esposito. I was wondering if I'd ever hear from you."

Hallie tugged on my sleeve, and we followed the old biddy in.

I'd expected Chez Esposito to be a hoarder's showcase, but apart from the felines and a multitude of litter boxes—a nose was all I needed to count them—the rooms sounded nearly empty, an impression that proved accurate when Mrs. Esposito sat us down on metal folding chairs in the center of a large, echoing room. "Cat dander," she told us. "Mr. Esposito was allergic to it, so I had to sell the upholstery and rip up all the rugs. Now that he's gone, I don't see any reason to replace them. It makes it so much easier to clean up after my babies. I'm sorry about the odor. With this many of them, you can't get rid of it no matter how much you try."

"Yes," Hallie said like she had no trouble believing it.

Mrs. Esposito apparently thought she was being patronized. "I'm not some crazy cat lady, if that's what you're thinking. This is a licensed cat foster home certified by the Illinois Department of Agriculture. I take in strays that the shelters don't have room for and take care of them until a permanent placement becomes available. You can read all about it on my website."

In other words, a professional cat lady.

Right at that moment, a large, soft lump landed in my lap, nearly knocking my cane to the floor.

"Whiskers, no," Mrs. Esposito said like she was remonstrating with a toddler. "We don't know if the blind man likes kitties. Get down and go play with your brothers and sisters."

Whiskers ignored her and made several turns before settling down in a way that suggested I was his personal property. "Nice boy," I said, finding his head and patting it. Whiskers commenced purring and kneading my thigh. "What kind of cat is he?"

"He's an orange tabby with a white face. That's why I named him Whiskers. Three or four years old. He was almost starved to death when they brought him in."

Malnourishment no longer seemed to be Whiskers's problem.

Mrs. Esposito sensed an opportunity. "He's very good with children and other pets. Fixed and has all his papers. All you need to do is complete the forms and undergo a home visit from one of our adoption specialists. Just to be sure the environment is suitable. And once the placement is approved, you can call him whatever you like."

I looked over to Hallie for help.

"Mrs. Esposito," she said. "We'd love to talk more about Whiskers. But to get back to Rachel Lazarus . . ."

"Oh yes, that's right. Well, as I was saying, I certainly don't suffer from dementia. But the police never pay attention to people my age. I was in business, you know. Before we retired in eighty-seven, Mr. Esposito and I ran a very successful H&R Block office. I told them that, but they still acted like I couldn't keep a figure in my head. I had to insist that they write it all down."

I heard Hallie draw in a breath. "Write what down?"

"The number of the license plate. On the car parked in Westlake's driveway. Oh, and the young person who was there. Poor Rachel. I always felt sorry for her. You didn't have to be a detective to know what was going on over in *that* house. But I know she wouldn't have done something so awful. Even if he was such a nasty little man. Why, do you know that he once complained to the police about my babies . . ."

With further prodding from Hallie—and several detours into the merits of cats in general, and Whiskers in particular—the following facts emerged: on the night Gunther Westlake was killed, Mrs. Esposito had just that afternoon taken custody of a litter of six kittens abandoned outside a Home Depot in Beverly. Being only four weeks old and seriously dehydrated, the kittens had to be nourished with a syringe every few hours, a task that had taken up most of Mrs. Esposito's time. It was a warm night, and Mrs. Esposito had put the shades up and opened the windows ("to let in a little fresh air"), giving her ample opportunity to hear, as well as glance at, the activity on the street, which was filled with groups of students rushing to and from the "Scav" exhibition area.

"I never liked that silly competition. Every year it's the same thing—noise all night, just like Halloween. It scares the babies and I'm always afraid one of them will be kidnapped and tortured in some kind of experiment. I wouldn't put it past the students I see around here. Every one of them a weirdo. You should see the clothes they wear!"

While nursing a kitten in her living room, Mrs. Esposito had observed a young man knocking on Westlake's door a little before 7 p.m. and being let in by the professor. The young man left a half hour or so later with an angry look on his face.

"Would you recognize him if you saw him again?" Hallie asked.

"I think so. I'd seen him come around here before."

"What about Westlake—did you see him again that night?"

"A little later. He made a big show of shutting the windows in the front of the house, like he was annoyed by how loud it was outside."

"What time was this?"

"Eight or eight-thirty. I can't remember exactly. I wasn't spying on the house. I respect people's privacy."

Shortly thereafter, with the kittens sleeping in a bassinet at her feet, Mrs. Esposito had switched on the TV and was fortunate to catch the last hour of one of her favorite movies, *An Affair to Remember*. "The heroine was handicapped too," she informed me. At the movie's conclusion, while crossing the room for a box of tissues, she noticed the car in Westlake's driveway, parked under the *porte cochere*. Night had fallen but the streetlights were on, illuminating the rear license plate, whose number she memorized out of habit.

Hallie typed the number into her phone and asked Mrs. Esposito if she could name the make and model of the car.

"Oh, no. I never pay attention to things like that. Just numbers. And of course, my babies. I always hear them the instant they start to cry."

Unfortunately, just after she noticed the car, one of the kittens had begun to do precisely that, requiring Mrs. Esposito to return to the kitchen in the back to prepare and warm another batch of formula. When she returned some fifteen minutes later, the car was gone.

"It had to be the killer. I told the police that, but they just looked at me like I was losing my marbles."

Hallie asked, "Did you see anyone else going in or out of the house that night?"

"No."

"What about Rachel later on?"

"If she came in her car, she would have gone in through the back door. The Westlakes always drove in from the alley, where the garage is."

Further questioning elicited no additional information from Mrs. Esposito, except that all of the kittens had subsequently found new homes.

"It broke my heart to see them go," she told us with a catch in her throat as Hallie and I were putting on our coats. "Though of course it was for the best. I only wish the older ones had such an easy time finding families to love them." She put a hand on my sleeve. "Will you think about Whiskers? He's such a loner. I don't think he's very happy here with all the others. Always escaping outside and staying away for days. He has a chip, but I still get sick with worry when he's gone. You're the first person he's met that he seems to like. Look, he's even followed you to the door."

As if participating in the sales pitch, the cat rubbed up against my leg.

"Please tell me you'll consider it," Mrs. Esposito said. "Pets can be such a comfort, you know. And," she added brightly, "I'm sure you could get him registered as a service animal."

Acquiring a nonhuman charge—of any kind—was literally the farthest thing from my mind, but I lied and told her I'd think about it. It seemed the polite thing to do.

TWENTY-SEVEN

I spent that night at my place after Hallie dropped me off. I didn't ask her in and she didn't seem to expect it, lingering in the MG only long enough to go over our plans and wish me a terse good night. It was better that way. Despite the thaw in our relationship, a whole *Encyclopædia Britannica* remained unsaid between us. We were in a warming trend, but an arctic chill could yet descend on us, wiping out any hope for the future. And there was a decision weighing on me, a decision I wouldn't be able to put off much longer.

I put the key into the lock of my unit—sometime in the last few weeks it had stopped acting like buried treasure—and stepped inside, hoping to find a package from the telephone company in the mail the postman had slid through the slot in the door. But apart from a few sales circulars and a letter addressed to me in Braille from the Lighthouse, there was nothing. Another issue I was happy to defer, if only for the time being.

Early the next morning, a Saturday, found Hallie and me once again at the Cook County Jail. Hallie had only been able to phone ahead that morning, and the guard on duty informed us we might have a thirty-minute wait. Rachel's daughter was also visiting.

"Are you thinking the same thing I am?" Hallie asked me as we sat ourselves in two of the hard plastic chairs populating the jail's waiting area.

I folded my cane and secured the sections in place with the elastic strap. "Why not? If we're right about Olivia, the danger of discovery is past. No one suspects her and Rachel isn't appealing. It's a whole lot easier to carry out a reunion here than in some dungeon in the nether regions of Illinois."

Hallie sighed. "You're being denser than usual. I was asking whether we should try to question her."

"Do you know what she looks like?"

"I've seen a photograph. She's quite tall, dark-haired like her mother. And probably better dressed than the average jailhouse visitor."

I considered it. The room was packed with weekend traffic, mostly women with small children in tow. The one playing a video game next to me seemed to have trouble staying still for more than ten seconds at a time. The music escaping his headphones was already driving me nuts. Synthetic speech was bad enough, but synthetic John Williams was over the top.

"I don't know. The noise in here would drown out any conversation, but what would we say? 'Hi, we were wondering if it was actually you who murdered your father?' Seems a trifle awkward."

"You're right," Hallie said. "I wasn't thinking it through. Except that I'd still like to think Olivia's innocent. What do you make of what Mrs. Esposito had to say?"

"Besides me being a prime candidate for cat parenthood? It tells us that at least two people besides Rachel—and maybe Olivia—were at Westlake's on the night he was killed. Can you put a reverse trace on that license-plate number?"

"It's not as easy as everyone thinks—you can't just find out with a search engine, and the online services charge an arm and a leg for looking through old, mostly unreliable databases. But I have a buddy in the legal department at the Secretary of State. I called him first thing this morning. It might take a while because their computer system is down for maintenance this weekend. The earliest he thought he'd be able to get back to me is Monday. Who do you think the young man Mrs. Esposito saw was?"

"I'd put good money on it being Lecht, the graduate student who nearly lost his lunch when we showed up at Blum's office."

"So he's looking even better as a suspect."

"Except that Mrs. Esposito was pretty clear that Westlake was still alive after he left. How reliable a witness do you think she is?"

"I don't want to fall into the trap of discounting somebody's word just because they're elderly. She was wearing glasses, but not the coke-bottle type. And she does run a business—of sorts."

"Did you get a peek out her front window?"

"Just before we left. The lots in that neighborhood are big, but not so big that she couldn't have seen Westlake shutting his windows, especially if there was lighting behind him. Forty, maybe fifty feet."

The child beside me had moved into high gear, bouncing up and down in rhythm to the *Star Wars* theme. I flipped the crystal on my watch. "How much longer do you guess?"

"God only knows. No—wait. There she is now," Hallie said, tugging on my sleeve.

"Olivia?"

"Uh-huh. And she's coming right this way."

I felt my muscles tense. Would I soon be coming face-to-face with a murderess?

Moments later, a diaphanous figure pulled up in front of us. Hallie and I pushed back our chairs and stood.

"Are you . . . ?" the girl began.

For a few seconds, I didn't know what to say. Hallie wasn't as diffident. "Yes, I'm your mother's lawyer. And this is Mark Angelotti, the doctor who testified on her behalf."

I stuck my truncated cane under my arm and held out my free hand. But Olivia didn't want a handshake. Before I knew it, she had thrown her arms around me, hugging me tight. Startled, my first impulse was to pull away. Our cheeks brushed briefly, and I realized hers were wet.

I fished in my trouser pocket for my handkerchief and handed it to her.

"Thank you," Olivia said. "I didn't . . . I don't . . . Oh God, why is all this happening to us?" she wailed at the top of her lungs.

Even with the decibel level in the room, I figured heads were starting to turn our way. I took Olivia by the shoulders and helped her into the seat I had just vacated.

"I'm going to get her some water," Hallie said to me.

Olivia continued to sob, a raw, wracking sound. I sat down beside her and sought to take her hand, but she pulled it away with a quick motion. "Don't," she said through her tears. "Don't. It's ugly."

Even with all my clinical experience, I felt helpless in the face of such distress.

Hallie returned with the water and knelt before the trembling girl. I gave her a look that said I had no idea how to deal with the situation, and she patted my knee to indicate she would take over.

Gradually, Olivia's sobs subsided and I heard her drink from the cup Hallie had given her.

"That's it," Hallie said. "Keep drinking and take some more deep breaths."

"I'm sorry," Olivia said at last. "I'm so . . . so ashamed of myself."

Because she had broken down in public, or put her mother in prison?

"It's OK," Hallie said. "Nobody minds a little crying. This isn't a happy place—for anyone."

"I shouldn't have come. Mom said not to, not until she's at that place they're taking her to. But it's all the way down near Carbondale and I just couldn't wait to see her again." Her voice choked in anguish once more.

"We should get her out of here," I said to Hallie.

Hallie agreed. "Olivia, why don't you let us take you home? My car is right outside."

Olivia didn't want to hear it. "No," she said, momentarily composing herself. "No. You're here to see Mom, right?"

Hallie must have nodded.

"Go to her, then. I'll be OK. Please. She's been expecting you."

In the end, we were able to persuade Olivia not to leave unaccompanied. I phoned Amanda Pearson, who agreed to come get the girl and perform watchdog duty that night. Being mostly a hindrance as an escort, I stayed in the waiting room while Hallie took Olivia outside to where Amanda was waiting. I used the time to leave a message for Alison, asking if she had time to take on Olivia as a patient. The girl urgently needed help, but I had serious doubts about Peter Crow, and I was too involved in the whole fiasco to assume the job myself. If Olivia had something to get off her chest, I was the wrong person to hear it.

When Hallie returned, I could tell she was just as troubled as I.

"How was she when you dropped her off?" I asked.

"Better," Hallie said. "But I'm still worried about her."

"Did she say anything about . . . ?"

"Uh-uh. Just asked me a lot of questions about the prison her mother is going to. What the food is like, how she'll be treated there, and so on. Do you still think—I mean she seems so sweet."

"Lizzie Borden's neighbors probably thought the same thing."

"That's not funny."

"I know. But I was making a serious point. I don't think there's such a thing as a criminal personality. Psychopaths come the closest, but not all of them engage in antisocial behavior. Given the right set of circumstances—fear, stress, grinding poverty—anyone can become a killer. Given what we know, if Olivia *did* do her father in, she was probably provoked into it."

"Or was acting in self-defense," Hallie said. "For all we know, he sexually abused her, too. Except for that hand, she's very good-looking. Not that it means anything."

"What's wrong with her hand?"

"You mean you didn't notice?"

I shook my head. "She wouldn't let me touch it."

"She has six fingers."

I thought that was interesting. "Polydactyly? Where's the extra one—on the thumb side or the pinkie?"

"Pinkie side on the right hand. And not some little thing, either. A fully formed extra finger. She's obviously self-conscious about it, keeps it covered up in her sleeve. It was only when she was getting into Amanda's car that I saw it."

Another reason to feel sympathy for poor Olivia.

TWENTY-EIGHT

Rachel's health hadn't improved since I was last with her. The same wet cough, the same chapped and spindly fingers. As we were shaking hello, I took the opportunity to test something, but as far as I could tell, she didn't share her daughter's abnormality. She took the seat opposite Hallie and me at the room's metal table and launched into a soliloquy.

"Thank you for coming. I've wanted to tell you how grateful I am for everything you did for me. Please don't think that I blame you for the verdict. I did a terrible thing, and I deserve to be punished. I'm not sorry about what's going to happen to me. I hope you'll understand why I've decided not to appeal. Please don't try to talk me out of it. I'm tired and I just want the whole thing to be over with."

"I can understand why," Hallie said.

Rachel missed her meaning and let out what sounded like a sigh of relief. "Good. I know you lawyers hate losing your cases. I thought you might have come here to get me to reconsider."

"Reconsider, no. But I would like an explanation."

"An explanation? It's what I just said. I'm tired and I want it over so I can get on with what little is left of my life."

"That sounds very nice, but I don't think it's the truth."

Rachel didn't say anything.

Hallie said, "Rachel, I know you've been through a horrible time, and the last thing I want to do is cause you any more upheaval. So I'm going to lay all my cards on the table. It comes down to this: when I became a lawyer, I took an oath to uphold the law and see that justice is done. If I'm going to violate that oath, I'd like to know that it's for a good reason."

Rachel continued to pretend confusion. "I don't understand."

"It won't change anything, but it would ease my conscience to know why an innocent woman has been taking the blame for her husband's death."

"'Innocent'? What are you talking about?"

"I'm talking about the fact that you didn't murder your husband. And that you did everything possible to make yourself look guilty."

Rachel grew heated. "That's a lie. It's all there in the record. I killed Gunther because I hated him. I'd do it again if I had the chance. I killed him and then I sliced him to bits so that the whole world would know how he treated me."

"So not because you were in some kind of PTSD-induced trance?"

Rachel realized her error and rushed to cover it. "I don't know. It was all so confusing. I really don't remember what happened. I—"

Hallie cut her off with a sigh to indicate she wasn't buying it. The psychiatrist in me approved. Though it might seem cruel, Rachel had lied before and would continue the charade until someone called her on it.

Hallie fell silent then, and so did Rachel. I tried to picture the looks on their faces: Hallie's filled with determination, and Rachel's reflecting . . . what? Surprise? Fear? Calculation? A combination of the three?

When at last Rachel spoke again, it was to take the offensive. "You have no right to be angry with me."

"I'm not angry with you," Hallie replied in a still evenhanded tone. "I'm angry at a system that failed to protect you, at police officers who looked the other way, at a society that implicitly—if not openly—allows violence against women and children to go unpunished. I'm angry at a lot of things. But not at you."

"But you still want to know why."

"If you're willing to tell us."

"I can't think of a reason why I should."

I couldn't help stepping in. "Really? I think we just met her outside."

Rachel laughed bitterly. "So that's why you're here. To help my daughter. You won't mind me saying that's rich."

Any number of bromides entered my head. None of them even began to deal with Rachel's predicament—a predicament no parent should ever have to face. There was only one thing I could think of that might get her talking.

I turned to Hallie. "Let's go. We're wasting our time. She's already told us what we came here to find out." I picked up my cane from the table. Hallie grasped what I was doing and made motions to leave also.

"No. Wait. What are you going to do?" Rachel hissed as fiercely as a lioness sensing a threat to her cub.

"Nothing," I said. "Except try to get Olivia into treatment. It would be helpful if I could pass on all the facts to a qualified therapist. But if I can't get them here . . ."

"Passive aggression," Rachel said with a sneer in her voice. "Is that what they teach you psychiatrists in medical school?"

"Happily, no," I said. "A few of us are even competent to spot potential suicides. What you're hiding from us won't save Olivia. In the end, it will destroy her."

"So you say. But how do I know you won't go to the police?"

"Because I'm still your lawyer," Hallie injected, sensing as I did that the tide was beginning to turn in our favor. "Anything you say to me stays inside this room. For as long as you instruct me to keep it secret."

"That's all well and good. But what about him?"

"I'm also bound by an oath. To do no harm."

"That's not good enough," Rachel said, "I want you to swear it."

Despite a world of misgivings, I gave her my solemn promise.

Gradually over the course of the next hour, the unexpurgated story of the Westlake marriage came out. Most of it wasn't new information.

I'd heard it on the tapes of Brad's sessions and in my own two-hour interview before the trial. What had changed was the way Rachel told it. Gone was the defeated attitude, the languid air of a weak and indifferent victim. In their place was anger of the purest kind, though not all of it directed at Rachel's husband.

"I wasn't lying when I said I deserve to be punished. I did everything to myself. What I can't forgive is exposing what I love the most. I should have left Gunther when she was young. As bad as he was, I thought he wouldn't touch a child, even one he hated as much as Olivia."

This was a completely foreign concept for Hallie. "He hated his own daughter? Why?"

"Partly for being a girl instead of the son he wanted. Partly because she wasn't like him. Stupid, he used to call her. And deformed."

"Because of her hand?" I said.

"Yes. He called it her mark of shame, as though it was her fault she wasn't perfect."

I couldn't help thinking of my own imperfection. "A man of his intelligence should have known it was nothing to be ashamed of. It's just a genetic mutation. And one that can be surgically corrected in infancy. Why didn't you have the extra finger removed?"

"Gunther refused to consent or pay for the surgery. I should have overridden the decision, taken her to the hospital myself. But by that time, I was a virtual prisoner in my own home. I had nowhere to go, no one to turn to. Everything I told you about my mother was true. She wouldn't have lifted a finger to help us and I had no other family. Gunther kept me on a tight financial leash. I had a monthly allowance for food and clothing, but no credit cards, and he set up our bank account so that withdrawals could only be made jointly. I didn't even have my own checkbook. It was exactly as you said at my trial. I was too ashamed to let the world know what I had gotten myself into. Me, a former PhD student, trapped like some concubine in a harem. And I was worried what he would do to retaliate if I ever tried to leave him. He used to threaten me with it. 'Do you think you're hurting now?' he used to say. 'Wait and see what happens when you lose custody of her.'

As long as he kept his hands off Olivia, I thought I could put up with anything."

"But that changed at some point?"

"When Olivia got to high school. She was a good student, very intelligent like her father, but also shy and withdrawn. Several of her teachers mentioned to me at conferences that they were concerned about depression. Then, during her third year, one of them called me in for a special meeting and showed me a poem she had written for a class assignment. It was . . . very disturbing. In it she expressed a wish to die."

"Do you still have the poem?"

"No, I burned it. Along with the journals I found when I searched her bedroom. Apparently she'd been doing this for several years, spinning fantasies of how she would kill herself and the suicide note she would leave, blaming Gunther."

A lot was starting to make sense. "Did you confront her?"

"Not confront. I took her aside one day while Gunther was away on a speaking trip and asked her what it was all about. She gave me a desperate look and said it was nothing. That it was all her fault anyway. That's when I realized just how much I had failed her by staying with him."

"But you didn't go to the authorities?"

"I'm not that stupid. I knew the ordeal Olivia would be put through if either of us even breathed the word *rape*. The lawyers Gunther would bring down on us, how he'd accuse her—and me—of fabrication and mental illness. It was just the kind of no-holds-barred attack Gunther relished. He would have said there was no proof, and he'd be right because I vowed then and there that it would never happen again. For the next year and a half, until Olivia turned eighteen, I made sure they were never alone together, even for a minute. That's when I moved out. Olivia was about to start her first year at the college and would be living in the dormitory. I thought we'd both be safe. The only mistake I made was in not filing for a legal separation beforehand."

The comment jarred a memory of the memorandum I had come across in Brad's files at the beginning of the case. What was it Rachel's divorce lawyer had said?

Hallie understood immediately. "Without a formal order, Gunther still had control of your assets."

"That's right. But even worse, I found out that unless he consented, I would have to wait two years for a divorce. That's the real reason I went to the house that night. To beg Gunther to set me free. When I got there and I saw . . ." Rachel seemed to have difficulty going on.

"Why don't we go back a few steps," Hallie said gently. "To when Olivia dislocated her shoulder."

"You know about that?"

"Yes, Amanda Pearson told us about it. How she reported it to you and you acted like it was Olivia's boyfriend. But it wasn't a boyfriend, was it?"

Rachel's breathing became ragged, like she was running a race. "As Olivia told it to me, she'd been lunching with a friend at Morrie's Deli. The friend had to leave to get to class, and since it was a beautiful day, Olivia decided to take the long way back to campus, along the path behind the Science and Industry Museum. She hadn't gone very far when she saw Gunther out walking too, about twenty yards ahead of her, and as usual with a scowl on his face. Olivia turned around, but not before Gunther had seen her. He caught up with her near one of the lagoons and demanded to have a word. Except for the two of them, the area was deserted. Olivia said she had nothing to say to him. He said, 'You little mongrel bitch. I know what you want and you're not going to get it.' Gunther grabbed her by arm. Olivia said he pulled it so hard she thought she would faint. But she managed to twist away and run, all the way to the Metra underpass at Fifty-Seventh Street, where there's a coffee shop popular with the students. Gunther didn't dare follow her in and continue what he'd started. Olivia managed to get back to her dorm safely, and spent the night in unbearable pain. Later, I chastised her for not phoning me. She said she was afraid of what I might do."

So both mother and daughter feared how the other would act if pushed to the brink.

"I wanted to report the incident to my lawyer, but Olivia said we shouldn't. That she had friends watching out for her now and would take extra steps to be careful. The important thing was staying out of his way until the divorce was finalized. Then we could both move to another part of the country and start a new life. But I didn't trust Gunther. Except for the assault on Olivia, he was being too quiet. I knew he had something planned."

"Like what?" Hallie asked.

"I don't know, but I was afraid for my safety. I asked my divorce lawyer what would happen if one of us died before the divorce came through, and she confirmed that Gunther would get everything. I thought if I could just get a final settlement, I could pay for Olivia to finish college at another school, a good school that I couldn't afford on my salary. I went back and forth about what to do, until there didn't seem to be any other choice. I had to go there and plead with him. Still, I procrastinated until Mother's Day weekend. Olivia and I were planning to go to brunch to celebrate, and I thought how wonderful it would be if I could tell her.

"When I walked in the door, I knew right away something was wrong. Gunther always hummed to himself while he read or worked, or had classical music playing. But the house was deathly quiet, and the carpet in the foyer was at wrong angles. Gunther always straightened it when he went by. He couldn't stand disorder of any kind. I pushed it back into place with my foot and stepped into the living room. That's when I saw him, propped up on the floor by the fireplace. At first, he didn't look dead, only dazed and expressionless. But as I got closer, I could see the blood on his forehead and his legs splayed out like a puppet's. That's when I realized he was gone."

"What time was this?" Hallie asked, barely above a whisper. It's one thing to imagine violent death. It's quite another to hear it in the tenor of another's voice.

"Ten, I think. I waited until later in the evening to come because I was expecting a fight and didn't want the neighbors to hear us at it again. It looked like Gunther had been reading the paper and drinking a scotch before it happened. The glass and the bottle were on a side table, and the papers thrown all over the floor. The glass was still half full. The first thing I thought was how upset Gunther would be if the police saw him like that, looking so silly and with the room all in a mess. So I started straightening up, the way I always did when I used to live there, like a good little housewife. Like I was in a dream. I put the bottle back in the sideboard and brought the glass back to the kitchen to wash it. I scrubbed and scrubbed it with a washrag until it was clean. It was just as I was crossing the room to put it away that I saw them."

"Saw what?" Hallie said in the same hushed tone.

"Olivia's keys to the house. They were lying on the floor, by the door to the backyard, attached to a key ring I had given her as a present. It had a little gold charm attached to it with her initials on it. O.W.W. Olivia Winona Westlake. I picked them up and realized they were covered in blood. That's when I knew."

Rachel went on almost proudly. "I became very clearheaded then. I used to watch television shows like *CSI*. I knew the police would be all over the house, searching with their crime kits. It wouldn't be enough to get rid of fingerprints. They'd find something. A tiny flake of skin or a hair or a thread from her sweater. No matter how small it was, they'd find it. I had to fool them somehow. I washed the keys under the tap until the water ran clear and dried them with a towel and put them in my purse. Then I went back to the living room and wiped the poker with the towel. When it seemed clean, I put my hands in Gunther's blood and smeared the poker all over again, pressing my fingers around the handle. I rubbed the end against his hair and all over my clothing. And then I went back to the kitchen for the knife."

Rachel stopped for a moment, and I asked one of my questions. "You remember it all then?"

"Yes. I'm sorry I lied to you before. Maybe now you'll see why I had to."

"And moving the body—was that also to fool the police?"

"I wasn't planning on it at first. But just as I was finishing with Gunther's corpse, I heard a group of students outside on the street, laughing loudly and cheering. It reminded me that the scavenger hunt was on. I thought how perfect it would be if I put him there, right in the middle of the exhibits for everyone to see. Gunther always wanted to be the center of attention, and now he would be!"

Rachel giggled off-kilter. "The life-sized vagina was just a bonus. How I laughed and laughed when I found it. Gunther laid to rest in the thing he hated most—a woman's body. And he no longer a man himself!"

Her voice rose in hysteria. "Everyone thinks I'm sick, don't they? Not sick enough to send to an asylum instead of prison, but a monster like those women you hear about in the news, the ones who drown their children in the bathtub to save them from the devil. Gunther was a Satan, but I wasn't crazy. Shoving his balls down his throat was the sanest thing I ever did!"

And at that she broke down completely.

A guard, hearing the commotion, opened the door to check on us. Hallie waved him away.

"Thank you," Hallie said. "Thank you for telling us. I think we understand now."

"If you repeat any of it, I'll report you," Rachel had recovered herself enough to warn.

"Yes," Hallie replied. "But there's no danger of that, is there, Mark?"

"No," I said, feeling a sorrow beyond words. "No, there isn't."

TWENTY-NINE

On the drive back, we didn't talk. I could tell that Hallie felt as I did: mentally exhausted but unable to avoid the questions that crowded our minds like a kettle of pitiless vultures. We were each bound never to reveal what we knew—Hallie because of her duty to her client, and I because I had given my word. But we could never forget what we had heard or wonder whether we had done the right thing in forcing Rachel to reveal her tragic secret.

Was Rachel sick in a medical sense? I didn't think she was psychotic, and I was no longer even sure about the PTSD. It didn't matter what the textbooks said. What she had endured would turn the sanest person in history into a short-term maniac. In a skewed way, she was right to be pleased with herself. Her quick thinking had made fools of the authorities. And it was no small irony that Brad Stephens—or whoever had doctored his report—had also been right. Rachel had been lying to everyone from the very beginning.

When Hallie dropped me off at home with promises to get in touch soon, the rest of the weekend lay before me like a barren desert.

I went upstairs and changed into jeans and a bulky sweater and came back down and poured myself a double. I wasn't hungry, but I forced myself to lunch on cold pizza from the refrigerator. I turned on the television and channel surfed for a while without finding anything worth dozing through. I thought about going for a walk, but when I checked the afternoon forecast it was out of the question. The temperature had been falling steadily all day and was expected to reach ten below—not counting the wind chill—by midnight. Even Tom Skilling seemed depressed by the prospect, which was producing a spate of urgent public-service warnings. Anyone not bundled up like Admiral

Peary with the excuse of a wife in labor and about to deliver should stay inside.

The only way to survive the tedium of being shut in was a good book.

I was often asked why I'd bothered to learn Braille when audiobooks were as plentiful as cornfields in Illinois. The answer was part ego and part aesthetics. When I finally admitted that my eyesight wasn't coming back—not for a while, anyway—I attacked the problem in the spirit of frank competition. Being sightless was just another post-graduate course I was determined to achieve high honors in. The aesthetic piece was more complicated. So much of my day-to-day information now came from my ears. I'd be damned if that was the only way I could entertain myself. And I missed the pleasure of reading itself, of getting mentally lost in an artfully constructed flow of words. For me, listening to someone else read a book, even a talented actor, was like having sex with a mannequin.

That didn't mean I read only on paper. Even my new space wasn't big enough to accommodate a broad selection of Braille books, which were both bulky and harder to come by. Nor was I as fast as I used to be. Though the most proficient Braille readers approach speeds equivalent to their sighted counterparts, I wasn't yet in that league. But a free service gave me digital access to most of the bestseller lists, which I could then enjoy with a tactile display attached to a tablet or computer. If I now read at more of a trot than a gallop, at least I was still holding on to the reins.

I poured another bourbon, retrieved my laptop from my study, and made myself comfortable on the sofa, away from the wind scratching at the windows like a noisome prowler. A few keystrokes through the spoken menus brought me to my search engine, and then to my blink "Amazon," where dozens of new titles awaited. I gave some thought to what might cheer me up. In my present state of mind, true crime was definitely out. History or biography might also be too heavy. I needed something light, but not so light that I would quickly grow bored. A spy thriller might fit the bill.

I selected one that seemed promising and downloaded it, switching the laptop from sound to Braille mode. The prologue instantly swept me in with its vivid descriptions of Stalingrad under siege, and of a young girl searching the bombed and rubble-strewn streets for her missing father. I read on, gathering speed. As always, the ingenuity of the Braille display impressed me, the tiny pins moving up and down in six-position patterns as my fingertips passed over them. The marvelous ingenuity of Braille itself. In its contracted form, which had taken me months to master, vowels were frequently omitted. A whole phrase might be indicated by just a few simple dots. A world of meaning communicated through the touch of a finger.

I stopped short suddenly, frowning.

Meaning from a finger.

Rachel's cold and fleshless ones.

Olivia's extra digit.

A series of seemingly random connections swept through my mind. Rachel Lazarus's abrupt marriage to Gunther Westlake. Her decision to take her case to trial instead of pleading guilty. The story she had told me about *A Tree Grows in Brooklyn*. Westlake's hatred for his daughter. An oddly shaped hand.

I shivered, and not just because of the draft escaping the windows.

Alison picked up on the first ring.

"I'm so sorry I didn't get back to you right away," she rushed to apologize. "We just got home. We were planning on taking Mika to the zoo. We realized when we got there that it was crazy to be outside and went shopping at the Water Tower instead. I'd be glad to help Olivia. How quickly do I need—?"

I interrupted her. "It may not be as bad as I first thought. Listen, do you still have that glossary you mentioned to me? The one you found Mika's name in?"

"Sure, but why—"

"I need you to look something up for me."

A few minutes later, I had at least one answer.

"Are you sure you're comfortable with this?" I asked Hallie.

I had caught her even before she had time to change out of her business suit, and we were now speeding down the Drive, once again headed to Hyde Park. Judging by how little Hallie was hitting the brakes—driving with her was always as pulse-pounding as a stock-car race—everyone seemed to be heeding the weathermen's advice.

"Swearing not to reveal my client's confidences doesn't mean I can't do something else to help her. And while I was home, Carter called. You want to guess what he found on the *Maroon* message boards?"

"Death threats?"

"You don't lack for a suspicious mind, do you? There were more than a thousand comments, most of them directed at either proving or ridiculing the idea that the school is a hotbed of racism, not a few politely calling on the administration to fire Westlake. But there was also a verbal fistfight between two parties calling themselves 'Son of Cato' and 'Billy Jack' that got nastier and nastier as the thread went on."

"Westlake and our new suspect. What did Billy Jack say?"

"That whites had been raping and murdering his people for genera-tions and that Son of Cato would pay for their crimes and more. Son of Cato wrote back that Billy Jack was a drunk and a sniveling coward, just like the rest of the genetic cesspool he climbed out of, and that he and his 'whore-squaw' had gotten just what they deserved."

"So Westlake didn't pull any punches. What did Billy Jack threaten him with?"

"He said he'd see who the coward was and warned Son of Cato to keep his doors locked at night."

"Timing?"

"The last exchange was two weeks before Westlake died. Carter also found out something else."

"Let's have it."

"That PhD student we met—or rather didn't meet—in Blum's office."

"Lecht?"

"Mmm-hmm. He was on the message boards too, writing under his own name and contributing long, complimentary posts about Westlake."

"So he's an ass-kisser."

"That's how it would appear, though it still doesn't answer the question why he ran away from us."

The sun was just starting to set when we pulled up to the courtyard building on South Kimbark.

"I'm not regretting the fortune it cost me to buy this fur," Hallie said as we exited her car. I agreed as a frigid zephyr nearly lifted me from the ground. We went up a walk to the building's vestibule and I waited, shivering and stamping my feet, while Hallie scanned the list of tenants. "This one," Hallie said, pressing the button. An ancient buzzer moaned inside.

Olivia Westlake's voice came over the intercom. "You're here already? I hope you won't mind. I'm not ready yet." In a stroke of good luck, she didn't wait for a response before buzzing the door open.

The lobby we turned into was wonderfully warm.

Less so Olivia's welcome when we turned out not to be the visitor she was expecting.

"Wha . . . what are you doing here?"

Hearing the door begin to close, I thrust my cane through the opening to stop her. "Olivia, we need to speak to you. It's important."

"No, I'm not supposed to talk to you anymore. It will just get us in trouble. He said so."

"Who said so?"

Olivia clammed up.

"Olivia," Hallie interceded gently. "We're not here to stop you from running away, if that's what you want. Please let us in. It will only take a few minutes."

"I . . . I don't—"

"Please, child," I said. "We won't do anything to hurt you."

I regretted the falsehood the instant it came of my mouth.

"Oh, all right. I guess so," Olivia said, moving aside to allow us in.

"You were right," Hallie whispered in my ear as we entered. "She's packing a suitcase."

"Ummm, so why are you here?" Olivia asked after Hallie had seated us on a sofa. "Did Mom send you?"

"In a way," I said. "Olivia, we came to tell you a few things. Some that will make you happy. And others that you won't want to hear about. I need to be honest about that from the start. Because without realizing it, you've been put in a terrible position." I hesitated, not knowing exactly how to say that she could save one parent, but only at the cost of losing the other.

"If it's about Mom being guilty, I know that already," Olivia said matter-of-factly. "She did it for me. She told me I shouldn't feel guilty or ashamed. He said the same thing."

"Your father," I said.

"Don't be silly, my father is dead."

"We both know that he's very much alive."

"That's a lie. I told you my father is dead. He's dead and my mother killed him."

Once again, I hesitated. If I had been her therapist, I wouldn't have dreamed of confronting her. I would have let her go on spinning her tale for as long as she wanted, until she was ready to tell me herself. *First do no harm.* But hers wasn't the only life at stake and we were running out of time.

"Olivia," I repeated patiently. "We know all about your father. What *you* don't know is that your mother is innocent and has been lying to protect you. Help us prove it."

"You don't know anything," Olivia said petulantly. "My father is dead and my mother killed him and I'm not sorry about it. The only thing I'm sorry about is that nobody ever did anything to stop it. That nobody would ever *listen* to us."

"Someone will now. I have a friend, a colleague who is waiting to help you. But first you need to tell us everything."

"I'm not saying anything," Olivia insisted.

"Because he told you not to."

"That's right."

"And why do you think that is? Come on, child, think. Why are the two of you running away? What does he have to be afraid of? Besides you and your mother, who hated Westlake enough to crack his skull open?"

Olivia was stubbornly silent.

"How did he react when you told him about the rape? What did he say to you? Did he just sit back and nod? What look did you see in his eyes? Was it the look of a man who was going to take it lying down?"

My frustration was taking over.

"He said not to worry. That he knew what to do and would take care of it."

"What did you think he meant?"

"I don't know. Go to the police."

"And is that what happened? When did you notice that your keys had gone missing? How did you think the murderer got in? Come on, Olivia, tell us."

"I won't. He didn't do it! He loves me!"

"What about your mother? Doesn't she love you too?"

"She loves both of us. I know she does. Or else she wouldn't have . . . But we can't be together again. It's too late. He explained it to me. After I saw you that day in the jail. Nobody can keep Mom out of prison now, but if we go away we can help her. Send her letters and books and things to make her feel less lonely. We're going to go away, just the two of us, and be a family. That's the only thing that will make her happy now. He said so and I believe him!"

I had almost forgotten Hallie was in the room. "Mark," she said, touching my sleeve. "Stop now. You can't see what this is doing. She's shaking all over. Don't make her choose."

She was right.

I was venting my anger on the person who least deserved it.

And there was still one thing left to try.

THIRTY

The dark shadow of Westlake's house loomed above us from the alley where we had parked so as not to be seen.

"Do you keep a flashlight in the car?" I asked Hallie.

"Yes, but you still haven't told me what we're doing here."

"Looking for evidence the police probably didn't think of."

"That seems far-fetched. I'm sure they went over the place with a fine-tooth comb."

"Would they have dusted every last object in the house for fingerprints?"

"Well, no. Their time isn't that unlimited."

"OK. Here's what I'm thinking. What's the one thing an alcoholic can't resist?"

"I hope you don't mean that as a trick question. A drink, naturally."

"Right. Now, do you remember what Lazarus told us she did right after she found Westlake's body?"

Hallie caught on quickly. "The scotch bottle on the table."

"Exactly. She said she put it back with the rest of the liquor bottles. Unless the police took all of them away, it might still be there. And if I'm right, it'll have more than just Rachel's fingerprints on it."

"And you don't want to turn the lights on while we're searching?"

"I don't see any reason to alert the whole neighborhood—including Mrs. Esposito—to the fact that we're breaking and entering."

"We could ask the police to search the house for us."

I gave her a look that said what I thought of that idea.

"OK," Hallie said. "You're right. They won't help. But how are we going to get in without a key?"

I held out the universal bike tool I'd brought along just in case. "I've

picked locks with this before." I was foolishly proud of the skill, which I'd
taught myself on another search mission a few years back. Apart from certain
other, obvious difficulties, I liked to think I would make a good cat burglar.

A few minutes later, I felt a little less sure of myself. Though the
wind had died down to a modest gale, Westlake's back porch was mired
in a deep chill. Within seconds of removing my mittens, my hands were
shaking and I worried about my fingers sticking to the lock. If the metal
was cold enough, I might not be able to pry them off again. Hallie came
to the rescue, digging in her handbag and handing me a small, squishy
package. "Hand warmer. Haven't you learned anything about Chicago
yet?" I applied it first to the standard lock and then to the deadbolt,
until they were both warm enough to work with a pick.

"You are a man of many talents," Hallie said when the door swung
open.

"It's only because I have Mary Poppins as an accomplice. Don't step
over the threshold yet—let's make sure an alarm doesn't go off."

When it appeared we were in the clear, Hallie pointed the way
with the flashlight, which zigzagged faintly ahead of us as we made our
way along the north side of the house through a mudroom, a kitchen,
and the side entry hall before turning to the right and into the living
room, where the furnishings lay covered under sheets. They reflected
enough of the ambient light that I could detect a few of the ghostly
shapes. Though the heat was on, the air smelled stale and damp. I poked
at one of the shrouded objects with my cane, finding a plush ottoman.

"Who gets all this stuff?" I asked Hallie.

"Now that she's been convicted, Rachel can't claim a penny from
the estate, so whoever's named in his will."

I'd lay good money on it not being Olivia.

I took on the role of sentinel near the door while Hallie searched
for the drinks cabinet. Except for the sound of rustling linens and the
humming of the refrigerator motor, all was quiet.

"Here's what we're looking for," Hallie said from a far corner of the
room. "A dry sink with a bunch of bottles in it. This one is scotch. But
we're going to need something to put it in."

I picked my way past various pieces of furniture over to where she stood. "With everything else that's in there, I'm surprised you don't have an evidence locker in your purse."

"Joker. I'm going to go see if I can find a plastic bag."

I heard her steps retreat, followed by the sound of drawers and cabinets being opened and shut in the kitchen. While I waited for her return, I explored the area around me with my stick, reflexively noting how the sound changed when I moved the metal glide from one surface to another. The slippery scratch of a hardwood floor here, the muffled thud of a carpet there. After three years, I barely had to think about what the cane was telling me. I moved on from the floor to the dry sink, curious about what else I could find out without leaving fingerprints. Boxy in construction, it stood on rolling casters and rattled loudly when I struck its side. Particle board, if I had to guess, and none too steady. I sniffed at the bottles it was holding, locating the one holding the scotch near the front.

Thus absorbed, I failed to notice that I was no longer alone.

An overhead light switched on.

"What do you think you're doing?"

"Hallie," I yelled. "Get out of here!"

"You're too late," Peter Crow said. "She's not going anywhere. And just to play fair, you should know that my two very large hands are around her neck. Tell him, sweetheart."

"He came in the back door," Hallie squeaked.

"So I'll ask again. What are you doing here?" Crow said.

My mind raced. Even with two good eyes, my chances of tackling him from ten yards away were zero. But unlike most people, I didn't need to see my phone to call 911. "We were driving by the neighborhood and thought we'd stop in for a drink. No, wait. That's your line, isn't it?" My back was still turned to the room. With my free hand, I reached for the pocket of my coat.

"Uh-uh," Crow said. "Throw the phone on the floor."

I did as I was ordered.

"Now turn around."

Once again, I complied, but not before tossing my cane away with a quick motion and grabbing the sides of the dry sink. I heaved it up and back with all my strength. It crashed into the wall behind with a loud bang, rattling the bottles and sending several toppling over the side. The sound of glass shattering filled the room.

"Nice," Crow said. "But no one's going to hear you make noise. The streets were completely deserted when I was driving over here. Try something again and I'll strangle her. Come out into the center of the room."

"Easier said than done. You know I'm blind, right?"

"My grip's getting tighter," Crow said.

I took a sliding step forward with my arms held out like a zombie in a B movie. If I remembered correctly, the carpet should be right ahead of me. I found the edge with my toe and tripped over it, landing on the floor in a tangle of knees and feet.

"Oh, for heaven's sake," Crow said. "No, don't get up. Just stay there and don't move while I take care of your girlfriend."

Crow pushed Hallie onto a chair. I heard a sound like adhesive tape being ripped, followed by a muffled cry. At least he no longer had a chokehold on her.

I pulled myself into a cross-legged position with my hands behind me. "How did you know to find us?"

"Winona called me on my cell and told me about your little visit."

"Winona?"

"Don't play dumb. I prefer to call Olivia by her Sioux name—first-born daughter. You should be ashamed of yourself, putting psychological pressure on a vulnerable young woman."

"Not as ashamed of myself as I would be if I'd put her mother in prison."

"You must think really ill of me. That wasn't my doing. In the morning, after I remembered what happened, I was all set to turn myself in when I heard about Westlake's body being dumped in the middle of Scav. Rachel had to go and screw things up even more by confessing before I could get to her."

"And it didn't occur to you to go to the cops then?"

"Oh, sure. And have us both arrested? After what that pig did to her, my daughter is a very sick young woman. Who would make sure she gets the care she needs if both of us were locked up? By the way, I'm not even sure I was the one who killed him. He could have bled out later, you know."

"Oh, it was you all right. Though you were probably too drunk to notice."

He'd finished trussing Hallie up and came over to haul me to my feet.

"Off with the coat," he said, helping me roughly out of it.

"I'm surprised your substance problem has escaped attention for so long."

"There wasn't one until Winona told me about the rape. Hadn't touched the stuff in years. The last time was right after my wife left me. I was in my first teaching position at the University of Minnesota. She took off with our two boys and drove to Canada. They were only three and five at the time. The courts up there always take the woman's side in custody disputes. I'm sure you wouldn't understand—sanctimonious pricks like you never do—but losing the kids in the divorce made me see the destructive path I was on. I got sober and went into counseling. Now, let's have it with the pants pockets. Pull the insides out."

"Is that why you abandoned Rachel—because you were married and had kids?"

"Uh-uh. I didn't know about the pregnancy. She never told me, and we only shacked up a few times before she went running back to Westlake. My wife and I were already on the outs, and I would have left her for Rachel if she'd said something. Rachel and I grew up worlds apart, me on the rez and she in some fancy suburb on Long Island, but we both had the same baggage. I bet you don't know about that either, what it's like to have a parent who beats the shit out of you every day."

My pockets stripped, Crow took me by the shoulder and hustled me over to where Hallie was seated.

"I loved Rachel, but I guess she didn't think I was good enough.

Turns out she was right. But that's all going to change now that I have Winona to think about. Hold out your hands." He started to wrap something that felt like packing tape around my wrists. I figured this was why Hallie was being so quiet—Crow had used it to gag her.

"Convenient that you came so well-equipped," I said.

"I was on my way to pack up some things for Winona when she called. Otherwise, I would have brought something heavier."

"When did you find out—about Olivia being your daughter."

"When Amanda Pearson sent her to see me. I knew right away when I saw the extra finger. You know what my old man did to me? Hacked it off with an axe six weeks after I was born. Said it must have been put there by evil spirits. Drunk as usual. I almost died from the infection. And Winona looks just like my mother in photographs. She—my mother—did what she could to shield me, but he went after her too."

He continued unhurriedly with his story. "Eventually she couldn't take it anymore and ran away in the middle of the winter. They found her body a year later, in a far-off corner of the reservation. They said she froze to death. That's why this whole thing makes me sick. History repeating itself. It doesn't matter where you come from or what tribe you belong to. It just goes on and on. I only wish there was some way we could get Rachel off so the three of us could be together."

"Is that why you talked Rachel into a Battered Woman's defense?"

"Yup. She was all ready to plead guilty when I went to visit her at Cook County. I told her it would add insult to injury, screw Winona up for life if she was convicted. Rachel argued with me but finally agreed it was the right thing to do. Winona's well-being was always the most important thing to us."

I marveled at Crow's ability to rationalize his cowardice.

"So you coached her about what to tell me?"

"Uh-huh. It must have been some blow to your ego when you figured it out. That's why you just couldn't let things be, isn't it? I looked you up after that other doctor got run over. White men, both of you. East Coast schools, the best of everything our country hands out to the privileged few. I admit it felt good pulling the wool over your eyes." He chuckled and nudged me in the arm. "C'mon, you have to admit that's a good one. Laugh with me."

"I would if I didn't feel the urge to vomit," I said.

"That's right. Keep up the sarcasm. It'll only make things easier. Any last words before I put the gag on?"

I wasn't about to give him the satisfaction.

Crow herded us through the house, out the back door, and down a short flight of steps. With my wrists bound in front of me, I misjudged the last step and pitched forward into Hallie, pushing both of us down into a bed of crusted snow. Crow picked her up and then me. "Guide him!" he snarled. Hallie complied by coming over and leaning into my shoulder. When we resumed walking, she was limping. We proceeded that way a short distance farther on.

I had assumed Crow was taking us to a car but realized otherwise when I heard the scrape of wood on metal.

"Nnnnnn," I heard Hallie protest through the tape sealing her lips.

"Yes, little lady, that's right. In you go."

He shoved Hallie forward, and I heard her stumble. Her muffled protests grew louder.

"You too, four-eyes."

He pushed me into an opening barely larger than I was. I stumbled over the threshold and landed against Hallie again, sending us both onto an uneven dirt floor. We stayed there, huddled in a heap while Crow shut the door behind us, cutting off the moan of the wind. In the sudden silence, I could hear Hallie breathing in and out. A bolt that might have been a two-by-four was put back into place with a thud. Moments later, I heard a car door snap shut and an engine growl to life.

It sounded just like Hallie's MG.

I realized then that Crow meant to leave us there.

As soon as the car drove away, I rolled over Hallie and then onto my side, coming up against a rough plank wall that tore at my sweater while I slithered into a sitting position. Crow had been stupid about one thing, leaving my fingers free. I set to pushing and pulling at the tape securing my mouth until I had worked a corner of it loose. It took a few more seconds to gain enough traction to tear it from my cheeks. "Keep still. I'm coming," I said to Hallie, who in the interim had also maneuvered herself into a sitting position. I dug my heels into the dirt and scooted back over to her. Hallie gathered what I was up to and inched her face over to where I could grope it.

When she could move her lips again, I asked where we were.

"In some kind of shed behind Westlake's house, by the alley. Probably where he stored his firewood. I saw a pile of it in the back before Crow shut the door."

"Did you see anything else?"

"You mean, like a set of keys? No such luck. But don't take my word for it. I'm as blind as you are right now."

"Do you have your coat?"

"Uh-uh. Crow took it. And my phone. All I have on now is a jacket and slacks."

Not nearly enough in such cold.

"You should stand up and move around, to keep your blood circulating."

"I can't," Hallie said. "I think I twisted my ankle when we fell down."

With some difficulty, I got into a squat and slid my back up the wall until I was standing. Where it met the wall, the roof barely cleared my head. "Here," I said. "I'm going to try to help you up." I squeezed my bound hands together and braced them under her armpit to give her a boost. "Can you put any weight on it?"

"I'm trying," Hallie said.

I felt her flinch in pain.

"No, I guess not," she capitulated, sinking heavily back down.

"All right. Just sit tight while I do something else."

"You're awfully relaxed for a person who's just been bound, gagged, and tossed into a coal bin," Hallie said.

In fact, I *was* operating on the calm, if unjustified belief that finding a way out of there would be a cinch—as soon as I got my hands free.

Hallie's view of the situation was more practical. "Shouldn't we be screaming for help?"

"Save your lungs while I try some other things."

Fortunately, Crow never noticed the shard of glass I had retrieved from the floor and tucked up my sleeve—with some risk to my brachial artery—after intentionally falling down in Westlake's living room. With some delicate shifting of my shoulders, I managed to work it back down to where I could grasp it.

"Stick your wrists out," I said to Hallie. "And yell if I start to cut you."

We took turns sawing each other's bindings off. When my arms were free, I pulled my sweater off and handed it to her. "Put this on while I take a look around. There's no light at all?" I asked, hoping for a window or a crack somewhere that I could leverage into an escape hatch. I knocked experimentally on one of the plank walls. Old lumber and probably as thick as my wrist.

"Uh-uh," Hallie said.

The dryness of the hut confirmed it. Though it felt every bit like a freezer, the air held barely a hint of damp. I doubted there was even a mouse hole. Using the back of my knuckles as a defense against splinters, I went all the way around the walls without finding anything besides a pile of dry logs in the rear and a plastic tarp in a corner. I brought it back to where Hallie was sitting.

"Find anything?" she said. Her teeth had begun to chatter.

"Not even a termite," I answered. "Here, wrap yourself up in this. It will help keep you warm."

I'd saved the door for last. Unfortunately, it appeared to be constructed from the same heavy lumber as the walls. I felt all around the edges, but it was set solidly in its frame on hinges that were only moderately rusted. Using my shoulder as a battering ram, I made several runs at it without producing so much as a shudder.

"*Madone*," I said, using a childhood expletive I resorted to when *shit* didn't seem nearly expressive enough.

Stubbornly I searched the floor and all around the walls again, finding nothing—not even an old nail—that I could use to pry us out.

"OK," I said. "We yell for help now."

But though we shouted ourselves hoarse for the next half hour, no one answered our cries. With all the warnings about staying inside, it was unlikely anyone was taking a stroll through the alley, and the shack's thick walls meant we probably couldn't be heard more than a few yards off.

"It's not working," I said to Hallie, when the futility of our efforts finally sank in. I slipped down to the floor beside her and helped myself to a section of the tarp. "We need to save our strength."

My next thoughts were about how to stay alive until help arrived.

You didn't live through a Chicago winter without hearing about them: the dozen or so victims who perished from the cold between the months of November and March. Though the risk was greatest for alcoholics and the elderly, it could happen to anyone. A slip and fall in an alley, a breakdown on a little-used road, a furnace that stopped working in the night. The next day, it would be all over the news, with renewed warnings about the deadly effects of prolonged exposure to severe weather.

As a doctor, I knew the progression only too well. Human beings are essentially tropical animals with few natural defenses against cold. When body temperature falls below normal, the nervous system, heart, and other organs react accordingly. Shivering is actually a good sign, because it means that the body is still trying to manufacture heat. But as core temperature continues to drop, the major blood vessels constrict, sending less and less oxygen to outer limbs and the brain. Lapses in judgment follow, along with a deterioration in motor skills and drowsiness. Eventually the victim loses consciousness, breathing ceases, and the heart stops.

When I was a Boy Scout, I'd also been drilled over and over about what to do if caught in a blizzard. Get out of the wind, remove wet clothing, cover yourself with blankets, leaves, or even snow. Don't waste energy, and wait quietly for aid to arrive. Good advice that only went so far. Though the walls of our prison reduced the danger of frostbite, they were no barrier to the steadily falling temperature. The cold was almost a tangible thing, penetrating the hut in ever-intensifying waves. Even under the cover of the tarp, the gelid air tugged at our skin, bit into our nostrils, and made breathing a chore.

I put my arms around Hallie and hugged her tightly to me. Two-thirds my weight, she seemed to be having a much harder time of it. Her limbs were wracked with tremors. Huddled together this way, sharing each other's warmth, we might survive for a few hours, but not indefinitely.

"How are you doing?" I asked her, through the staccato of my own teeth.

"All right. But the next time we go winter camping, remind me to bring some matches."

"I could start a fire without them."

"Hmmm. Smoke inhalation might be a problem."

"As would being roasted alive."

"Too bad we don't have any marshmallows."

"Are you hungry?"

"Famished."

That was another problem, along with dehydration, both of which would hasten our end.

As the first hour passed into the second, and the second into the third, I grew more and more pessimistic about our chances. Even if we were reported missing, no one knew where Hallie and I had gone or would think of looking for us in the yard behind the deserted Westlake mansion. If Crow had half a brain, he would destroy our cell phones and abandon the MG in some faraway place, in a body of water or across state lines. It would be a simple matter to tell Winona to follow him in his car—as simple as coming up with an explanation the confused girl wouldn't question. If so, it might be months before our bodies were found, when the odor from our thawing corpses became too strong to miss. By that time, grass would have grown up over Brad Stephens's grave. Rachel Lazarus would have spent her first months in prison. And with no one there to remind him, Louis would begin to forget he ever had a natural father.

"Are we going to die?" Hallie whispered to me. In the last half hour, her speech had slowed and she had stopped shaking, a bad sign since it meant her body was giving up the fight.

"No," I said. "Though it might be time to say our prayers."

"I don't want to pray. I just want you to kiss me."

I obliged her, feeling with a shudder another kind of kiss on her lips.

"Mark?" she said from far away.

"What?"

"If we don't make it—"

I put a finger over her mouth. "Don't talk. Just stay with me."

Not long after, I stopped shivering too and my thought processes became muddled. Cold, I thought farcically. Why did cold have to feel so much like fire? Wasn't that an oxymoron? Cold burning me up while I was freezing. Cold that wouldn't go away. Cold that never relinquished its grip, that felt like a hot lick of flame on my cheek. Come to think of it, there *was* something on my cheek. I batted at it with numbed fingers, but it came back, sending a hot, foul smell into my nostrils. "Damn it!" I murmured, pushing it away again. "Why can't you just let me die in peace?"

The cold returned, pushing at my face with a tiny palm. A soft palm with disconcertingly rough edges. Pushing ever so slightly and then more insistently. I heard a sound like a clock ticking next to my ear and felt the sensation of something moving restlessly above my chest. The cold come to taunt me in my final moments. It hovered there, circling around and around, before landing like a barbell on my throat.

I shot up in shock, clawing at the air.

And being clawed in return as the equally surprised animal leaped over my ear and into the dark.

"Meow," it said.

"What the—?" I said, my brain fog lifting ever so slightly.

"Meow," it complained again.

No, I thought. It couldn't possibly be. "Whiskers?" I said experimentally. He—or she—responded by returning and rubbing my leg.

The sudden rush of adrenaline had put a temporary halt on my mental decline. I lowered my ear to Hallie's chest and felt for her wrist. She was still breathing, but her pulse was faint.

Curious about what I was up to, the cat drew nearer to where I could touch it. "Whiskers, or whatever you're called," I said. "How the hell did you get in here?"

The cat swished its tail in response.

"Come on, show me."

The cat trotted away to the woodpile at the back of the shed to where I could hear it scratching around. The only place I hadn't searched for an escape hatch was behind it.

Later, I would remember tearing at the logs with my almost comically useless hands, weeping real tears of relief when I'd pushed the last of them away and felt the current of fresh air on my face. It was only a hole near the ground, the size of a small animal, and the earth around it was too frozen to enlarge. But when I screwed my head into the dirt and pressed my ear to the opening, I heard footsteps crunching through the snow toward us and recognized the voice of Mrs. Esposito.

"Whiskers? Is that you? Bad boy, making me come out looking for you on such a dreadful night. I don't know what I'm going to do if you don't stop running away."

THIRTY-ONE

"Y ou got custody?" Hallie said in disbelief.

"Amazing, isn't it? I think what won them over was showing I could keep him at a healthy weight."

It was the following Thursday and we were sitting down to dinner at a much-touted new restaurant in Bucktown specializing in all things brined, locally sourced, and hormone-free.

"Why? Feeding a cat isn't rocket science."

I took a sip of my handcrafted, small-batch bourbon. "The adoption specialist acted that way. And seemed amazed that I could actually open the can. I only have one more home visit to go before I can officially call him my own."

"And they were OK with the name change?"

"Mrs. Esposito was disappointed but said she understood."

Following forty-eight hours of intense scrutiny, which included proof of employment, an overnight trial, and my notarized promise to keep him indoors, Whiskers—whom I had rechristened Top Cat—had taken up residence in my home. When I left him that morning, he was sleeping contentedly in my bed, no doubt dreaming about his next jail break.

There were other things to celebrate, not the least of which was Hallie's rapid recovery, leading to her discharge from the hospital with a clean bill of health two days before.

"How are the toes?"

"Still a becoming shade of purple. But it's a small price to pay for still having all ten of them. How about you?"

After we were rescued, I experienced a brief scare about my fingers.

But they emerged from our ordeal with only superficial frostbite, though the tips were still roughened and sore.

"OK, though I won't be tackling *War and Peace* anytime soon. More importantly, how's Rachel?"

"I had a long visit with her this morning. She's . . . I don't know. Overjoyed that it wasn't Olivia, of course. But still feeling responsible for everything that happened. I told her she shouldn't. Many young women in her position would have decided to keep the baby, and it wasn't until after Olivia was born that she knew without a doubt the child was Crow's."

I fiddled with a piece of bread. "Westlake suspected it, too. I'm guessing that's one of the reasons he abused her."

"Who knows what goes on in the heads of men like that. What we do know is that she was being systematically terrorized for most of her adult life and too frightened about losing her daughter to leave him. The saddest thing is that she'll always blame herself when it's the system that failed them both."

"When will they free her?"

Hallie was quiet.

I frowned. "You have something bad to tell me."

"It should happen automatically, but I've been a lawyer too long to think that it will. The police and prosecutors don't like to be proved wrong. I've seen them fight tooth and nail to hold on to a conviction even when DNA evidence leaves no doubt about a defendant's innocence. They have Crow in custody, but that's no guarantee they'll reopen Rachel's case."

Acting on our report, the police had picked Crow up on I-80, just as he was crossing the Iowa border. With Olivia beside him in the passenger seat, Crow hadn't resisted arrest on assault and attempted-murder charges.

"Wait. You're saying they may not prosecute him for Westlake's murder?"

"I'm afraid so," Hallie said.

"But what about the fingerprints? And Mrs. Esposito?" I had naively assumed that the police would go hunting for remnants of the scotch bottle. And that the old woman's story would now get the credit it deserved. As soon as the DMV's computers were back up and running, Hallie's friend was able to confirm that the car parked under Westlake's *porte cochere* that night belonged to Crow. "And I've got to believe the police will find further evidence that Crow was in the house if they go looking for it."

"That's the big 'if.' I'm preparing a motion demanding that they conduct another, thorough search of the property. But even assuming Crow left behind some of his DNA, his defense lawyers will dispute when and how it got there. If the evidence isn't airtight, O'Malley could easily decide she's better off sticking with the attack on us."

The meal was beginning to seem a lot less celebratory.

"What about O'Malley?" I said. "She's always struck me as honest. Can we go to her with our suspicions about Di Marco?"

"I've been thinking about that," Hallie said. "The problem is the same one we started out with: finding the original police notes and tying their disappearance to Tony. I've got to think he covered his tracks well. And O'Malley can't very well launch an investigation into one of her senior ASAs without some serious cause."

"So he gets away with it." Not to mention the possible murder of my friend.

"I haven't given up completely, but it looks that way."

Our main courses had come and we picked at them in silence. I hated thinking we had come this far with so little to show for it. True, we had put Rachel Lazarus's mind to rest about Olivia, and the girl was now under Alison's care. Overcoming her trauma wouldn't be easy, but I had every confidence in my colleague's ability to start her down the path to recovery. And there was still hope that O'Malley would put aside petty concerns about her office's track record and agree to vacate the conviction.

If only I could believe it.

When the waiter came to collect our plates, I held out my credit card and told him we wouldn't be needing desert.

"Are you on some kind of diet?" he asked. "'Cause you didn't eat anything the last time, either."

"The last time?"

"At the Outpost. A couple of weeks ago. I was your bartender," he said, as though this was something to be proud of.

I thought his voice sounded familiar. "So you've moved up in the world."

"Yeah. Gotta friend who works in the kitchen, and she put in a good word for me. Beats having to wait on drunks all the time. And the money is good enough that I could afford to go back to school part-time. I'm getting my degree in photojournalism from Columbia. The one here, I mean. Which reminds me. You know that chick you were with—the hot-looking one?"

I figured he meant Michelle. "What about her?"

"You know she wasn't in love with you, right?"

My jaw must have dropped. "In love with me?"

"Yeah. I saw her at the Outpost with another dude, back in December. Middle-aged guy with a cane, just like you. That's why I remember her so well. That and the big tip."

"What are you talking about?" I asked, with a sudden ill feeling.

"You sure you want to hear about it? I mean, it looks like you've found yourself another lady—and a much nicer one, too."

"I'll take that as a compliment," Hallie said, making no effort to hide her amusement.

I put my hand on her forearm to alert her that this was no laughing matter. "I'm not worried about my feelings. Tell us about the other man she was with."

"It's like this. First the two of them come in and have this super intense conversation over beers. Kinda like the one she was having with you, though she didn't cry half as much. About an hour into it, they leave. Then, about twenty minutes later, she comes back through the door, all nervous and looking over her shoulder. Throws herself on a stool and asks me to pour her a double vodka, which she downs in one swallow. Right away, she asks for another shot. So I ask her if something's wrong."

"Go on."

"First, she tells me she's OK, but then it's like the whole story starts pouring out. So she's been seeing this guy—the one she just left with—and she's really in love with him and he loves her back but he's married and his wife is a crazy bitch. And the guy's got some kind of disease—I could see that—and can't afford to pay alimony on top of all his medical bills. And now she thinks the wife has hired a private detective and she's being followed all the time. And she thinks it was happening a few minutes ago, which is why she came running back to the bar. And if somebody ever asks would I please, *please* not tell them that she and her boyfriend were here."

"And that was it?"

"No. Then she passes a fifty-dollar bill across the bar, winks at me like it's our little secret, and walks out. So I'm like, this is a bit strange, but I'm not gonna pass up the spending money. Then, a few weeks later, she shows up again, this time with you. At first I thought you were the same dude, but then I realized you looked a little different and uh . . ."

I said, "I know. Just finish the story."

"Well, that's pretty much it. Except that this time I'm beginning wonder if she's some kind of con artist. If she was so in love with the other dude, why was she back at the Outpost, putting on the same sad face with another handicapped guy? And so soon. Afterwards, I was sorry I didn't say something to you. I hope she didn't cheat you out of anything. 'Cause if she did, I'd be glad to tell my story to the cops."

I did some rapid thinking. "Thanks," I said. "I may have to take you up on that offer. What's your name?"

"Wayne."

"So Wayne, would you recognize this 'other dude' if I showed you a photo of him?"

"Yeah, but I could do even better than that." He sounded nervous bringing it up. "I mean, it's probably illegal, but maybe I could get some kind of immunity in exchange for helping you?"

"What do you mean?"

"Well, it's like this. Most days when I was working the bar at the Outpost, the place was really slow, and I'm not that into watching TV, so I passed the time with a hobby of mine. Actually, more than a hobby since I'm hoping to get my own show one of these days. You're not supposed to do it without permission, but I thought the patrons there wouldn't mind. Most of them were passed out when I took the shots anyway. And I thought it could be really cool artistically—what people do in bars when they think no one's watching them . . ."

THIRTY-TWO

We drove to Sauganash on Chicago's far northwest side. To steady my nerves, I checked the name online on the way up and discovered it meant "English-speaking." It was named after a Native American leader of the Potawatami tribe, Billy Caldwell, also known as "Sauganash." In exchange for negotiating a treaty between the United States and his people, the federal government granted him the hundred acres along the Chicago River that still bore his name. Thanks to the number of municipal employees and cops living there, it was considered one of the safest neighborhoods in the city.

Tony Di Marco was waiting with an unmarked cruiser when we arrived. "Why don't you ride with us?" he said when Hallie rolled down the window of the rental car she'd been driving since her MG was discovered, stripped down to the chassis by opportunists, in a cornfield in Grundy County. "It'll be more fun that way."

After Hallie parked in his driveway, the three of us—Di Marco, Hallie, and I—piled into the backseat and Di Marco introduced us to the two detectives who would be accompanying us.

"Skip the red lights," he told them. "But no lights or sirens. I want this to be a surprise."

"Sure, boss," the driver said.

We took off in a screech of burnt rubber that had me clinging to the armrest.

"OK, let's see what you got on film," Di Marco said to me as soon as we were on our way.

I showed him the photograph Wayne had sent to my phone in the restaurant, which bore a date and time stamp showing it had been snapped thirty minutes before Brad Stephens's "accident."

"Oh, yes," Di Marco chuckled malevolently. "That's our Michelle, all right. Who would've thought she could pull it off?"

"Do you think she acted alone?"

"No more than you do. I'm just saying it must have taken a lot of nerve. More than I would have given her credit for, even with my boss's encouragement."

"You must have really done something to piss O'Malley off," I said. "Unless it was just being your usual charming self."

"You know what they say about taking one to know one," Di Marco said. "But no, *Dottore*, it wasn't only me getting on O'Malley's nerves. You ever heard of the *Shakman* decrees?"

I shook my head no.

"Hallie can tell you more about it later. But the short version is that starting in nineteen sixty-nine—yeah, that's right, corruption has been going on in Cook County for half a century—a civil-rights lawyer named Shakman brought a bunch of lawsuits against the city and state for filling civil-service jobs with patronage workers. Shakman argued that it screwed up the election system because folks in government who wanted to hang on to their jobs were forced to support Machine candidates and get all their family and friends to vote for them. Sometimes they were doing campaign work right at their desks. The federal courts got interested and entered a series of orders prohibiting hiring or firing based on political affiliation. And it wasn't just the Democrats, by the way. The Republican organizations in the collar counties were just as active in filling government jobs with political cronies. You might say it's the bipartisan way. So you want to guess what O'Malley's been doing ever since she got her hands on a seat that's been held by the Democrats practically since the Fort Dearborn Massacre?"

I nodded. The temptation to fill her office with political allies would be almost irresistible. "And you found out about it?"

"Yeah. But that's not everything. *Shakman* gets violated all the time. It's not a crime—just the basis for a civil suit—and there isn't an Illinois politician who hasn't been accused of it at some point in their career. But accepting 'donations' from job candidates is. I can't go into the details because the feds are investigating as we speak. But you can take it as a given that I was the person who brought it to the attention of the US Attorney and will be called as a witness when the grand jury is convened."

"So O'Malley had an interest in discrediting you."

"And in getting me fired so that there'd be another senior position she could fill with a friend. So you see, *Dottore*, we were both set up."

"O'Malley was banking on me tracking down Brad's original report."

"You have to admit you're the dogged type. And anyone can see that there's no love lost between the two of us. How much you want to bet that report will mysteriously show up in your mailbox one day?" Di Marco gave a cynical little laugh. "That's the only thing that upsets me—how you thought I was behind it."

"The rumors, Tony," Hallie pointed out. "The rumors."

"I'm not talking about the police scribbles. I'm talking about how Michelle mishandled the cut-and-paste job. It's Evidence 101 that an expert can't openly call somebody a liar. *If* I had wanted Stephens's report to come out a different way—and I'll deny I ever felt that way—I never would have been so stupid. Or so crude."

It was after 10 p.m. when we pulled up at our destination, a bungalow in West Rogers Park. Tony sent one of the detectives to watch the back door while we proceeded up the front walk and rang.

The young man who answered—presumably Michelle's husband—was in the middle of telling us she wasn't home when Di Marco cut him off.

"Five to ten," he said.

"Excuse me?" the young man stuttered.

"That's the penalty in Illinois for helping a fugitive evade justice. Now be a nice little boy and step aside."

Just as we were about to enter, the second detective dragged Michelle Rogers from the back of the house, crying and screaming, "It wasn't me! It was her! It was her! She made me!"

Di Marco said, "That's being a doll, Michelle. Keep singing like that at the station house, and I'll do what I can to get you into one of the more luxurious correctional facilities." Then to the detectives: "Get the girls and boys with the baggies down here and go over every inch of her car before you impound it. And bring the hubby in too, in case he's stupid enough to try and provide an alibi. It's late, but I'm afraid I'm going to need you there for a while too," he said to Hallie and me. "To give statements."

"That's all right," I said. "Because there's something you're going to do for us in return."

Several days later, the news flash came on the television just as I was leaving for work. In what WGN was calling a "shocking setback" for Republicans hoping to reclaim the governor's mansion, State's Attorney Linda O'Malley was expected to announce her resignation at a press conference later that morning. Though the reason was yet unknown, several prominent party members pointed to an at-risk pregnancy and O'Malley's agonizing decision to put her family first. Other, more credible sources claimed it was related to the fact that a different suspect was now under arrest for the slaying of University of Chicago professor Gunther Westlake, along with rumors that an unnamed lawyer in the State's Attorney's office had confessed to the contract killing of the expert witness originally hired to evaluate Rachel Lazarus.

In a side note to the unfolding scandal, a spokesperson for the University of Chicago reported that the school was opening an investigation into a PhD candidate who had allegedly stolen one of Westlake's unpublished papers and submitted it in place of his dissertation. The theft was discovered when the student's odd behavior aroused the suspicions of Erik Blum, the head of the Sociology Department, who was said to be "dismayed by the culture of laxity" among today's graduate students, even while acknowledging that a "breakdown in oversight" may have contributed to the young man's problems.

Ambling into the office coffee room an hour later, I discovered a minor celebration underway.

"Woot, woot, here he is!" Josh exclaimed, taking my arm and ushering me to a table where a number of my colleagues were gathered. Several of them came over to offer their congratulations and pound me on the back. I assumed they were talking about Rachel's release, which Di Marco had informed me would take place as soon as his appointment as acting State's Attorney was made official. Though Rachel would still have to answer for the mutilation of Westlake's corpse, the misdemeanor carried only a minimal sentence that could be taken care of by time served.

"Thanks, guys," I said. "But you didn't need to throw me a party. And it's way too early to open a bottle of champagne."

"*Au contraire*," Josh said, handing me a glass of the bubbly stuff. "Who wants to tell him?"

"I will," Alison said, audibly beaming.

I had no clue what was going on. "Did I forget it was my anniversary?"

"Better than an anniversary," she said.

"Oh yeah? Has Jonathan announced where he's sending me next? If it's Siberia, I can just walk outside."

"Not Siberia. But you're getting warm."

"What are you talking about?" I demanded.

"Switzerland, home of the Appenzell Institute, what some consider the finest psychiatric hospital in the world."

"Great. I'm being committed."

Alison said, "Don't be such a goof. I'm not talking about you. I'm talking about Jonathan. Guess who an international search committee has tagged to become the Appenzell Institute's next director? He's moving the whole family to Lausanne next month."

"How did you—?"

"Engineer it? I got wind of the opening, and a number of us took the opportunity to submit Jonathan's résumé to the search committee, along with our heartfelt letters of recommendation. But it was Sep's connections that really cinched the deal. He was hopping mad when he heard how Jonathan treated you. He couldn't be here this morning, but he wanted us to tell you that he's also put your name in as a possible replacement."

I couldn't have been more stunned. "Me?"

"But only, to quote Sep, 'if he promises to work on his interpersonal skills.'"

"So we're stuck with you," Josh said.

"And couldn't be happier about it," Alison added.

I didn't have the stomach to argue with them.

I asked Hallie to give me a lift home that night, using the weather as an excuse. Though the days had lengthened considerably and signs of spring were everywhere—Top Cat's launching himself at the windows to get at the birds outside being just one example—it was still too early to call it a winter.

The drive was just long enough for me to get some questions out of the way.

"So Michelle claims she was paid to run down Brad?"

"That's her story. Says she was promised a promotion in exchange for making 'something happen' to your friend that could be later pinned on Di Marco. The means was left up to her. She admits she lured Brad out to the bar that night on a pretext similar to the one she gave you: that she had suspicions about Di Marco and was concerned about Brad's safety. When they were done, she followed him home from the bar and waited to hit the accelerator until he was crossing a street with no one around. Not exactly a foolproof plan, but the only way she could think of to make the death look like an accident. And if Brad did survive, he could testify about what she told him."

"So the part about the affair was just something she made up."

"Uh-huh. She was worried Wayne could identify the two of them if the police came around, asking questions. She figured he'd be scared enough about taking a bribe that he'd keep his mouth shut."

At least I had one good piece of news to deliver to Inga Duckworth.

"What about O'Malley? Will she be tried for the murder?"

"According to my sources, the only question is where. Right now, as you'd expect, O'Malley's attorneys are promising a fight—nothing on tape, the word of an admitted felon against hers, and so forth. If the case is tried in state court, they'll fight like hell to keep the federal corruption charges out of it. But the US Attorney is pushing to charge O'Malley with conspiracy, and this may be the one time Di Marco will willingly step aside. I hear he's already planning a run to make his acting position permanent in the special election."

"And Brad's original report—did Michelle say where it was now?"

Hallie chuckled. "Just as Di Marco predicted. On its way to you in the US Mail. The FBI put an intercept on it, but I was asked to tell you to call if it arrived on your doorstep."

This time when Hallie dropped me off, I asked her if she'd like to come in and see the place. It was early enough in the evening that the invitation wouldn't be misconstrued, and I wanted her to see how I was changing for the better: no longer so in thrall to my demons that I chose to forgo all creature comforts. I gave her directions to the alley and the ground-floor garage I didn't need and hopped out ahead to open the door.

I took her around the first floor, the room I'd once planned on turning into a home theater—if I couldn't see anything more than the glow of a television screen, I could make up for it with surround sound—the spacious laundry, and the yards of storage space, still filled with the movers' boxes that would now go unopened. I showed her my bicycles and my stationary trainer and took her upstairs to where Top Cat rushed up to greet us. I showed her the Jetson-like kitchen and the gas fireplace and the little office den where I had sweated out the details of my Lazarus testimony. Playing the host, feeling an owner's pride, recognizing for the first time that these four walls—and the city outside them—had become my home, made me regret all the more what I had to do.

It was while we were touring the third floor that Hallie grew suspicious.

"Is this the room where Louis will be staying when he comes to visit you?"

"That *was* the plan."

"Was?"

The time had come to fill her in on what was happening. So I took Hallie through my last meeting with Annie, the written demand from her lawyers, and my intention to seek shared custody in court.

"The ironic part is that I've always hated my name. And now I'll be fighting just so that he can keep it," I said, as I was finishing up my story.

"But it isn't just about the name, is it?"

"No," I admitted. "It's much more than that."

"What does your lawyer think about your chances?"

"She's not being Debbie Downer, but even a paralegal would know the odds are against me. I walked away from him at birth. And that's before we even get to *this*." I waved a hand in front of my eyes.

"That's not a reason to deny you custody," Hallie said quickly and heatedly.

"You can say that because you were brought up to believe it. How many family-court judges will feel the same way? And to be honest, I'm not all that confident myself. I manage OK on my own, but how will I do with a little child? I know blind people can be good parents, but I'm still so new—to both games. I'm worried about losing him in a crowd, of getting lost somewhere when I'm supposed to be picking him up from school, of his friends not wanting to play at our house. Maybe it's unfair of me to even want it."

"Don't ever think that. He needs you. And you'll have other people to help you—your friends." She didn't need to say the words. *And me.*

We'd come to the nub of the problem and I shook my head. "If by some miracle I win, I can't stay in Chicago. I'll have to move back to Greenwich." I looked straight at her. "It will improve my chances if I do it before the court gets around to deciding."

And that would be the end of us. Hallie had a well-established career here. A large and loving family. I could never ask her to move halfway across the country to take a chance on a shithead like me.

Hallie was quiet while my words sank in.

"I've been putting off making a decision, but now that this business with Rachel is over, it's time to face reality. So I won't be holding on to this place for much longer." I tried to sound lighthearted. "It's a shame. I was just starting to find my way around."

"How long . . . ?"

"As soon as I can find another job. My lawyer cautioned me about being unemployed when we go to hearing. Another strike against me. But I still have a connection or two back on the East Coast. Maybe they'll be willing to overlook . . . well, things. If I'm lucky, I can be on my way in a month."

"But there's no guarantee—" Hallie started to say.

"I know. But after everything I screwed up before, what would you think of me if I didn't go for broke now?"

That put an end to her protests.

"We could still see each other. I mean, before you take off."

"Nah," I said in my best Queens accent. "As they used to say where I grew up, time for you to go looking under another bridge."

We embraced, probably for the last time.

As she was pulling out of my garage a few minutes later, my eyelids were moist and my chest felt like I had swallowed a brick. I told myself to pull it together. If Rachel Lazarus could sacrifice her life for her daughter, I could give up Hallie for my son.

I hit the garage-door switch and lumbered wearily back upstairs.

Only then discovering the pile of mail by the front door. I picked it up and carried it to my study, smiling to myself at the presence of a manila envelope that I judged to be just the right thickness to contain a copy of Brad Stephens's missing report. Underneath it was another eight-by-twelve envelope with a cellophane window in the upper left corner. With a quickening heartbeat, I placed it on my scanner and waited for the machine to read the return address.

New England Bell.

I took a deep breath to calm my nerves.

What I heard some ten minutes later was this: included among Annie's repeated calls to me that night were four, the last occurring two hours before I burst shamefacedly through the door. It was a number I knew well.

A wave of comprehension swept over me, causing pinpricks to form behind my eyes again.

Until they turned red with rage.

I wasn't the only doctor who misdiagnosed Jack's fever.

So had my father-in-law, Roger Whittaker.

ACKNOWLEDGMENTS

I would like to express my appreciation to the YWCA Evanston/ North Shore for allowing me to serve on its Board of Directors and as a member of its Advisory Council, and for its tireless advocacy and support of women who find themselves in abusive relationships. It was through my association with the YWCA, its outstanding staff, and its talented director, Karen Singer, that I first came to understand domestic violence as a tragedy affecting women from all walks of life. Though, as here, I sometimes leaven the dark subject matter of my novels with humor, there is nothing humorous about violence against women, and it is my fondest wish that readers of *Dante's Dilemma* will come away with fresh awareness of a social problem that affects an estimated 1.3 million women and their families in the United States annually. To learn more about domestic violence and the work of the YWCA Evanston/North Shore, visit its website at http://www.ywca.org/evanston.

As always, I owe a huge debt of gratitude to my editor, Dan Mayer, and all of the staff at Seventh Street Books for bringing the novel to life. A special thank you also goes to Robert Rotstein, James Ziskin, and Allen Eskens for reading and commenting on early drafts of this work, and to my agent, Brooks Sherman of the Bent Agency, for his ongoing advice and support. And once again, a big shout-out to my cover designer, Jackie Nasso Cooke, and to Jade Zora Scibilia, copy-editor and proofreader extraordinaire!

ABOUT THE AUTHOR

LYNNE RAIMONDO is the author of *Dante's Wood* and *Dante's Poison*. Currently a full-time writer, she was formerly a partner in the Chicago law firm Mayer, Brown & Platt, the general counsel of Arthur Andersen LLP, and the general counsel of the Illinois Department of Revenue. To learn more about Lynne Raimondo, visit her website at http://lynneraimondo.com.